UNHOLY

A WITCHBANE NOVEL #5

MORGAN BRICE

UNHOLY

By Morgan Brice

ebook ISBN: 978-1-64795-000-2
Print ISBN: 978-1-64795-001-9

Cover art by Lou Harper.

Darkwind Press is an imprint of DreamSpinner Communications, LLC

1

EVAN

"IT FEELS GOOD TO BE BACK ON THE ROAD." EVAN MALONE WRIGGLED TO get comfortable in the front seat of the black Silverado. He laid a hand on his partner's thigh and gave a squeeze.

Seth Tanner took one hand off the steering wheel and reached down to twine their fingers together as Evan sat back to enjoy the view. Seth's dark blond hair still looked sleep-mussed, and he hadn't completely lost the flush to his skin from a round of wake-up sex before they got on the road. Evan's heart pounded a little faster at the thought that he had put that look on Seth's face. The glint in Seth's chocolate brown eyes suggested that there would be another round once they were done with the day's drive.

"I missed this."

Seth raised an eyebrow. "The road trip part or the almost-getting-killed-by-witches part?"

Evan gave him a look. "The road trip. The other stuff just goes with the job."

"I have to admit, it was nice staying in one place for a few months," Seth replied. "We put some money in the bank, rested up, and did some great hikes on those trails." They had taken time off and stayed for a while in the Blue Ridge Mountains of North Carolina after finishing their last hunt.

"When all this is over—hunting the witch-disciples—I really want to take the RV around the country just for fun. Are you still on board with that idea?" Evan couldn't help sounding a little wistful. They still had a lot of dangerous work ahead before they could make good on that dream.

"Sure. There's a lot to see, and I promised you we'd go all the places you wanted to visit," Seth reminded him. "But eventually it would be nice to have a house. A home base to come back to. We could still take the RV out when we wanted, but it would give us a little more elbow room...maybe even a yard with a garden." The fifth-wheeler RV they towed was their home for now, inherited from Seth's parents.

Evan smiled. "I like that. But it could be a while...I have a long bucket list."

"Bring it on." Seth grinned. "I'm up for the sightseeing challenge."

Moments like this made it difficult for Evan to remember that he and Seth had been a couple for less than a year. They had fallen in love fast, outwitted a killer, and gone on the road together after only four days. Then they started the harder work of getting to know each other, while continuing Seth's quest to track down the men responsible for a century of murders—including Seth's brother, Jesse.

Sometimes Evan couldn't quite believe this was his life. He'd been a bartender back in Richmond, not a warlock hunter. Then a dark witch kidnapped him to sacrifice in a ritual. Seth had saved his life and destroyed the witch.

Nearly a year later, here they were, still together, still alive, and still hot on the trail of yet another murderous witch.

"I've never been to Charleston," Evan said. "Do you really think Simon's cousin will be willing to help us?"

"According to Simon, she and her friends have tackled much bigger bad guys. I guess he didn't quite realize what all Cassidy was involved in until just a few months ago."

"It'll be nice to meet Teag face-to-face, after all the times we've emailed and called," Evan replied. "I'm looking forward to that, even if I'm not exactly excited about going up against another witch-disciple."

Seth snorted. "You'd have to be crazy to be excited about that. Nice to know you're still reasonably sane."

"As sane as I can be, given what we do."

Three years ago, Seth had celebrated coming home from the Army by going camping with his younger brother, Jesse, near a supposedly haunted underpass with the goal of drinking some beer, making a spoof video, and debunking the ghost stories. Then something dark and terrible attacked in the middle of the night, dragging Jesse away and leaving Seth wounded and unconscious. When Seth came around, he found Jesse's mangled body. The cops blamed it on drug dealers, but Seth knew what he'd seen hadn't been anything mortal.

Legend had it that one hundred years ago, a sheriff and his posse killed dark warlock Rhyfel Gremory. Gremory's witch-disciples scattered, but they swore vengeance on the sheriff, his posse, and their descendants. That began a cycle of ritual killings that led to Jesse's murder, and nearly cost Evan—one of those descendants—his life.

Seth spent almost two years after Jesse's death learning about the supernatural and how to fight things most people didn't believe existed. Then he went looking for the witch-disciples, to stop the cycle and avenge Jesse. That led him to Evan, who was the first of the descendants he saved. Falling in love was a bonus.

"I know we've got a job to do in Charleston, but I couldn't help looking up places to eat and things to do," Evan confessed. "I read a couple of books that were set there, and I've always wanted to do some sightseeing. It's supposed to be a real foodie city, too."

Seth chuckled and gave his hand a squeeze. "Does this mean you've already put your list together?"

Evan felt his cheeks heat and grinned. "Maybe."

"Please tell me we're not going on any ghost tours." Seth sighed. "Those are either disappointing because there aren't any real ghosts, or the guides get pissy with us for banishing the spirits if they show up."

"That only happened once." Evan couldn't hide his grin. In hindsight, it was pretty funny, although the tour guide probably didn't think so.

"Just sayin'. Charleston's supposed to be one of the most haunted cities in the U.S., and that's without a psycho witch-disciple on the loose."

"I want to go see some of the old mansions." Evan turned to see Seth better. "There's a huge live oak tree that's supposed to be over five hundred years old. And a tea plantation. Oh, and we could take a boat ride out to Fort Sumter. Or we could see that Civil War submarine they recovered." He bounced with excitement, like a kid at Christmas.

Seth gave him a fond look and rolled his eyes. "That doesn't sound too bad. How about the food?"

Evan gave a dreamy sigh. "Fresh seafood. You know how much I love that. Good barbecue, although it would be hard to beat what we had in North Carolina."

Seth groaned, and the sound went right to Evan's cock, although it was food, not fucking, on his mind. "You've got that right. I didn't know barbecue could be that good."

Evan chuckled. "That's because you grew up in Indiana. Not a state known for culinary excellence."

Seth's fake-offended expression made Evan laugh harder. "Watch it! We had corn. Lots and lots of corn. And popcorn! We were the home state—"

"—of Orville Redenbacher!" They said in unison.

"I know! You've told me so many times!" Evan wiped a tear from his eyes. "Next you're going to tell me about persimmon pudding—"

"Don't knock it until you've tried it."

"And sugar pie."

"My grandma made a really good version of that pie," Seth said with a wistful note in his voice.

"And Wonder Bread."

"You've got a point there," Seth conceded. "Now that we know who the food snob is, what else do you have planned?"

Evan hadn't been kidding about making plans. "I want to try shrimp and grits. And fried green tomatoes. She-crab soup." His stomach rumbled, although they had finished breakfast less than an hour before. "Not to mention fried oysters."

"Oysters, huh?" Seth gave him a wicked look. "Aren't those supposed to put you in the mood?"

"Seriously? I don't think we need any help in that department." Evan was twenty-five, and Seth was twenty-seven. More than physical attraction fueled their relationship, but combustible sex certainly helped.

"Maybe you're right," Seth replied with a smirk.

Before he'd met Seth, Evan hadn't had much luck with relationships. Actually, when he thought about it, "disastrous" wasn't too far off the mark for some of them. His high school boyfriend had outed him to their conservative church and gotten Evan kicked out of both the church and his home. Another boyfriend-turned-stalker had tried to kill him.

That just made it all the more remarkable that he and Seth had found such amazing chemistry from the start. More importantly, Evan knew that Seth had his back. Seth had risked his life to protect Evan more than once, and Evan had done the same in return. The circumstances that brought them together might have been highly unusual, but Evan thanked his lucky stars for the man he'd fallen in love with.

"You're such an adorable dork." Seth's soft smile and the tone in his voice managed to be sexy and sweet at the same time. "I'm just shocked you didn't sign us up to tour the Old Charleston Jail." At Evan's look of surprise, Seth shrugged. "Hey—you're not the only one who knows how to research."

"That's one place where I definitely wouldn't want to run into any ghosts." Evan shuddered. "And to be honest, if any of the spirits could tell we're hunters, it might cause more activity than the tour guides bargained for."

While he and Seth pledged to go after the witch-disciples, that didn't stop them from handling the occasional vengeful ghost or marauding monster when they came upon a problem. Most spirits weren't aware enough to realize that Seth and Evan could send them packing, but a few angry ghosts who weren't ready to leave had recognized the danger and put up a fight. Evan definitely didn't want a repeat of that, especially with an audience of tourists.

"You know what else I want to do?" Evan asked. "I want to go to the City Market and buy one of those woven sweetgrass baskets. Just a little one. I know we don't have room for a lot of knickknacks," he added. Living in an RV and staying on the move made for a very streamlined life. "But I got paid from that big project I just finished, and I thought a basket would be a nice souvenir. They're supposed to be good luck."

"Was that the project for the museum? The commemorative booklet for their anniversary?"

Evan nodded. "Yeah. They were really happy with the way it turned out, and they knew I put in a lot of extra time. I was glad they paid fast."

Evan's graphic design business was portable, allowing him to work from anywhere—much like Seth's job as a "white hat" hacker for a computer security company, stress-testing networks to find vulnerabilities. That meant they didn't have to worry about keeping food on the table or hustle poker games to pay for gas.

"You earned it—if you want a basket, get one. It's nice to have some decorations. And a basket won't break if it falls off the shelf," Seth said.

"I'm gonna hold you to that," Evan replied with a grin. "You can help me pick it out."

"Deal. And if we go to that tea plantation, maybe they'll have some special flavors we can buy. That's my kind of souvenir—something I can drink!"

"Sounds like a plan to me."

They rode in silence for a while, the kind of comfortable coexistence that Evan had never experienced before he met Seth. Spending time with boyfriends in the past always seemed to require staying constantly busy. They had to be doing something—going to a movie, watching TV, playing video games—all the time. Conversation had been awkward and silence even worse. But with Seth, Evan didn't feel pressured one way or the other. Whether they talked or didn't, it felt *right*.

"I'm kind of surprised that the witch-disciple's gotten away with things as long as he has, if Simon's right about his cousin being some kind of badass supernatural vigilante," Seth mused after they had driven several miles. "I would have thought she and her friends would have cleaned house."

"Like you said, Charleston's a haunted hotspot," Evan replied. "That might take a while to clear out all the bad actors."

"I hope we're right about being ahead of the curve this time," Seth said. "We know the witch-disciple is calling himself Michael Longstreet. We know he's going after Blake Miller. And if Simon's right about Cassidy and her friends, maybe we can take Longstreet down without nearly getting killed ourselves."

"Working with Travis and Brent in Pittsburgh certainly helped," Evan replied. "And I'm not sure what we would have done without Milo and Toby in Boone. Which makes it all the more amazing that you took out the first one all by yourself."

"Both of us almost died."

"But we didn't." Although Evan had to admit, silently, that it had been a near thing.

"We still don't know where Longstreet's anchor is, or what he uses for an amulet," Seth pointed out.

"We'll find them," Evan replied confidently.

Evan's phone rang, and a glance told him it was Simon Kincaide. "Hey, Simon. What's up?"

"Where are you? Is Seth with you?" Simon's voice had an urgent edge to it. That sobered Evan immediately.

"We're in the truck, driving to Charleston. Is there a problem?"

"I had a vision. A warning." Simon's abilities as a psychic medium were the real deal. "You and Seth are both in danger."

"Not to be a smartass, but we kinda knew that," Seth replied. "Seeing as how we're going after another witch."

"I think it's more immediate. I saw broken glass and blood...a flash of something pink...and something about a UFO."

Evan and Seth exchanged a look. "A...UFO?" Evan echoed.

"Alien hitmen?" Seth sounded incredulous.

"I know how it sounds. I wish visions were more complete. But this was strong enough that it almost knocked me off my feet. That usually means whatever I saw is going to happen soon."

Evan opened his mouth to say something, just as Seth gripped the wheel with both hands, and the truck swerved. A pink delivery van careened across the median strip, heading straight for them.

"Hold on!" Seth yelled. Evan braced himself.

"What's going on?" Simon shouted over the phone.

Hitched to the RV, the truck couldn't maneuver. The van crashed into the driver's front corner, twisting metal and shattering glass, drowning out Seth's cursing and Evan's cry of alarm as the airbags deployed with a bang like a gunshot.

"Guys? Seth, Evan—" Simon called through the phone.

Evan's world went black.

2

SETH

"WHEN CAN I SEE HIM?" SETH'S HEAD THROBBED, AND HIS BODY FELT LIKE he'd been in a fight, but the Emergency Room had cleared him of any serious injuries. A cut on his temple itched where sutures pulled, and his ribs ached from the airbag, but all things considered, Seth knew he'd been lucky.

He just hoped that luck extended to Evan.

"Mr. Tanner, we're still running tests. We will let you know as soon as he can have visitors," the harried nurse replied to Seth's question.

"Just tell me...is he awake? How bad is it?"

"We'll know more when the tests are complete. Please, have a seat in the waiting room, and someone will come to get you." The nurse's tone was patient but made it clear that patience had a breaking point. Reluctantly, Seth went to the waiting area and found a place to sit.

At least we filled out those Power of Attorney forms, and I had them on my phone, or they wouldn't tell me anything. Like I'd let his family get within ten feet of him.

Seth pulled his phone from his pocket. Evan's phone was still somewhere in the Silverado. *Fuck! Where are they going to take the truck and the RV?* He'd been out of it when the police and ambulance reached the scene. Then again, he hadn't been able to focus on

9

anything except the rise and fall of Evan's chest. Panicking, he searched his pockets and began to breathe again when he realized the cops had given him a card with the name and number of the towing service.

There'd been so much blood…

Still, they were both alive. From the glimpse Seth had as the EMTs hustled him into the ambulance, the driver of the delivery van hadn't survived. The airbags in the Silverado had kept their injuries from being much worse, although Seth wasn't sure his hearing would ever be the same. *I never knew airbags were so damn loud.*

Simon's vision was spot on, except for the part about UFOs, which eluded Seth. He stared at his phone, thinking he should call Cassidy, but he couldn't concentrate and didn't figure that would change until he could see Evan. The next hour crawled by until he saw another nurse coming his way.

"Mr. Tanner? I can take you back now."

Seth's heart was in his throat as he followed her. He and Evan had been taken in different directions when the ambulances brought them into the hospital, and Seth hadn't seen Evan since. His control nearly snapped as he endured the doctor's questions, poking, and prodding. They'd given him something for muscle aches and a printout on symptoms to watch out for; then he'd been pulled aside to fill out paperwork and talk with the police. All the while, he'd just wanted to see for himself that Evan was still alive.

"How is he?" Seth's mouth was dry.

"His doctor will be in shortly to talk with you," she said, avoiding an answer. "We're still waiting on a few more test results." She led Seth to the outpatient recovery area and pulled back a curtain to reveal Evan, lying in the bed, eyes closed.

He's breathing. That's a good sign. Why isn't he awake?

The nurse was gone before Seth could ask. *She probably wouldn't have answered me anyhow,* he thought.

"Evan?" Seth approached the bed hesitantly. Evan stirred, opening his eyes, and Seth's heart soared.

"Hey." Evan's weak voice worried Seth, but he'd still take this as a win.

"Hey, yourself." Seth reached for Evan's hand, and held it in both of his, then bent down to brush a kiss to his lips. "You scared the crap out of me, babe."

"Sorry."

Seth blinked back tears and swallowed hard. "Don't be. You're here. I'm here. That's all that matters."

"My head hurts."

"I haven't been able to get a straight answer, but I think they're trying to make sure you don't have a serious concussion or internal bleeding. At least, that's my guess."

"You okay?"

"I feel like I was on the wrong end of a cage match, but I'll recover," Seth replied, managing a wan smile. "Gonna have some spectacular bruises."

Evan's eyes widened. "The truck—"

"It didn't look good." Seth shook his head. "I didn't get a whole lot of answers from the cops at the scene, but I have a card for where it and the RV were towed. I think the RV was okay."

"The van? The other driver?"

Seth glanced to the side, not wanting to share the bad news. "Not sure." He looked around for Evan's clothing. "Do you still have your saints' medallions? And the woven bracelet Teag made?" They had given each other protective silver necklaces and bracelets for Christmas and birthdays and usually carried several other items to ward off supernatural attacks. Seth still wore his two bracelets—one with silver and onyx, and one of woven string—but Evan's jewelry was gone.

Evan's other hand went to his throat, but there were no chains beneath his thin hospital gown, and his wrist was bare. "I had them. I hope they're here...somewhere."

They were vulnerable in the hospital, especially if Longstreet had, somehow, been behind the accident. Seth kissed Evan's knuckles before letting go of his hand just long enough to look for Evan's personal items and found them in a bag on the nightstand on the far side of the bed.

Before Seth could retrieve them, the temperature in the room plummeted, and a shadow passed over them. A frisson of energy slithered across his skin, wrong and foul. Evan paled, and Seth could tell his partner had felt the change, too.

"What the fuck?" Seth muttered. He grabbed the bag with Evan's belongings and dug out the necklaces and bracelet. "Here. Put these back on." He held the chains for the two silver saints' medallions to slip over Evan's head and had the woven bracelet in his fist. But when his skin touched Evan's, pain seared through him, as if he'd pressed against a hot iron. He recoiled, as Evan jolted. The items dropped into Evan's lap.

"What just happened?" Evan asked, breathless and frightened.

"I don't know." The prickle of energy vanished, leaving a psychic stain Seth wasn't sure he could scrub clean. He reached out gingerly to lay a finger on Evan's bare arm.

"Ouch!" Evan winced and jerked his arm away. Pain radiated up Seth's hand and arm, and he stepped back instinctively.

"Try putting the necklaces back on by yourself."

Evan complied, then nodded once the saints' medallions lay against his chest, and slipped the bracelet onto his wrist. Seth touched him again, with the same results.

"This isn't good," Evan murmured.

"There's got to be an explanation," Seth said, hoping his voice sounded steadier than he felt. "We'll call Simon. Or Cassidy. We'll figure it out."

The curtain rattled as it was pulled back, and a doctor in scrubs walked in. "Mr. Malone," he said, acknowledging Evan. "And Mr. Tanner?" Seth nodded. "I have the tests back. Evan has a slight concussion and two bruised ribs. The hearing loss from the airbag inflation should fade over time, but it is a dangerously loud noise in a confined space at close range, so there may be some permanent damage for both of you." He glanced up from his clipboard, looking from Evan to Seth for acknowledgment.

"Really?" Seth felt like his head was wrapped in cotton. Good hearing could be a lifesaver on a hunt, and he really hoped the effects were temporary.

The doctor nodded. "The benefits of the airbags outweigh the disadvantages, but the volume definitely comes as a surprise, on top of everything else when you're in a crash."

He stepped toward Evan and set his clipboard on the stand. "Let me check your vitals again, and we should be able to start working up your discharge." The doctor took his stethoscope from around his neck and reached to lay the metal disk on Evan's chest. Evan flinched at the cold but didn't pull away. Evan met Seth's gaze, and the truth was clear to both of them.

Only Seth's touch burned.

The doctor continued his examination without noticing their silent conversation. "Everything looks good—with the exceptions I noted. We'll print out some notes for you so you know how to care for those ribs and watch for problems with the concussion." He turned to Seth. "He shouldn't drive until the symptoms resolve. It will all be in the handout."

"I'll drive. We live together. I'll take care of him." Seth promised, though his thoughts spun at the implication of the strange aversion to touch. *It has to be something to do with that shadow. We were fine before then.*

Had Longstreet engineered their crash, and then taken advantage of a vulnerable moment to lay a curse on them? Seth feared that might well be true.

"Very good. I'll authorize his discharge. You can go ahead and help him get dressed. He might be a little wobbly." With that, the doctor left them alone, pulling the curtain behind him.

"Seth?" Evan sounded scared.

"We'll figure it out," Seth assured him, but he knew Evan could see he was just as freaked. "First, let's get your pants on. Maybe if we don't touch bare skin…" He laid out Evan's clothing on the bed, and then pulled the thin blanket off the bed and wrapped it over his hands. "Try this. See if I can steady you."

Evan laid a hand over Seth's blanket-covered fist. Nothing happened. Seth let out a breath he didn't know he'd been holding.

"Let's get out of here." Seth felt exposed, and he hated that he'd been unable to protect Evan.

Evan dressed slowly, moving as if everything hurt. His hand

slipped as he put on his shoes, touching Seth's bare arm and sparking pain for both of them. Evan shied away, nearly losing his balance and knocking a cup to the floor in the process. Seth grabbed for him, managing to catch him with his covered hand.

A nurse poked her head in. "Is everyone all right?" She frowned at the blanket in Seth's hands. "You do know that concussions aren't contagious, right?"

"My hands are cold," Seth said with a smile he hoped looked genuine. "I don't want to give him a chill."

The nurse's skeptical expression said she didn't buy his explanation, but she walked away, apparently convinced that no one was in danger. Evan eased into his jacket, and Seth put the blanket back, keeping a guiding hand on Evan's denim-clad elbow.

"They've got a wheelchair ready. I'll push you out to the car."

"What car? Seth—the truck is a wreck, and our 'house' got towed. We don't have anywhere to go."

The same nurse they had seen before returned and pulled back the curtain completely. "Here's your discharge packet," she said to Evan, handing him a plastic pouch. Her fingers brushed against his, but nothing happened. "And your friends are waiting out by the nurses' station. They said to tell you that Cassidy and Teag are here."

Seth's eyebrows rose, but he figured he might as well roll with it. "Great. They got here sooner than I expected." A glance to Evan silenced any awkward questions.

Seth pushed the wheelchair as they followed the nurse out to the lobby, where a woman with strawberry blonde hair waited, accompanied by a tall, slender man. Both appeared to be within a few years of Seth's age.

"Take care," the nurse told Evan. "And there's a number to call in your packet in case you have any questions." With that, she headed back to her station. That left Seth and Evan staring awkwardly at the newcomers.

"I'm Teag Logan," the man said, greeting both Seth and Evan with a handshake and a hug. They knew each other from phone calls and email, but this was their first chance to meet in person. "And this is Cassidy Kincaide, Simon's cousin," Teag added, smiling. He didn't appear to be fazed by their wariness. "We have ID. And you could video call Simon and have him vouch for us."

"How did you know to come here?" Seth asked, still off-kilter from the crash.

Cassidy's smile was kind. "Simon called me. He heard everything in real-time. Scared the crap out of him. We knew you had to be around Bowman from the UFO clue, and Teag found where you'd been taken from the police scanner."

Seth's thinking felt foggy. "What did UFOs have to do with it?"

Teag chuckled. "There's a guy who built a 'UFO Welcome Center' in Bowman. It's been there for over twenty-five years. Everyone around here has heard of it."

"Thanks for coming," Seth said. "But the truck might be totaled, and the RV got hauled away. So I guess we need to find a hotel."

Teag and Cassidy exchanged a glance. "Let's talk in the car," Cassidy replied.

She brought a silver RAV4 up to the circle in front of the lobby. Seth helped Evan into the passenger seat, being careful not to touch bare skin. He and Teag folded themselves into the back.

"Your truck is being looked at by a body shop we trust," Cassidy told Seth without taking her eyes off the road. "They'll give you a fair estimate, and make sure that there aren't any 'extras' added—like runes or hex bags. The RV is being towed to the St. Expeditus Society's safe house. No one with ill intent will be able to get to it."

Seth felt overwhelmed. He longed for the comfort of Evan's hand but made do with gently gripping Evan's shoulder through the denim jacket. "Thank you. I can't believe you arranged all that so quickly."

"Connections come in handy," Cassidy said with a grin. "If it's alright with you, I'd like to take you to my house, where you can get cleaned up and rest a bit. It's heavily warded, so you'll be safe. I thought I'd order pizza, and let you tell some of our 'fellowship' of friends and allies what brought you to Charleston."

"Thank you. That sounds good." Seth cleared his throat. "Something else happened in the hospital. We both felt a dark energy in Evan's room, and since it left, we can't touch each other—bare skin—without pain."

"I think it's getting worse," Evan added. "It seemed to hurt more each time."

"Sounds like something Rowan would know how to deal with," Teag replied. "She's a powerful witch—and what she can't do alone, her coven can probably handle."

"Witch?" Seth said, wary.

"One of the good ones," Teag answered.

"I hope you're right," Seth said. "Because we can't stay like this." The thought of never being able to touch Evan again knotted his stomach.

Cassidy pulled into a curbside parking space next to a tall, narrow white house positioned so that the side, instead of the front, of the house faced the street. A door opened onto the sidewalk, leading to the porch.

"It's called a 'single house,' and it's a Charleston thing," Cassidy said, in response to Seth's questioning look. "Back in the day, having the porch—we call them 'piazzas' here—face the garden gave people a bit of privacy to loosen their collars and hike their long skirts before there was air conditioning."

Evan moved stiffly, but he managed to get out of the car on his own and walk unassisted. As they passed through the door, Seth felt a tingle of magic.

"What was that?"

Cassidy turned. "Wardings. Several different magical traditions, reinforced frequently. This house is one of the safest places in the city."

They climbed four steps to the wide porch. Seth caught himself reaching out a hand to help Evan, and exchanged a helpless look with his boyfriend. Evan got by using the railing, but Seth could see the strain in his face.

"Your garden is beautiful." Seth looked out over the walled area that was filled with azaleas, camellias, and boxwood. High-pitched barking sounded from inside the house.

"That's Baxter, my Maltese," Cassidy said with a smile as she unlocked the front door. A white ball of fur came charging at them, yapping its displeasure.

"Heart of a warrior, body of a guinea pig." Cassidy scooped the little dog into her arms. He quieted immediately and licked her nose. "No one is going to sneak up on us with Bax around."

Evan came up beside Seth and bumped shoulders. The brief contact grounded Seth. He'd never realized just how often he and Evan touched—a brush of fingers, holding hands, rustling hair, a peck on the cheek. Now that he wasn't able to, all he could think about was making that connection between them.

"I love the house," Evan said, looking around.

Seth took in the view of the foyer and living room. The home had an elegant feel, although nothing about its furnishings or decorations was stuffy or pretentious.

"It's been in my family for a long time. Antiques are the family business, so you'll see a lot of them—but everything's either usable or it's a reproduction. My parents sold the house to me when they moved to Charlotte several years ago," Cassidy replied.

Cassidy showed Seth and Evan to the guest bathroom and offered the adjacent bedroom if they needed to rest. "We won't get everyone together until after dark, so you can lie down for a while if that would help. You've been through a lot today. I'll order pizza after everyone gets here. If you're hungry now, I have sandwich fixings in the fridge."

Seth knew he should be starving, but with all that had happened, he felt nauseous. "I'm alright." Evan nodded to agree. "But I might be in better shape to tell our story if I lie down for a bit—my head is pounding, and I can't take another pill for several hours."

"Make yourselves comfortable," she said. "There are towels in the bathroom, and we keep a supply of T-shirts and sweatpants in several sizes in the closet, since it's not unusual for folks to come back covered in blood."

Seth took note of how the way Cassidy had said that made it sound completely normal.

"Thank you," he told her. "I can't tell you how much we appreciate all you're doing for us."

"You've been working with Simon and Teag for a while now. I realize I haven't met either of you before this, but I feel like I know you from what they've said," Cassidy replied. "Get some rest. You're among friends."

She pulled the door shut after her, and Evan lowered himself into a chair by an antique dresser. "I feel like we've fallen through the looking glass even more than usual, and that's saying something."

They shed their bloodstained clothing and found temporary replacements in the closet. Seth did his best to help Evan change, but doing so without touching skin made the process difficult.

"Do you want me to run you a hot bath?" Seth offered and hated how useless he felt. "Or get your shoes off so you can lie down?"

"Shoes, please. I don't even want to think about getting undressed and dressed again."

Seth helped Evan out of his sneakers and then toed off his own. He padded over to the bed, which had four tall corner posts and looked like it might be mahogany. "Pretty fancy, huh?"

"Hasn't her antique shop been around since forever?" Evan asked. "I imagine that makes it easier to find good stuff." He managed a tired smile. "I don't think that bed will fit in the RV."

Seth pulled down the covers and crawled in, then patted the mattress for Evan to join him. Evan moved stiffly, and the way he squeezed his eyes closed told Seth just how bad he felt. When he finally stretched out on the comfortable mattress, Evan sighed in relief.

"How are you holding up?" Seth asked, gritting his teeth to keep from brushing a strand of brown hair off Evan's face.

"About as well as you can imagine. Everything hurts. But we're both alive, and we're safe—for now."

"I'm sorry I let you down," Seth said quietly. "If I'd had the truck warded better—"

"The wardings we had are the reason we're still here," Evan argued, not bothering to open his eyes. "And even Simon can't predict everything. Apparently he didn't see the 'curse,' either."

"Maybe." Seth wasn't ready to let himself off the hook just yet. "But I've never wanted to touch you more in my life than I do now."

Evan smiled. "Me, too. Guess that'll make everything even hotter once we break the spell."

"Go ahead and get some sleep," Seth urged. "I'll make sure to wake you up when dinner's ready. And I'll be right here if you need me."

Lying down eased his tired body, but Seth's thoughts were too scattered to let him sleep.

He lay still, listening to Evan breathe, and expressed his gratitude to any power that might hear him. Normally, they would be pressed together shoulder to knee, hands linked. Now, several inches separated them, and it felt like a gulf to Seth.

What if they can't break the curse? What if I can never touch him again? Seth tried to force down the panic he felt. He loved Evan with all his heart, and thinking that they might not be able to be together broke something inside him.

Not being able to touch each other threw everything off-kilter. Seth and Evan trained together to stay in shape and enhance their fighting skills. That usually carried over to an equally energetic round of sex. But now, both sparring and making love would be impossible. That meant they'd be off their game going up against Longstreet, which was probably exactly what the witch-disciple had in mind.

We live in an RV, practically in each other's pockets. How many times each day do we brush against each other? It's not physically possible to avoid contact long-term. And if the pain gets worse the longer the curse lasts? Does it end with one of us killing the other with just a touch?

Seth couldn't imagine never being able to kiss Evan, or touch his face. Not being able to reaffirm their connection in bed. They'd be cut off from each other, each in his own enforced solitary confinement.

As much as I love Evan—and he's it for me, I know that—I couldn't do that to him. Not when someone else—anyone else—could give him what I can't. We'd be miserable trying to stay together, but it will rip my heart out to let him go. I hope Cassidy's witch friend can figure out a way to get us out of this mess. Because I don't know what will be left of me if I lose him.

3

EVAN

"EVAN, WAKE UP."

Evan heard Seth's voice, but throwing off the haze of sleep seemed almost too hard to manage.

"Come on. People are waiting, and the pizza's on its way."

Evan opened his eyes and blinked hard. The bedside lamp shone painfully bright, and he looked away. His head throbbed in time with his heartbeat. "Where—"

"Cassidy's house. Remember?"

Evan's thoughts cleared slowly, but the memories returned. "Oh." He recalled the crash, the hospital—and the dark magic that stole away the comfort of the person he needed most.

He forced himself to get out of bed on his own, feeling every bruise and aching rib. "When we come back up, can you read the discharge instructions to me? I tried in the car, but I kept seeing double."

"Of course. Why didn't you mention it?'

Evan shrugged. "I just did. There's nothing to be done about it except what we're already doing."

Evan went down the steps slowly, with Seth right behind him, close enough to catch him if he fell. When they entered the dining room, they saw several people they didn't recognize sitting at the large cherrywood table. Pizza boxes sat in the middle, offering choices with a variety of toppings.

"Everyone—this is Seth Tanner and Evan Malone," Cassidy said, which gained nods and smiles in response. She turned to them. "Go ahead and help yourself to pizza and sweet tea, and I'll introduce you to the others once you're settled."

"Sit," Seth murmured to Evan. "Just tell me what you want, and I'll bring it to you."

Evan opened his mouth to protest, but the look in Seth's eyes told him that this was his boyfriend's way of showing affection, now that other avenues were unavailable. "Thank you," he said, giving Seth a fond smile.

Moments later, Seth returned with water and cheese pizza for Evan, then went to get two slices of pepperoni pizza and a sweet tea for himself. He bumped Evan's knee when he sat and gave him a reassuring smile as they faced an audience of strangers.

"Father Anne arranged to tow your RV to the safe house," Cassidy said, with a nod toward a woman in her thirties with short, spiked dark hair. Portions of richly colored tattoos peeked from below her black T-shirt, and she wore a white clerical collar.

"Thank you," Seth replied. "I can't tell you how much we appreciate that."

Father Anne inclined her head in response. "You're very welcome. Glad we could be of assistance," she added with a smile.

Teag turned his attention to another woman in her early thirties with shoulder-length blonde hair and picked up on the next introduction. "Rowan is an exceptionally skilled witch," Teag said. "She's very interested in hearing about Rhyfel Gremory and his disciples, and I've told her about the spell you encountered in the hospital."

Rowan gave them an appraising look, and Evan thought he saw a flash of alarm in her eyes. "I can see the spell binding both of you. Before I say more, I need to hear your story."

Evan felt exposed by her appraisal, as if she could see down to his bones. He started to reach for Seth's hand and jerked back before they could make contact. Seth's sorrowful gaze suggested that he wanted the grounding connection of touch just as much as Evan did.

Cassidy's expression made Evan wonder if she read more into Rowan's comment than Evan had understood. "Then let me finish up introductions, and Seth can get started. Alicia is a psychic medium, whose talents are very similar to Simon's," Cassidy took over from Teag, indicating an unassuming woman in her late thirties with light blue eyes and black hair who sat next to Rowan. "Since the murders have been going on for a century, Alicia may be able to gather information from the ghosts of the victims to help."

"Hi, and welcome to Charleston," Alicia said. "I've heard a lot about both of you."

That left one other person. He looked to be in his late twenties, with blond hair in a trendy cut, high cheekbones, and gray eyes the color of the sea after a storm. Unlike the others, he didn't have a drink or a plate in front of him. The man's appraisal made Evan shiver, although nothing in his manner seemed hostile.

"This is Sorren," Cassidy said. "He's my business partner, and he and my ancestor founded Trifles and Folly—my shop—back when Charleston was first chartered."

Seth and Evan exchanged a glance. "But Charleston is over three hundred years old," Seth protested.

Sorren smiled, and Evan caught his breath as he glimpsed the tips of fangs behind his lips. "You're correct. And I am nearly six hundred. I am deeply interested in finding out about this witch-disciple you hunt. He has, apparently, gone to great lengths to avoid my notice."

As soon as Sorren spoke, Evan wondered how he could have thought the man was close to his own age. Sorren had a presence that made it easy to believe he was immortal. Instinct warned him not to meet Sorren's gaze, and he remembered stories about a vampire's ability to glamour mortals and bend their will.

"Don't worry. You're safe here," Sorren said, apparently noting Evan's uneasiness. "You are guests in Cassidy's home, and allies. That puts you under my protection—something I take very seriously."

Evan pasted on a smile and nodded. *Holy shit. What have we gotten ourselves into?*

"You already know Teag, and I believe he and Seth have bonded over hacking to get information on some of the cases we've worked on. But his ninja computer skills are really an outgrowth of his Weaver magic," Cassidy said, "which you know at least something about, from the spell-woven braided bracelets you gave each other for your birthdays."

She sat at the table beside Teag. "Eat first, and then we all want to hear your story."

Evan wasn't sure what might pass for normal conversation with this crew, but the banter felt comfortable and familiar. They obviously knew each other well and were friends as well as colleagues. While they ate, the conversation drifted to local happenings, upcoming events, and the shared frustration that went with having to avoid road construction. Even Sorren commented now and again, and Evan noticed that no one at the table seemed to regard him fearfully. Evan glanced at Seth and knew from the look on his boyfriend's face that the mental wheels were turning, appraising their new allies.

When everyone had their fill of the pizza and had topped off their drinks, the chatter stopped, and they all looked to Seth and Evan. Teag stepped away and returned with his laptop.

"We know a little bit about your hunt for the witch-disciples from the information Teag helped you find in the past," Cassidy said. "But since your search has brought you to Charleston, we can help you better if we all know as much as possible. So if you could tell your story from the beginning, it would help a lot."

Seth swallowed hard and nodded. Evan chanced reaching over to give his thigh a reassuring squeeze, counting on the denim of his jeans to blunt the curse. He knew that recalling the details of Jesse's murder still hurt Seth, and probably always would.

"It all started when my brother Jesse and I thought we'd go legend tripping," Seth began. Their audience listened with rapt attention as Seth told about the night Jesse died, the shadow of suspicion that fell on him as the cops tried to explain the inexplicable, his parents' questionable deaths in a car accident, and the fire that destroyed their home.

Evan kept his hand on Seth's leg in silent support, grateful that the dark magic at least permitted that contact. Seth teared up a couple of times but kept his voice steady as he explained how Toby and Milo Cornell, two experienced hunters, had become his mentors and taught him how to fight an enemy his Army training had never prepared him to face.

Seth's recap of the fight against the first witch-disciple in Richmond, when Evan had nearly been sacrificed, made Evan's throat tighten with remembered fear. Briefly, Seth ran down how they had tracked the second disciple in Pittsburgh, with the help of Travis Dominick and Brent Lawson, two more hunters, and then the third in North Carolina, teaming up with Milo and Toby.

"The witch-disciples have to change their identities every few decades to avoid suspicion, but we know he's calling himself Michael Longstreet now, and the descendant of the sheriff's deputy who is the chosen sacrifice for this round is Blake Miller," Seth said.

"We know *who* he is, but we still have to figure out his anchor—where he stores extra magic—and his amulet—usually a charm he wears to be able to tap into that stored magic," Seth added.

"Tell us how this sacrifice works." Interest glittered in Rowan's eyes.

"The witch-disciple creates a warded circle and recites an incantation," Seth replied. "Then he stabs the sacrifice in the heart and a rift opens, allowing the disciple to receive more energy from his master, while the master feeds on the sacrifice. At least, that's the way it's supposed to go." He paused and rubbed the back of his neck.

"Apparently, no one ever threatened the disciples before," Seth continued. "So when I went after the disciple in Richmond to save Evan, the witch didn't realize I was after him until too late. The disciple in Pittsburgh also didn't seem to think he could be stopped. The one in Boone might not have liked or trusted his old associates, but he kept tabs on them enough to know two had been killed. He tried to scare us off, and when that didn't work, he sicced his helpers on us. I think that Longstreet knew he'd be next and tried to kill us by somehow causing the car accident."

Rowan leaned forward, frowning as she concentrated. "So the witch-disciples of a powerful dark warlock each chose one of the deputies who killed Gremory, and worked some kind of ritual that let them feed off their dead master's magic to power their immortality?"

Seth nodded. "I think the disciples divided it up that way so that they didn't have to cross paths with each other. We got the impression there wasn't any love lost among them. Until we started hunting them, they each killed their sacrifices every twelve years. But when the disciple in Pittsburgh knew we were coming after him, he panicked and moved up the timetable. So did the one in Boone. So we've thrown off the cycle—and I don't know how that affects their magic, or whether their rituals work as well to power them up."

"Interesting," Rowan mused. "And each cycle has a specified victim?"

"That's been the pattern," Seth replied. "But they've made some mistakes. Technically, they go after the oldest living direct descendant. But in my case, it should have been my father, or me. But he took Jesse by mistake. I think Jesse and I happened to be in the wrong place at the wrong time, and the disciple seized an opportunity—and picked wrong."

He swallowed hard, obviously still upset over Jesse's death. "Then he killed my father to try to fix his error, but he only worked the ritual with Jesse. So I don't know how that affected his recharge. In Boone, we were able to keep the disciple from getting the descendent he wanted, so he took me instead. That's when I realized any of the disciples could have come after any of the descendants—they picked territories and laid claim to specific families to keep from squabbling, I guess."

"Did the disciples sacrifice their victims all in the same year?" Rowan asked, intent on Seth's story.

Seth shook his head. "No. They staggered it one year each, so the entire cycle took twelve years."

"But you've thrown that off," she clarified. "They've moved up their kills by one or more years from when they would be due, is that correct?"

"Yes. And the part I've never been able to understand is why, if they have so much power, they didn't just bring Gremory back? Where is he that they can keep tapping into his magic? Three times now I've seen the ritual almost completed," Seth told her. "When the disciple works the spell, a rift opens up in the air, and if the sacrifice isn't made, the disciple gets pulled inside instead of getting a recharge."

"Magic has rules," Rowan said, sitting back in her chair. "Spells and rituals are meant to be precise. Improvising or substituting has consequences."

Her smile looked predatory. "But I think you've had one thing all wrong. Gremory isn't their patron. I think the disciples turned on their master when he was weakened and worked a spell to bind his soul and magic, keeping him from dying. Each year, one of them gets to drain Gremory to juice themselves up. He's not their god—he's their prisoner and their drug."

Seth and Evan looked at each other in horror. "Holy shit," Evan gasped, wide-eyed. Seth looked as if the world had shifted under his feet.

"From what you've said, I would agree." Everyone turned to look at Sorren. "Since I know something about immortality." A wry smile quirked at the corner of his lips. "It sounds to me like the disciples are bleeding off Gremory's magic to sustain themselves—not receiving a gift. That might have worked for quite some time—not indefinitely, but perhaps another century or so—if they had stuck to the plan."

Sorren looked at Evan and Seth. "But the two of you threw off their game. The Pittsburgh and Boone disciples panicked. They were afraid they wouldn't get their refill if they waited, so they went early. But that endangers all the others because Gremory needed that year between rituals to replenish his power. Tapping him early presents the very real possibility that Gremory could be drained dry."

"And that would be the end of the disciples," Teag replied.

"Sacrificing the descendants isn't an offering to a god," Sorren said. "It's part of a protection spell that keeps Gremory from killing the disciple who opens his 'cell.' Until you two came along, all the disciple had to worry about was getting his fix before the protection spell wore off. Which is why when the sacrifice couldn't be made, bad things happened—to the disciple."

"Exactly." Heads turned toward Rowan again. "And that explains the curse. It's a particularly nasty variation of a 'touch-me-not' spell. Touch-me-nots have been around for a long time. They're usually used by jilted spouses to get even with cheating partners. Normally they wear off after a period of time. But not this one. This one is different."

"It's getting stronger, isn't it?" Evan asked. Seth sat right beside him but felt like he was miles away. "We figured Longstreet meant to distract us, make us more vulnerable."

"Oh, the curse will do that—but if it isn't lifted, it will kill you," Rowan replied, and Evan wondered what the witch saw when she looked at them. Could she see the spell itself, wrapping around them like barbed wire? Or could she see the effect as it leeched away their energy?

"Explain." Sorren sounded concerned, and Evan didn't think that boded well.

"I'd need to study it to know more, but I believe the curse works on two levels," Rowan said, looking at Seth and Evan like a scientist with a puzzle. "Obviously, there's a psychological component. They're isolated, and not being able to be together will break their spirits. But I think the physical part—slowly draining their life force, is intended to provoke a confrontation."

"Longstreet wants to force us to fight him?" Seth echoed, incredulous.

"On his terms, in his timing. It's a fight to the death. Kill him, or he kills you—either way, the curse is lifted. I don't think it can be broken any other way," Rowan replied.

"How long?" Evan's voice was a croak. His mouth had gone dry, and his stomach twisted into knots.

"Days. A week at most," Rowan answered.

Seth moved close enough that their shoulders bumped. Evan wondered if it was his imagination that he felt a prickle at the contact. Would the curse escalate until any connection at all caused pain?

While the conversation went back and forth, Teag had started typing on his laptop. He looked up. "What did you say the name of the intended sacrifice was?"

"Blake Miller," Seth replied.

Teag pursed his lips and blew out a long breath. "That's not good. I'm looking at a police report that says Blake Miller from North Charleston went missing two days ago...and his mutilated body was identified this morning by family after it was found on the riverbank." He looked up. "Longstreet's already powered up. You're too late."

4

SETH

Teag's announcement made bile rise in Seth's throat. He moved around the table to stand behind Teag and looked over his shoulder, hoping that the "wrong" Blake Miller might have been the victim.

"Can you find an address for him?" Seth watched as Teag's fingers flew over the keyboard. A new screen gave a street number that matched what Seth's hacking had turned up.

"Shit," he muttered. "It's the right guy."

"There's something else," Teag said, glancing over his shoulder at him. "Blake had a younger brother who's also gone missing—no body found."

This just gets worse and worse.

Seth straightened and went back to his seat beside Evan. He thought that the last time they touched, he had felt a sting even through their clothing. If that was the case, Seth wanted to ration their remaining touches, savor them while they lasted. He couldn't bear to think about that, so he forced himself to focus on the murder.

He looked up and saw the others watching him. "Can I ask a question? And, um, don't eat me," he added, with a nervous look at Sorren.

Everyone else stifled a chuckle. Sorren rolled his eyes. "You are quite safe, I assure you," Sorren replied.

"How does a guy like Longstreet manage to fly under your radar, if you're the guardians of the city?" Seth asked, made bold by the tangle of emotions in his gut.

Cassidy cleared her throat. "It's a little more complicated than that."

"Allow me." Sorren folded his hands in front of him on the table. "The Alliance is a coalition of mortals and immortals—like the people here at the table—who do their best to get dangerous magical items out of the wrong hands and protect the world from supernatural threats. And that's where the problem arises. A dark witch like Longstreet never threatened the city or the world. A murder every twelve years—especially if the bodies aren't found—probably doesn't even show up as a pattern to the police."

"If he was smart enough not to challenge the established magical dynasties, or cause trouble here in the city, he could have easily been overlooked," Rowan added.

"You have magical dynasties?" Evan looked a bit gobsmacked.

"Charleston as a city is a bit hung up on pedigree," Cassidy replied. "Especially the old, moneyed families that have been here running the show for centuries. That goes for the mortals as well as the magical players."

"As immortals go, Longstreet isn't very old," Teag mused. "If Gremory died in 1900, then Longstreet might be at most, what, one hundred and fifty? By immortal standards, that's barely legal to drive."

Sorren laughed at that. "I wouldn't have put it that way, but Teag's right—those of us who are much older may have also overlooked him because we, mistakenly, disregarded the potential threat. Now we have a chance to fix that—with Longstreet—and by providing support to find and destroy the other disciples elsewhere."

Despite everything, the possibility of help with their quest lightened Seth's heart, just a little. "That would be great," he replied. "Thank you. Of course, Evan and I have to live through fighting this one."

"I have him." Alicia Peters had been quiet up until now. She straightened in her chair, and her eyes widened. "Blake Miller's spirit would like a word."

Seth stared at Alicia, dumbfounded. He knew his friend Simon could see and talk to ghosts, but he'd never witnessed Simon doing so. Seth had a rote magic spell that enabled him to summon ghosts, but he felt certain that Alicia's mediumship went far beyond what he could do with a memorized incantation.

"Please, let him speak," Cassidy encouraged. "We want to hear what he has to say."

The temperature in the room dropped from comfortable to cold. Seth expected the ghost to take form near where they sat. Instead, a shift came over Alicia.

"My name is Blake Miller, and I was murdered." The voice was Alicia's, and yet it wasn't. The pitch deepened; the cadence changed. Even the medium's features had a different set to them.

"Who killed you?" Cassidy asked, watching Alicia closely.

"The warlock. He put a spell on me and took me away. Please, find my brother, Logan. He's in danger."

"What kind of danger?" Teag pressed.

"The warlock saw him. Logan tried to follow the van. My killer won't give up until he finds him. I don't want Logan to die."

"Where were you killed?" Seth asked, finding his voice. The transformation that came over Alicia was incredible, and he found himself in awe of her ability.

"I don't know. He knocked me out, and when I woke up, I was in the place where he killed me. Inside a small, old building. I could hear birds...and frogs."

"Was the warlock wearing a necklace with an amulet?" Evan spoke up.

Alicia looked puzzled. "No. I didn't see anything like that. All I saw was a ring. He said a spell, and a strange light came out of nowhere, and he started to glow. I don't remember anything after that."

"If you think of something important, will you come back?" Cassidy asked. "We want to stop the man who did this from hurting anyone else."

"Yes. Just please...protect Logan. He's all alone." Alicia's voice had grown softer, and signs of strain showed in her face, as if keeping the connection with Blake's spirit had grown difficult.

"Thank you," Seth said. "We'll find him and stop the killing."

Alicia nodded and slumped in her chair, looking drained. Teag ran to the kitchen and returned with a small bottle of juice, while Cassidy and Rowan moved quickly to help Alicia sit up, and Rowan placed a hand on the medium's face.

"She's exhausted, but not harmed," Rowan said after a moment. Teag passed the juice to Cassidy, who helped to steady Alicia's hand as she drank.

"Thanks. I'm okay," Alicia said in a shaky voice. "Did Blake say anything helpful?"

Seth and Evan must have looked confused because Teag saw their expressions and answered their unspoken question. "Alicia doesn't always remember what the spirits say when she channels them," he explained. "It's really surprising that such a new ghost could even manage to manifest, let alone speak through her."

"He was driven," Alicia said. "Worried about his brother. If I hadn't let him speak, he probably would have found a way to write on the walls or something."

"I think I like him," Cassidy replied. "If he's that determined, maybe he can be of help—an inside man, so to speak."

"What do we do next?" Evan asked. Seth could see that his boyfriend looked tired, and the pain medicine for his ribs had probably worn off, given how he held himself.

"Rest, for now," Cassidy replied in a voice that didn't sound like she would take no for an answer. "You've had a very long day." She glanced at Rowan and Sorren. "I think we've got enough information to make some inquiries in our circles. Tomorrow, we start tracking Longstreet and see what we find."

"I'll see Alicia home," Rowan offered.

"And I can take Seth and Evan to their RV unless they're staying with you," Father Anne said with a look to Cassidy, who nodded. "You'll be in warded areas, no matter which you choose."

"You're very welcome to stay here," Cassidy offered.

Seth's gaze went to Evan, who shrugged. "I'd like to stay here tonight if that's okay," Evan said.

"I'll help you up the steps," Seth volunteered. He paused and turned back to the people around the table—strangers—who had nonetheless offered to help with his very dangerous quest. "Thank you all. Everything you've done and offered to do—it's a lot. And we appreciate it."

"Longstreet's overdue to be stopped," Sorren said. "We'll find him and help you break the curse."

Evan managed the stairs by himself, although Seth hovered just a step behind him. Seth hadn't been hurt as badly in the crash, but he ached all over, and the emotional impact of the day had taken a toll.

Neither of them spoke until they had shed their borrowed T-shirts and sweatpants for bed. A nightlight in the bathroom kept the unfamiliar space from being completely dark. Once they were settled in bed, Evan shifted to be able to see Seth, grunting a bit as he jostled tender ribs.

"I'm scared," Evan confessed in a voice just above a whisper.

Seth wanted to stroke his fingers across Evan's cheek, or take his hand, or kiss him senseless. The intentional cruelty of Longstreet's curse just made Seth angrier, but he knew that right now Evan needed comfort, not a vow of vengeance.

"We'll figure it out," Seth said, hoping that was true.

"What if we don't?"

"Then we go out together," Seth replied. "Believe me, babe, I want a lifetime with you. I want us to get fat and old and be sneaking dildos into our room at the nursing home."

"Now I've got that image stuck in my mind," Evan groaned. "Eww."

"What? You don't think I'll be a silver fox?" Seth asked in joking outrage.

"I'm sure you'll be a very handsome geezer."

"The dildos are for when the Viagra doesn't kick in right away," Seth said, running with the joke because it made Evan laugh. "Because I wouldn't want you to feel bad, if you couldn't, you know."

"Who says I'll be the one who can't get it up? You're older than I am."

"I'm just trying to cover all the angles because I'm that kind of caring partner," Seth joked.

"Hold me."

"Babe, I don't want to hurt you." Seth didn't care how much it stung; he'd gladly give any comfort he could to Evan. But he knew that Evan felt the pain as well when they touched.

"If I wrap up in the blanket, we'll have layers between us. I just need to feel your arms around me."

No way could Seth refuse. He waited while Evan rolled up in the blanket, and then inched backward, so his back was to Seth's chest.

"It's kind of like hugging a burrito," Seth murmured as Evan snuggled into him.

"But less messy, and I don't make you fart."

Seth appreciated the humor for the effort it required to put on a brave face. He pulled Evan close, wrapping his arms around him. He hungered for the warmth of Evan's skin, but at least they were close.

"Talk to me," Evan said, as they lay in the dark. "I know you're upset about Blake Miller being dead, and the Alliance letting Longstreet get away with everything for so long."

"Right under their noses." Seth tried not to give voice to his anger, but he knew Evan saw through the attempt. "It's like it wasn't important enough to notice all those people over the years."

"Maybe it's more like the difference between the FBI and the local cops," Evan mused. "I mean, I wish the Alliance or at least the other witches in the area had caught on, but think of how many times someone turns out to be a serial killer and their neighbors lived next door for years and never suspected."

"Maybe," Seth admitted grudgingly.

"And if you think about it, the FBI goes after certain types of criminals, but not others. So if the Alliance stops the really big world-ending kind of things, they're not chasing missing person reports."

"I guess." Seth didn't want to argue. His gripe certainly wasn't with Evan, and he wasn't sure it was actually with Cassidy or her Alliance friends. It just seemed like such a missed opportunity.

"I hope we can find Blake's brother," Evan murmured. "We don't know whether Longstreet took him as a backup plan, or whether he's in hiding."

"Blake's ghost seemed to be pretty sure Logan was in danger," Seth replied. "I'd feel like I didn't let Blake down completely if we can save Logan."

"You didn't let him down at all," Evan countered. "It's not your fault."

"Feels like it."

"Well, it's not." Evan was quiet for a while, and Seth fancied that he could feel the beat of his lover's heart, even through the blankets.

"Why would someone want to be immortal?" Evan asked when Seth had almost been sure he was asleep.

"Because they're scared of dying? Or they think they'll go to hell for what they've done?"

Evan started to shake his head and then thought better of it. "Is that enough to want to live forever?"

"I can't say I ever thought about it," Seth admitted. "Why?"

"It just seems like the disciples go through an awful lot to stay immortal. Especially now that we know they're using Gremory like some weird soul-battery."

"Yeah, I didn't see that coming."

"I mean, when I think about what I want to do, just in a normal life-span, it's things like seeing the world and reading books, going to concerts and getting a dog. Bucket list stuff. But the disciples have had almost two lifespans already, and people like Sorren have had even more. How many times can you be a tourist?"

"I guess things would change over time, and it wouldn't be the same as when you saw it the first time." Seth had never thought about what the disciples might want out of their longer lives, aside from even more time.

"But we don't know if the disciples could travel that far," Evan pointed out. "Their power seems to be connected to where they make their sacrifices, so maybe they can. So...do they read a lot? Or is living longer just another way to make even more money?"

Seth grimaced, even though Evan couldn't see his expression. "I guess it is for some people. I mean, billionaires want to be trillionaires, right? Too much is not enough?"

"I just wondered if we're missing something that might be important for figuring out how to find Longstreet."

"It sounded to me like he'd already figured out how to bring us to him." Which brought them back to the whole curse thing again.

"I'm not sorry," Evan said, resolve firm in his quiet voice. "About any of it. If you hadn't saved me, I'd already be dead. This whole year we've had together, all the things we've done...loving you. I'm not saying that I'm ready to die—because I'm not—but if we do, I wouldn't trade what we've had for the world."

Seth had to swallow hard to find his voice. The darkness gave the conversation a confessional feel, secrets traded in the night. He was glad Evan couldn't see the tears on his cheeks. "I'm not giving up, babe. Not until the last breath. So don't you give up. We'll find a way out."

"I believe you," Evan murmured. "And I believe in us. Simon believes Cassidy and her crew can help. That's a whole lot of believing. But it doesn't make it any less scary."

Seth took a chance and pressed his lips lightly against Evan's hair, grateful to escape with only a slight sting. "It's okay to be scared. You'd have to be crazy not to be. Doesn't mean we won't kick Longstreet's ass."

Evan gave a final wiggle, pressing against Seth as tightly as the blanket allowed. "I love you," he whispered.

"Love you, too." Evan finally gave in to the pain medication and his exhausted body. Seth thought fatigue would make sleep come quickly, but he lay awake for a long time, listening to Evan breathe, struggling with the fears he couldn't say out loud.

THE NEXT MORNING, SETH WOKE SLOWLY. HE WATCHED EVAN SLEEP AND debated trying to doze longer himself, until he remembered that the curse meant time was limited. Seth moved carefully so as not to wake

Evan, then dressed and headed downstairs. He had expected to find the house empty, with Cassidy at her shop, Trifles and Folly. Instead, Cassidy and a man Seth didn't recognize were in the kitchen cooking pancakes and bacon, while Teag had a tall mug of coffee and his laptop at the dining room table.

"Um…good morning?" Seth said, still groggy.

"Hi, Seth! Come get coffee. We'll have breakfast ready in a few minutes," Cassidy called. "I'll save some back for when Even comes down." Seth followed the aromas into the kitchen, and the man he didn't know handed him a mug.

"I'm Kell Winston. Cassidy's boyfriend. Videographer by day, paranormal investigator and Alliance apprentice by night."

Seth shook hands. "Seth Tanner. Witch hunter and hacker. Pleased to meet you." He poured a cup of coffee, dumped extra sugar in it, and ambled in to take a seat at the dining room table across from Teag.

"You feeling any better?" Teag asked, looking up.

"I've felt worse, so there's that," Seth replied. "Evan's still sleeping. I figured he needed it. I woke him up often, because of the concussion." He noticed a glint of metal when Teag reached for his cup. "Is that an engagement ring?"

Teag grinned. "Yep. Best birthday present ever. And come Christmas, Anthony and I are going to England to stay in a real castle to celebrate!"

"Congratulations," Seth replied, genuinely happy for his friend. *Will Evan and I have a chance to get engaged? Will we live long enough to get married?* His worry overshadowed the joy he felt for Teag and Anthony.

"I can't believe after all the times we've talked on the phone that you and Evan are here in Charleston," Teag added, staring at his screen as he typed.

"It's nice to meet you and Cassidy and everyone in person," Seth agreed. "But don't you guys need to be at the store?"

Teag chuckled. "Our assistant, Maggie, is covering for us. She's a godsend. And yes, she knows about our 'other' job. So does Anthony. He's off doing lawyer stuff—a continuing ed retreat—so I figured it made the most sense for me to hang out here and help work your case." He paused to take a long gulp of his coffee. "We've had some other problems going on that I need to research anyhow."

Seth savored a mouthful of coffee before he answered. "What kind of problems?" He needed something to take his mind off curses and witch-disciples for a few minutes.

"As cities go, Charleston has a relatively low crime rate," Teag replied. "The cops keep a close eye on things since tourists want to feel safe. But the supernatural community polices its own pretty strictly— obviously, with some lapses," he added, mindful of Longstreet's subterfuge. "That's especially true when disagreements between different groups get ugly. Lately, there've been some issues."

They paused when Kell and Cassidy called for them to fill plates in the kitchen, and returned with pancakes and bacon that made Seth's mouth water.

"I mentioned last night that Charleston can be a bit preoccupied with social status," Cassidy said, then took a bite of a pancake covered with butter and syrup. "It goes with having a lot of old families with old money—and old magic. Magical dynasties like the Pendlewoods and the Etheridges are very influential, and tend to be pretty exclusive."

"What Cassidy is saying, very politely, is that the magical one-percent are just as snooty as their non-magical counterparts," Teag jumped in. "And that tends to rankle some residents who have less powerful talents or aren't as well-connected. So from time to time, there are flare-ups."

"I'm having difficulty picturing a magical protest march," Seth admitted.

"Oh, nothing that visible," Cassidy said. "More like the have-nots go out of their way to annoy the crap out of the haves. And maybe cause some minor magical vandalism."

"But over the last year, it's been worse than usual," Teag added, after swallowing a big bite of pancake. "The vandalism has been nastier, the magic is darker, and we aren't sure how the low-level witches are pulling it off."

"Outside agitators?" Seth asked.

"That's what we've been trying to find out," Cassidy replied, making short work of her breakfast. Kell offered to carry her empty plate out to the kitchen and refill her coffee, and she thanked him with a quick kiss. They were so stinkin' cute together, and their casual contact made Seth ache for Evan's touch even more.

"It makes a difference whether someone from outside Charleston is trying to set supernatural factions against each other, or whether it's an internal fight for more inclusion," Teag said.

"Sorry to hear there's trouble in paradise."

Cassidy shrugged. "Maybe not exactly paradise, but it's in everyone's best interest to keep tempers cool—especially when magic's involved."

"Some of the issue is that powerful dark magic relics and cursed objects have been finding their way into the hands of what are, for lack of a better term, witchy street gangs," Teag added. "So are spells that no one in the gang had the experience to write. That lets the gangs cause more dangerous trouble."

"So you've got a dark magic arms dealer out there somewhere," Seth summarized.

"That's what we suspect. And since the gangs have gotten worse, there's also been an uptick in people going missing. They aren't showing up dead like Blake Miller. We don't know what that means— or if it's related to Longstreet—but since it's happening at the same time, we don't think it's a coincidence," Teag replied.

Seth had finished the food on his plate. As good as it tasted, the pancakes felt like a rock in his stomach. He needed to figure out how to beat Longstreet at his own game before he and Evan ran out of time.

"I want to go to the places Evan and I identified as belonging to Longstreet and his past identities—his old homes," Seth said. "Maybe I can pick up a clue to help us find him."

"How about I go with you?" Teag offered. "I've got more defensive magic, plus I know the area. And you need transportation."

"What about me? I'm not going to just sit on the couch and wait for the curse to kill me."

They looked up to see Evan, still sleep-rumpled, at the bottom of the steps. Seth got up to greet him and made do with an air kiss by Evan's cheek. "Hey," Seth said quietly. "I figured you needed your rest. Go take my chair, and I'll get you some breakfast."

Evan seemed to be moving a little better today, Seth noticed as he went to the kitchen to fix a plate. He brought it and a cup of coffee back for his boyfriend, who thanked him with a longing look.

Not being able to touch each other sucked.

"I didn't know how you were going to feel today, so I didn't want to drag you around the city," Seth answered Evan's original question.

"We don't have time to waste. We need to find that bastard and break the curse."

"I have an idea." They all looked to Cassidy. "What if Evan and I go over to the St. Expeditus safe house compound and talk to Father Anne and some of her colleagues, see what they make of the whole witch-disciple thing? They might have some lore that would be helpful. And that way, Evan could also get anything you both might need from your RV. You're welcome to stay here as long as you want."

Evan considered the suggestion. Seth knew his partner hated being sidelined. "Do you really think they might be able to help?"

Cassidy nodded. "I do. There are different magical factions in the city—Rowan's coven, the old families, the St. Expeditus people, the Alliance, the shifters, and a few more."

"Other vampires?" Seth couldn't help being curious.

"No. Sorren made it clear a long time ago that Charleston was his to protect. He's rather territorial." Teag's tone made Seth suspect that there was a long story for another day.

"And of course, there are the ghosts," Kell spoke up. "After all, Charleston's one of the most haunted cities in North America, and our ghosts definitely have their own opinions about the way things should be done."

"What we want to avoid are the outside groups like C.H.A.R.O.N. getting involved," Cassidy said. "There are paramilitary groups from the government and the Vatican that try to step in and take over. We really don't want to attract their attention."

"We heard a little about those groups when we worked with Travis and Brent in Pittsburgh," Evan replied. "I'm all for steering clear."

"Which means we have to clean up our own messes." Teag gestured for Seth to come around the table so he could see the laptop screen. "Do you know the addresses of the places you want to go?"

Seth pulled out his phone and opened a document. "Yeah. Here's the list, and the names the properties were bought under. Longstreet's old aliases." He handed the phone over, and Teag glanced over the information.

"Well lookie here," Teag murmured, glancing up with a glint in his eyes. "Two of these properties match ones we tagged for a connection to the black-market relic trade."

He looked back to Seth. "A friend of ours, Erik Mitchell, used to help museums catch art thieves and track down cultural items that had been misappropriated. He's out of that business—runs a store a lot like Cassidy's up in Cape May now—but he still keeps his ear to the ground. Erik thought that some 'hot' occult relics may have passed through Charleston recently."

"We just wrapped up a situation with stolen magical objects— Simon and Erik helped a lot with that one." Cassidy picked up the story. "And I know Seth did some hacking for us on that, too. At first we thought the new pieces Erik was talking about were part of the cargo that hadn't been gathered up. But they weren't. So…who's procuring dangerous magical items and providing them to the witchy gangs?"

Evan and Seth exchanged a glance. "Longstreet's been in Charleston for over a hundred years, but from what you and Sorren said, he's never been part of the inner circle," Evan mused. "That kept him off the Alliance's radar, but I can't imagine he liked being an outsider."

"You think there's a connection?" Cassidy asked.

"Maybe. I got to thinking last night about what someone who was immortal would do with all that time," Evan said. Seth moved to stand behind him, making do with putting his hand on the back of his chair, wishing for more. "What if Longstreet resents the witch dynasties and old families? He probably knows that they'd never accept him. Maybe a guy like him enjoys supplying the rabble-rousers to stick it to the elites."

Teag nodded. "It's possible. And if he plays arms dealer, he might figure the Alliance wouldn't trace the weaponized relics back to him. Maybe he does this kind of thing in other cities, too, and is just getting cocky, thinking we won't notice."

Cassidy shrugged. "It's as good a theory as we've had. Definitely worth looking into."

"Maybe we can float that by Father Anne and her friends when we go over," Evan added, and Seth thought his boyfriend perked up a bit with the thought he could do something useful.

"I'll text Rowan and Sorren, and see if they think a connection is possible. We'd been lacking a motive—other than money or undercutting the status quo—but Longstreet makes an interesting suspect," Teag agreed.

"Sounds like a plan," Cassidy said.

"Have you heard anything about the truck?" Seth asked.

Teag nodded. "Our friend sent the estimate over this morning." He motioned Seth over to look at an email.

Seth stared at him, confused. "I don't understand. It should be much more—I was honestly afraid the truck would be totaled."

Teag grinned. "Told you we had connections. For whatever isn't covered by insurance, our friend offered to just charge for the parts, not the labor. I, uh, took the liberty of telling him to get started. He should have it done in a few days."

"Wow. I mean, thank you," Seth said, surprised and grateful for the unexpected generosity. "Oh, can you ask him to keep an eye out for Evan's phone?"

"He dropped it by this morning," Cassidy said. "It might not have a charge, but it didn't look damaged. She looked to Evan. "I'm ready to go whenever you are."

"Give me a chance to wash up, and I'm good to go," Evan replied. He looked to Seth. "Be careful."

"You, too," Seth replied, stepping in close for a goodbye kiss before he remembered, just in time, and drew back. He saw longing and frustration in Evan's eyes and felt the same. "I'll see you back here tonight."

Seth forced himself to turn away and join Teag, who had grabbed his keys and stood near the door. "Come on," he said to Teag. "We've got a witch to hunt."

5

EVAN

"When you said 'safe house,' I wasn't sure what to expect. It wasn't...this." Evan got out of Cassidy's SUV and put his hands on his hips, surveying the green expanse of lawn and the spreading canopy of old live oaks. A large, white two-story wooden house sat at the end of a long lane, with broad porches that encircled it on both levels.

"It looks more like a plantation, only not quite as fancy as you see in the movies," he added.

"The land has been in the Dawson family for a very long time," Cassidy told him as they walked toward the grand house. She casually matched her speed to his, and Evan knew she was accommodating his injuries. "It's been a lot of things over the years—a rice plantation, a hospital during the Civil War, and more recently, a spiritualist retreat center. The last owner willed it to the St. Expeditus Society, and they turned it into a safe house, a training center, and an archive."

"What kind of archive?" The idea of an arcane library caught Evan's attention. "Do you think it might have something that would help us break the curse?"

"It can't hurt to ask—although I imagine Father Anne already has people looking into it." Cassidy pointed toward a shady area beneath a grove of trees. "Is that your RV?"

The relief that flooded through him at the sight of the home he shared with Seth took Evan by surprise. Although he had lived in several apartments over the years, the RV was the first real *home* he'd had since his parents had kicked him out.

"It doesn't look damaged," he said, as he and Cassidy walked in a slow circle around the fifth-wheeler. "At least there's that." With so many things gone wrong, Evan was thankful for anything going their way. "And Seth's bike is okay." He gave the black Hayabusa motorcycle on the lift at the back of the RV a careful once-over.

"Father Anne assured me that she's had people go over it carefully to make sure there aren't any nasty surprises like hex bags or runes," Cassidy told him. "If they've allowed it inside their compound, it's safe."

"Thank you," Evan said, feeling a bit more hopeful. "Having it back means a lot."

"Do you want to go in now and check things over, or stop on our way out so you can grab clothing and anything else you need?" Cassidy asked. "That is, unless you and Seth want to stay in the RV?"

"We don't want to inconvenience you." As lovely as the compound was, Evan knew it meant being farther from town, and without the Silverado, investigating would be difficult enough.

"It's no inconvenience. I've got plenty of room. But it's entirely up to you and Seth."

"I think we'd like to stay with you for now, if that's okay?"

Cassidy smiled. "That's entirely all right. We'll stop back at the RV before we leave. Let's go inside. They're expecting us."

Evan followed her up the broad front steps. The door swung open as they approached, and Father Anne met them in the entranceway. "Welcome! Come on in. I've got some folks who are looking forward to meeting you."

She led the way to what might have once been a formal dining room but now looked like it served as a strategy center. Three strangers were already waiting for them.

"Cassidy and Evan, I'd like you to meet Father Barbara, Father Clemons, and Beck Pendlewood," Father Anne said.

Evan startled at the last name. "Pendlewood? Isn't that one of the witch dynasties?" He'd gotten the impression from their earlier discussion that the Alliance and the dynasties weren't exactly on the same page.

Beck chuckled ruefully. "A rather defunct dynasty. Which is a good thing. I'm the last direct Pendlewood heir, and I gave up my magic along with the demon box curse. A good trade, if you ask me." Beck was in his early thirties, with dark hair and brown eyes. He wore a T-shirt and jeans, both of which Evan thought looked expensive but well-worn.

Beck was the first to come around the table to shake hands. Father Barbara was next, a tall, sharp-featured woman with short gray hair and a no-nonsense demeanor. By comparison, Father Clemons reminded Evan of the depictions he had seen of Robin Hood's Friar Tuck, round-faced and good-natured.

"Father Barbara has a unique skill set," Father Anne continued. "Before she joined the Episcopalian priesthood, she was an analyst with the CIA. The St. Expeditus Society has found her talents to be very useful."

Evan had absolutely no idea how to read the older woman's expression, thin lips pressed together in a line, and light blue eyes that made him feel like a rabbit with a hawk. Her slightly-boned hand was ice cold, with a strong grip.

"Father Clemons left the Catholic Church and the Sinistram, and brings his extensive knowledge about the occult to help the Society," Father Anne added.

Father Clemons beamed at Evan and clasped both of his meaty hands around Evan's. "It's good to meet you, m' boy. Travis Dominick speaks well of you, and that's all the endorsement I need!"

Evan found himself surprised again at just how small the shadowy world of supernatural hunters really was. "Um, thanks. Seth and I really appreciated everything Travis and Brent did to help us."

An assistant brought in a tray with a coffee pot, cups, cream, and sugar and placed it on the table. "To get started, grab some coffee if you'd like and let's have Evan give us a recap of the Longstreet situation," Father Anne said.

Evan wasn't sure what coffee did for concussions, but he needed the warm cup in his hands to steady himself. He accepted the steaming mug from Cassidy with a grateful smile and then gave an overview of the witch-disciple problem, including the insights gained from the previous night.

"We believe Michael Longstreet is the current ID of the witch-disciple originally known as Albert Mosby," Evan concluded. "And we think he's laid a curse on Seth and me to stop us before we can stop him."

Beck canted his head to one side. "Longstreet? Do you know his other recent names?"

"Like the other witch-disciples, he changed his name roughly every twenty years. Before he was Longstreet, he called himself Braxton Pickett. Seems he had a fondness for Confederate generals." Evan listed off the other names they had found as the researchers took notes.

"I recognize some of those names." Beck leaned forward as the others looked to him. "My father sent me away from the rest of the Pendlewoods when I was twelve in hopes that I'd outrun the family curse. But before he did that, I overheard a lot of conversations. I guess no one figured I'd remember, or understand."

"Your family mentioned Longstreet?" Evan looked up; hopeful Beck's memories might provide a clue.

"Both Longstreet and Pickett, but I didn't know they were the same person," Beck replied.

Evan suspected there was a long story associated with why the scion of a powerful supernatural dynasty was present at a safe house.

"They knew about Longstreet, but they dismissed him as an unimportant social climber," Beck added, looking chagrined at the pretentiousness. "The phrase that sticks in my mind is 'no talent Johnny-come-lately,' which is very much something my uncle would have said. The point is, if the Pendlewoods knew of Longstreet, you can bet the Etheridges and the other old families did, too."

"Meaning that they would have ignored him?" Evan asked. His own family had been solidly middle class. Jockeying for social position hadn't been part of his upbringing.

"Socially? Yes. But they'd have kept an eye on him if they thought he could be trouble, and no matter how much disdain they had for him, it wouldn't have stopped them from using him if he could benefit them." Beck's cheeks reddened, and Evan had the sense that the other man felt ashamed of his family's actions.

"That's a very helpful insight," Father Clemons remarked. "It wouldn't be the first time we've seen an ambitious witch decide to upend the established order."

"Do you know anything about his original identity, this Albert Mosby?" Father Barbara asked, eyes narrowing, which told Evan she was processing the information.

"Not much. From what Seth and I could find searching the land records, his family had a small plantation and lost everything in the Civil War."

"Interesting," she said. "So a family of lesser magical talent lost their position, while the old families managed to ride out the war and come out ahead."

"By blockade running, smuggling weapons, and selling magic to the highest bidder—on both sides," Beck objected.

Sounds like there was no love lost between Beck and his relatives. Maybe that explains why he's here.

"Which is exactly what we're thinking Mosby...Longstreet...might be doing now, supplying the witch gangs to cause trouble for the old families," Cassidy said, excitement sparkling in her eyes. "Maybe he learned by example."

Father Barbara arched an eyebrow. "Perhaps. If so, then I doubt after a century he intends to supplant the established forces. But he may see gain to be made by embarrassing them or undercutting their power."

"Or maybe he just wants to stick it to the man." Father Clemons leaned back and folded his hands on his sizable belly. "The question for me boils down to whether Longstreet is acting on his own, or whether he's being paid by or manipulated by another force to be an agent of chaos." He took an inelegant gulp of his coffee, which earned him a fondly reproving glance from his colleagues.

"Back in my Sinistram days, it wasn't unknown for the Vatican—or the government—to do something similar to keep the old families from getting too powerful. We weren't looking to get rid of them, because they were a bulwark against loose cannons like the witch gangs," Father Clemons went on. "Just to keep them on their toes, remind them not to get too comfortable."

"You think the Sinistram is connected to Longstreet?" Father Anne didn't hide her surprise.

Father Clemons frowned. "No. Sacrificing descendants to remain immortal isn't their style. But if he's behind running relics and selling spells? He might be getting used without his knowledge. I still have some contacts. Let me put out a few feelers." The crafty light in the man's eyes seemed at odds with his jolly demeanor.

"Knowing the other names this Longstreet has used is a starting point," Father Barbara said. "The Society has a long memory."

Evan wrote the names on the whiteboard, and the others checked the spelling in their notes. "Right now, what would help Seth and me the most is finding Longstreet's anchor, the 'battery' he uses to store extra magic. Especially since he's just powered up with a sacrifice, he's going to be harder than usual to kill. If we can find his anchor, we can weaken him, at least to a degree."

"I suspect that his anchor is more than just a battery," Father Barbara replied. "While it may help him store magic, my guess is that it also plays a part in keeping Rhyfel Gremory's soul trapped in the pocket dimension they've constructed for his prison. So every anchor you've destroyed also loosens their hold on the spirit they're sucking dry to maintain their immortality."

Evan's head came up sharply. "Really? What happens if we destroy all of them? Does Gremory go off into the ether—or come back looking for vengeance?"

"Since you've destroyed Gremory's captors along with their anchors, we can hope he has no reason to return," Father Clemons replied.

"But that's another reason for Longstreet to want to stop Seth and Evan," Cassidy said, making eye contact with Evan as she spoke. "Because they're putting the entire setup at risk."

If he didn't have a strong enough reason to kill us before, he does now.

"What can we do about it?" Evan's nerves were at the breaking point, between the curse, the pain from his ribs, a throbbing headache, and a souped-up warlock who wanted to kill them. He had no more fucks left to give. "I don't know if Seth and I can take down a witch-disciple after he's leveled up. We'll need help."

"We intend to protect you while we gather information so we can launch the best attack possible," Father Anne said.

"We're only going to get one shot," Father Clemons added. "Especially since Longstreet knows you're coming after him, and he may have friends we don't know about yet. But thanks to you and your partner, we've got him in our sights."

Evan practically bit his tongue in frustration. While the others had time to strategize, the clock was ticking for Seth and him.

"Just remember, Longstreet's curse means Seth and Evan don't have time to waste," Cassidy cautioned. Evan could have cheered.

"We will not forget," Father Barbara replied.

A knock at the door had heads turning. Rowan and a dark-skinned older woman entered.

"Rowan, Mrs. Teller. I think you know everyone here," Father Anne greeted them.

"I haven't met this young man," Mrs. Teller said, eyeing Evan.

"Evan Malone, ma'am," he answered.

"If we're done strategizing, I asked Rowan and Mrs. Teller to see what they made of the curse and perhaps do a bit more to speed Evan's healing," Father Anne said.

Beck and the other two Society members rose and gathered their things, leaving them alone with the newcomers.

More healing? Evan wondered. His memories of that first night at Cassidy's house weren't clear.

"Can you see it?" Rowan asked the older woman.

Mrs. Teller walked closer to Evan, moving around him slowly. "Oh yes. Like briars. That's dark magic, no doubt about it."

"Can you do...something?" Evan asked, making no attempt to hide the pleading in his eyes.

Mrs. Teller laid a hand on his shoulder. "Yes, but maybe not quite what you're thinking. I can't lift it. No one can but the witch who laid it on you, by intent or dying. But the stronger you are, the harder you are to kill, isn't that true?" He saw a glimmer of defiance in her dark eyes that gave him hope.

"Anything," Evan said. "Just help me be able to stand with Seth and take on Longstreet when the time comes."

Cassidy stepped back to give Rowan and Mrs. Teller access, but she stayed in the room, for which Evan was grateful.

"What did you mean, 'more' healing?" he asked as the two women scrutinized him.

"I used my magic to speed your healing a bit," Rowan explained. "I'm not a healer, and I prefer not to use magic to do the body's work for it unless it's an emergency. But a little nudge now and again doesn't hurt."

Evan frowned. "Why not just use magic to heal it all?"

"The body's a complicated machine," Mrs. Teller replied. "It does best when it heals itself. Interfering can make other things go wrong. But sometimes there's just no choice."

"Are you part of Rowan's coven?" Evan asked.

Mrs. Teller laughed, a deep, rich sound. The look that passed between her and Rowan suggested a private joke. "Oh no, boy. I'm a root woman. Hoodoo. Whole different kind of magic. But sometimes a different path is what's needed."

Rowan laid a hand on Evan's shoulder. "I'm not going to try to heal your ribs completely. But I can help some, and that should ease the pain, let you sleep better. Which lets the body do its own work."

"If I live long enough." Evan could almost imagine hearing the curse count down the hours of his life.

"That's enough of that." Mrs. Teller gave him a light smack on the shoulder. "All the healing in the world won't help if you go digging your own grave."

"Let me see." Rowan's voice drifted off, and Evan felt warmth diffuse through his body. Moments later, he swore it was easier to take a breath and move in his chair without pain.

"My turn." Mrs. Teller set her hand on his other shoulder and shut her eyes. Her lips moved silently, and her face took on an expression of rapt attention. When she opened her eyes, she looked at Evan with concern.

"I did what I could to ease the grip of the curse for now," she said. "I brought mojo bags for you and Seth, and a specially-made uncrossing powder I want both of you to use when you bathe. It's not a fix—just a way to buy a little time."

"Thank you," Evan told them. "We're both grateful for your help."

"We might not be able to lift the curse itself, but we're looking for ways to find the bastard who set it on you," Mrs. Teller told him with a stubborn set to her jaw. "I've got no patience with people who use magic like that."

"Magic leaves traces," Rowan replied, looking bemused at Mrs. Teller's language. "Now that we know his 'signature,' we're going to hunt him. I know it's hard to be patient, but remember that Longstreet put the curse on you to force your hand and set the timetable. If you allow that, it's to his advantage."

Evan nodded. "I'm trying to remember."

Once they left, only Cassidy remained. "Let's go get your things from the RV. Normally, I'd offer to stop for lunch somewhere, but given the circumstances I think you're safer if we go straight home."

"On top of everything else, that damn warlock is making me miss out on Charleston's food," Evan grumbled.

Cassidy laughed. "Once we're finished with him, Teag and I will take you and Seth on a foodie tour you won't forget. I promise."

"Didn't you say something about an archive? I know Father Anne and the others have probably looked, but maybe I'll see something they didn't since we've been going after the disciples for a while now." If there was a chance that Evan could do something helpful to stop the curse and bring down Longstreet, he was willing to try.

"Sure. Let me see how we get access." Cassidy stepped out for a few minutes, then returned with Father Anne, who led them to a large upstairs room.

"Take your time," Father Anne told them. "You can't remove anything, but you can photograph whatever you find that's interesting. Just, obviously, don't post it anywhere." She headed for the door and then turned. "In case you're hungry, there are sandwiches, drinks, and snacks in the kitchen. Help yourselves."

Evan looked to Cassidy. "Do you mind? I'm keeping you from doing your own stuff."

"Maggie's got the store covered—and it's warded, so she's safe. So is her house," she added before Evan could ask. "Teag's off with Seth, and we all want to get this settled as quickly as possible. So just let me know how I can help."

They stopped in the kitchen for a quick lunch and then headed back to the archive.

"When Seth and I worked the last two cases, we focused on property each witch-disciple owned in his various personas, and places near the city that he might have been associated with where he either might have made the sacrifices, hidden his anchor, or buried the bodies," Evan said. "Seth and Teag are looking at the places Longstreet used to live."

He pulled up a document on his phone and handed it to her. "That's the list of places we thought might be important and a list of the names he's used. So we're looking for anything that might relate to those things, as well as curse breaking."

"You know, Mrs. Morrissey at the Historical Archive might be able to help us with some of this," Cassidy said after they had spent two hours paging through old volumes.

Evan sat back and ran a hand through his hair. "It would help if I had a clear idea of what I'm looking for. It's more of an 'I'll know it when I see it' kind of thing."

"Tell me how it worked for you before." Cassidy turned to look at him, closing the book she'd been scanning.

"We looked for ruins or abandoned buildings, usually where the disciple had worked. At least the first two disciples seemed to stick with familiar locations. Since the places weren't being used anymore, there wasn't any reason for people to be near them," Evan replied.

"We've found the anchors hidden in those places, and gotten clues from the ghosts of people they killed, who must have just gotten in the way," he continued. "But the more I look into the locations for Longstreet, it just doesn't seem like they'd be a fit. The most likely one is the old Santee Lumber Company, in what used to be Ferguson—but it's underwater, flooded when they built Lake Marion."

"I've seen video from people who go out there to explore," Cassidy said. "There's not much left above the surface of the lake, and I don't think Longstreet's going to go scuba diving to make his sacrifices. There are also enough people who go out there, so I don't think much would stay hidden for long."

"That's what I mean," Evan replied, utterly frustrated. "This guy seems to flip the script on everything. If Seth and Teag don't have any better luck, we're going to be in trouble."

"Don't give up yet," Cassidy said. "Ruling things out is still progress. Longstreet might have been more savvy than some of his fellow witch-disciples, especially if he originally came from a wealthy family."

"The disciples so far had all worked for other companies, even the one who was a doctor. Everything we could find seemed to point to Longstreet being in business for himself throughout the years. We just weren't sure exactly what his business was."

"Maybe that's the clue," Cassidy said. She checked the time. "It's still early. Let's go by the Archive. I can introduce you to Mrs. Morrissey, and you can give her Longstreet's aliases. She might have records that aren't online that could help figure out what he's done for a living all these years."

Evan frowned, worried. "Do you think that's safe?"

Cassidy shrugged. "Not completely. But much safer than a busy restaurant. There aren't likely to be many people at the Archive at this time of day. I think it's worth the chance. And before we leave, I'll mention it to Father Anne, too. That way they can look for those connections as well."

"Thank you." Evan could hear the tiredness in his own voice, and he felt sure he looked worn out from the after-effects of the crash as well as the drain of Longstreet's spell.

They walked back to the RV together, and Evan unlocked the door, motioning for Cassidy to come inside.

"This is nice." Cassidy looked around. The slides that expanded the dining area and living room were pulled in for travel, which made the main space seem smaller than usual.

"It's very comfortable," Evan replied, feeling better just being home. "When we park, we can move parts of both sides out so that there's more elbow room. There's even an electric fireplace." He started to move through the space, gathering their ebook readers and a few other items that would make their stay at Cassidy's easier.

"Seth's parents were going to take a grand trip when they retired," Evan told her. "And then…"

"Yeah. That's rough," Cassidy agreed.

"You can have a seat if you'd like," Evan offered. "I'm going to go get some clothes out of the bedroom, and I'll be right back."

He dodged into the bedroom, grabbing a duffle bag, and began to stuff shirts, pants, briefs, and socks into it for both him and Seth, enough for several days. Evan felt close to overwhelmed, but he tried to tell himself that if he just kept moving, he could handle it. He changed out of his borrowed sweats, shoved them in the bag, and pulled on a pair of his own jeans.

He held it together until he went into the kitchen. A photograph of him with Seth against the backdrop of the Blue Ridge Mountains lay on the floor, its glass cracked, likely knocked from the counter by the jolt of the collision.

Tears sprang to his eyes, and Evan stifled a sob as he picked up the broken frame. *I'm being stupid. It's just a photo in a cheap frame. It can be replaced.*

But it wasn't just the shattered glass. Everything seemed to hit him at once: the crash, the hospital, Longstreet's curse, not being able to touch Seth, and the reality of a magical death sentence.

Evan drew in a shaky breath and leaned over, planting his hands on the counter and letting his head hang down as he struggled for control.

He heard Cassidy come up behind him. She laid a hand on his back. "I can't imagine how hard this is on you and Seth. You've been thrown into this whole supernatural thing head-first, and then the accident and everything. It's okay to be overwhelmed."

Evan squeezed his eyes shut, but the tears still escaped. He didn't mind crying in front of Seth, but Cassidy was almost a stranger, and Evan didn't want her to think him weak.

"It's all just been so fast," he said, so quietly he wasn't sure she could even hear him. "Not even an entire year that Seth and I've been together, and so much has happened. The whole world turned inside-out."

He shuddered with the effort to regain control. "It's fucking terrifying, going up against the disciples. But we were doing a good thing, saving people, stopping killers. And I told myself that one day it would be over, and we could be normal again. But now, if we can't get to Longstreet before he gets to us, there won't be a 'later.' And even if there is, I don't think we can ever be normal again."

Cassidy's hand rubbed circles between his shoulder blades. "You can't unsee what you learn in 'the life.' You see things and know things that regular people would never believe, and they sleep better because of that. We take the hits so they can be blissfully unaware. And it's hard. But you and Seth aren't alone. I realize that you don't know us well, but when the chips are down, I'd bet on our group every time."

Evan nodded miserably, wishing he could be more butch and failing completely. He sniffed back tears, and Cassidy stepped away for a moment, only to return and shove a handful of tissues where he could reach them. Thankfully, she stayed behind him, where she couldn't see his face. Evan knew what he looked like when he ugly cried.

"I keep thinking, what if we die and I never get to touch Seth again? I miss that so much, and it's not even two days." He snorted again, and dabbed at his eyes with the tissues, knowing there would be no hiding the blotches he always got when he cried hard. Even dousing his face in ice water wouldn't help. "I just want to hold his hand. And I can't."

"We're going to beat Longstreet," Cassidy said in a low voice filled with lethal intent. "We'll destroy him and his curse and his psycho ritual. You'll be able to be with Seth again. Just don't give up."

Giving up was never really an option. Evan knew that. He'd reached the end of his rope for keeping his emotions in check, but that just hardened his resolve to find the fucking son of a bitch responsible and make him pay for all of it—Blake Miller's death, a century of murders, the curse, and whatever else he'd done. Saving Blake's brother, Logan, that was another reason to keep going. Anger was all

Evan had left, and he let it flow through him, drying his tears and slowing his rapid breaths.

I'm not giving up, Seth. I won't go down without a fight. And if that warlock bastard thinks he's broken us, he's got another thing coming. This isn't over—not by a long shot.

∾

Cassidy drove from the safe house compound into Charleston's Historic District and parked near a stately old house in a neighborhood of beautifully restored homes. A sign on the wrought iron fence confirmed that they were in the right place.

The interior looked just as elegant as the outside, and Evan worried that his jeans and T-shirt weren't appropriate. Cassidy bumped his arm with her elbow and gave him a reassuring smile.

"It's okay. The Historical Archive is open to the public, and so street clothes are welcome. You'll find this is a different kind of 'archive' than the one we were just at. A lot of local families have willed journals, diaries, and business documents to the organization, to preserve a side of history that doesn't usually show up in a regular museum."

No one sat behind the reception desk, but Cassidy knew where to go and gestured for Evan to follow her back a hallway. Evan noted the oil portraits and landscapes adorning the walls, and the vintage Oriental carpet runner, and figured that the Archive was well-funded.

Cassidy stopped at an open door and knocked on the doorframe before poking her head around. "Mrs. Morrissey?"

"Cassidy! What a wonderful surprise." An impeccably dressed woman in her later years rose from behind an antique desk and came to welcome Cassidy with a hug and an air kiss to one cheek. Evan didn't know much about fashion, but he felt certain that the older woman's jewelry was real and that her knit suit was expensive.

"This is my friend, Evan Malone," Cassidy introduced him. "Evan, this is Mrs. Benjamin Morrissey, the Archive director."

Mrs. Morrissey's handshake was firm and businesslike, and she looked at Evan with curiosity. "What brings you here out of the blue,

Cassidy? When it's a social call, you bring me coffee," she added with a wink.

"Busted!" Cassidy replied. "Evan is visiting from out of town, and we're trying to research some provenance. He's come up dry online, but we thought maybe the resources here might be more helpful."

"This has something to do with the store?" Mrs. Morrissey raised an eyebrow. Evan wondered if she knew or suspected what Trifles and Folly really entailed.

"Yes, and we've got a time crunch."

"That's not a problem." Mrs. Morrissey went to her desk and used the phone to call someone to her office. A few minutes later, a fresh-faced young woman appeared in the doorway.

"This is Emily, one of our interns. She's an excellent researcher, and I'll make your project her top priority. Just tell her what you need, and I'll call you when it's done."

Cassidy and Evan thanked both Emily and Mrs. Morrissey, and Evan shared the list of Longstreet's past identities. "We believe these men were business owners of some kind, during the dates marked, but we can't confirm the name or type of companies or their locations," Cassidy said. "Anything you can tell us would be helpful."

Emily looked excited. "I'll start on it right now, and that way I'll have everything ready to go in the morning," she said. "I love a good mystery."

She headed down the hallway at a brisk walk. Cassidy turned back to their host. "Thank you so much."

Mrs. Morrissey made a dismissive wave. "Not a problem. It's why we're here—and everything we learn about the city's past improves the historical record. If I know Emily, she'll come in early. Once she's on the trail of missing information, she doesn't stop until she finds it. You're in good hands."

"I promise to come back with lattes for both of you!" Cassidy vowed as they said goodbye. Evan found his spirits rising as they headed back to the car.

"Does she know?" he asked.

Cassidy shrugged. "I'm not completely sure, but I think so. She did a lot of work with my uncle, who willed the store to me, and they might have even been an item, because Mr. Morrissey has been gone for a long time. So...maybe."

As they reached the sidewalk, a man in a dark jacket with a cap pulled low on his forehead approached. Evan felt a sudden tightness in his chest and he gasped for air, staggering. Then he felt the invisible grip slide away, and he remembered the new mojo bags Mrs. Teller had given him.

If Cassidy felt the attack, it didn't slow her down. She stepped in front of Evan, and a wooden stick fell out of her sleeve and into her hand. Evan saw a flare of white, and then the stranger flew backward, knocked off his feet and into the brick wall surrounding the garden of the home next door.

"Stay behind me!" She ordered Evan, advancing slowly on the man, who was already scrambling to his feet and starting to twitch his fingers.

Once again, Evan felt invisible bands tighten around his chest, making him gasp for breath. Cassidy's hands went to her belly, and her knees buckled, apparently struck by whatever magic the stranger had thrown. The street was unusually deserted, and Evan wondered if the stranger's magic dissuaded people from coming this way.

Evan's anger flared at being jerked around by yet another witch, and he used his fury to gather his thoughts, despite the pain. He spoke an incantation, loosing a stream of fire from his outstretched palm in the same instant Cassidy sent another blast of cold power from her wand. Their attacker yelped as his jacket caught fire, beating at the flames with his hands as Cassidy's blast threw him down the sidewalk. Something small and dark clattered against the cement, but the man didn't stop to retrieve it before he took off running in the other direction.

Evan helped Cassidy to her feet.

"We need to move," she said. Cassidy hurried in the direction the stranger had gone and bent down to examine something on the ground. She pulled a cloth from her bag and dropped it over the item.

"Given my kind of magic, I'd rather not pick that up, at least, not here," Cassidy said, as Evan walked to stand behind her. "The cloth has Teag's magic woven into it, so it should be safe to touch—if you're not a psychometric. Would you mind?"

Evan reached for the item, bracing himself for a jolt, and felt...nothing. He made sure to keep the cloth wrapped around the piece as they walked back to Cassidy's car. "What is this?"

"I'm pretty sure it's an object of power that helped our attacker harness more magic than he'd normally have. A magical amplifier, of sorts. We can take a closer look once we're in a safe place." She gave a worried glance in the direction their attacker had gone.

"Let's get out of here." Cassidy and Evan headed to her car. She set her wand down on the center divider, and Evan got a good look at it.

"You use a wooden spoon as a wand?"

Cassidy nodded, still carefully watching the traffic around them and her rearview mirror for danger. "My specialty is touch magic, remember? I pull from the memories and resonance in an object or its magic. That spoon belonged to my grandmother, and there are a lot of powerful, good memories connected to it. That works for me."

"Interesting."

She stole a glance in his direction. "I didn't know you could do magic."

"I mostly can't," Evan replied. "Seth calls it 'rote magic'—helpful little spells that can be memorized word-for-word. Getting them to work requires practice and intention, but no personal magic."

"I'm intrigued. I can't say I've ever heard of that—but I'm going to look into it."

"Who was that guy?" Evan asked, with a glance over his shoulder as if he expected the attacker to be right behind them.

"No idea. Obviously not a friend. But did Longstreet send him? Or is he connected to the witch gangs?" Cassidy wondered.

"I felt his magic hit me, and then it sort of slid off."

"Good protective charms can do a lot, especially against low-level magic. He wasn't throwing around big power—but he still could have done damage. And you held your own." Cassidy flashed him an affirming grin.

"I hope Seth and Teag had better luck than we did." Evan looked out the window as they headed back to Cassidy's house.

"Don't write today off before we know what Father Anne's people and Mrs. Morrissey's intern find out. We set things in motion. Longstreet might be better at hiding his trail than the other witch-disciples you've encountered, but if he's been in the area for a century, he has to have left footprints. We've got good people helping us. Give it a chance."

Evan nodded but did not reply. His ribs were tender, his head ached, and the curse still separated him from Seth. All he wanted was a warm dinner and a night spent protected in Seth's arms, but thanks to Longstreet's magic, only one of those could happen.

What if we kill Longstreet, and it doesn't break the curse? We can't stay together without ever touching, especially when it could get bad enough to actually kill. I promised I'd stick with him, and I want that with all my heart, but if we can't get rid of the curse, we'll have to separate.

Evan remembered how lonely he had been before meeting Seth, and how as crazy as their first days together were, Seth had still made him laugh and woken his heart from its long slumber. Evan couldn't go back to his family, and his friends in Richmond had moved on. Although he and Seth hadn't been a couple long, Evan just couldn't imagine being with anyone else.

I refuse to give up. Not on Seth, and not on having a future together. Even if it means we lose, I'll be beside him all the way. Because I'm not going back to how it was without him.

6

SETH

"I THOUGHT WE MIGHT WANT TO START BY LOOKING FOR LOGAN MILLER," Seth said, pulling up the information on his phone. "If Longstreet didn't grab him, then he's out there, somewhere, and whether he knows it or not, he needs our help."

"Do you think Longstreet will still come after him?" Teag asked as he followed the instructions from Seth's phone GPS.

"If we've upended everything like you and Rowan said, Longstreet may want 'insurance' with another descendant. Some of the other disciples killed additional people—either witnesses or maybe for some kind of blood magic," Seth replied. "Blake was worried about Logan, and Logan may have seen something that might help us find Longstreet."

"That's good enough for me." Teag navigated through the streets of a neighborhood outside of Charleston's historic district. "I downloaded the police report that I hacked into late last night," he added. "Blake's body had multiple stab wounds. Cause of death was a knife in the heart, although the autopsy pictures looked like something out of a slasher film."

"I'm curious about why he showed up on the riverbank," Seth said.

"All of the other disciples have buried their sacrifices—I'd think finding Blake dead like that would attract unwanted attention."

"Unless the attention is exactly what Longstreet wanted. Not from the cops—from you and Evan," Teag countered.

"Cocky bastard."

"He's gotten away with murder this long, and now you two show up and threaten to ruin everything. Maybe Longstreet's willing to take some risks to stop you and save his shot at immortality."

The GPS brought them to a ranch house in a tidy suburban neighborhood. Most of the homes looked to have been built in the sixties or seventies. While they weren't huge or opulent, the trimmed yards, fresh paint, and tended gardens suggested owners who took pride in their homes.

"How do you want to play this?" Teag asked as they found a parking space along the curb a few houses down.

"I'd say we go up, ring the doorbell like we expect someone to answer," Seth replied. "When no one does, we go next door and say we're friends of Logan, and we heard about Blake and wanted to see if Logan is okay. And see what we can find out."

Teag nodded. "Sounds like a plan. Do you think it's worth it to come back at night and try to get into the house?"

Seth thought for a moment, then shook his head. "Nah. Blake's just a regular guy with the shitty luck to be related to someone who helped kill Gremory a long time ago. But if we could find a house that Longstreet's been living in recently, that's a whole 'nother story."

They got out of the car. Teag had glanced frequently in the rearview mirror to assure no one was following them. Even so, Seth was ready for trouble. He had a silver knife in a wrist sheath beneath his jacket sleeve, and Teag carried several knives inside his coat.

Seth approached the Miller house on high alert, the way he'd been trained in the Army to sweep a potentially hostile building. Teag's gaze looked unfocused as they walked up the sidewalk, and before they could reach the front porch steps, Teag put out his arm to stop Seth.

"Wait. There's a magical trap."

Seth stopped in his tracks. Teag reached into his pocket and pulled out a small cloth bag tied at the top with a drawstring. He dropped it on the sidewalk, ground it open with his heel, and untied a knotted cord that hung from his belt, letting the knot fall atop the mix of powders that spread from the open bag.

"That should neutralize the trap long enough to get in and out," Teag said. "I don't think the magic is looking for us—but there's no sense in taking chances."

Seth felt a frisson of power as they crossed the place Teag had marked, which only heightened his wariness. Nothing about the house looked amiss, except that it had the feel to it of a place where no one was home.

Teag knocked on the door, and for good measure rang the bell. They waited, putting on a show of worried expectation in case the neighbors were watching. Seth glanced at the doorbell and made eye contact with Teag, noting that the button had a security camera.

"Logan, if you are watching this, we came to help you. We know who killed Blake, and you're also in danger. We want to keep you safe." Seth spoke quietly, addressing the doorbell/camera/microphone.

After a few minutes, they turned and walked back to the main sidewalk. Teag stopped to pick up the knotted cord he had dropped and to scatter the powder. "Makes it harder to pick up a signature on my magic," he said in a low voice to Seth, who had watched him with curiosity.

Doing their best to look friendly but harmless, they went to the house on the left, which had the best view of the Miller's front porch. Seth rang the bell, and he and Teag stood far enough back from the door to look non-threatening. A woman in her middle years gave a cautious glance out the window and opened the door just as far as the security chain would reach.

"I'm not looking for a new church, and I don't need more magazines," she informed them.

"We're friends of Logan Miller, from next door?" Seth said quickly. "We heard about what happened to Blake—so awful—and we wanted to check in on Logan and make sure he's all right. No one's home. Have you seen him lately?"

The neighbor gave them a look up and down and then relaxed as if she had concluded that they weren't going to cause a problem. "No, I haven't, and I'm worried," she replied. "Logan and Blake were good boys, and I felt so bad for them, what with their parents and all."

"I'm not sure I understand," Seth replied.

"Well, their mama passed when the boys were young—cancer," she said. "And then their father died nine years ago, some kind of industrial accident, I think. They've been on their own since Blake was eighteen, and he stepped right up to take care of Logan."

She shook her head. "I mothered them as much as they'd let me—brought over a casserole or a cake from time to time, let them know I was here if they needed something. You know how teenage boys are—want to show everyone that they're all grown up. But me and some of the other neighbors, we tried to help where we could."

She seemed sincerely distraught, and Seth's heart ached for Logan. He understood all too well what it was like to be the last in his family.

"He didn't happen to say when he'd be back, did he?" Seth asked.

"No. I didn't know he was gone until the mailman said their box was full. I told him I'd hold onto it until Logan came home, but I worry that he's going to be late on his bills if he isn't back soon."

"If we hear from him, we'll let him know," Seth told her. "Thank you for being such a good friend to him."

She shrugged and looked away, embarrassed at the praise. "Oh, it's nothing, really. Just what anyone would do."

They thanked her and headed back to the car. "It's not really true, you know," Seth mused. "That 'anyone' would do what she does for them. I thought our neighbors were like that, but then when everything happened...they weren't."

Seth did his best not to think about how it was after Jesse's death, his parents' accident, and the house fire. Instead of support, there had been sidelong glances, rumors, and accusations that he must have had something to do with it, that he was "crazy," or maybe just evil. When he'd finally been cleared by the police and the doctors who evaluated his sanity, Seth had been happy to leave Brazil, Indiana, behind him forever.

"I read the police report on Blake Miller's murder—and that included their interview with Logan," Teag told him when they were back in the car. "Logan said a man he'd never seen before spoke to Blake at the coffee shop while Logan was waiting in line to get their drinks. The next thing Logan knew, Blake followed the man out of the shop, got into his car and drove away. Logan ran after them and tried to call him, but Blake was gone."

"Hex bag, maybe, or some kind of compliance spell." Seth winced, remembering when a similar spell had nearly cost him his life in North Carolina.

"That was my thought." Teag slid him a look. "I'm guessing you've run into something similar?"

Seth nodded. "Yeah. And when you're under its influence, you can't break out. You know you should, you want to, but you can't." He could imagine Blake's terror all too well.

"The police didn't completely believe Logan's story. They named him as a 'person of interest.'"

"So he's smarter than I was if he ran. I stuck around, got interrogated, and then sectioned to the psych ward until I learned to tell them what they wanted to hear," Seth replied.

"Did your research turn up anything else that might help us find Logan?" Teag asked.

Seth shook his head. "Evan and I spent most of our time looking at Blake. Logan went back to school, living at home—probably to save money. He took five years off between high school and college, working at one of the gift shops downtown. He still worked evenings and weekends for them while he was in school. Blake was the night manager at one of the hotels nearby."

"They had to be close if Blake forced his way back as a ghost to ask us to protect Logan."

Seth swallowed. "Yeah. I got that feeling from everything we could find about them. Two years age difference, both stayed in town, still living together in the family house."

"You see a lot of yourself in Logan?"

"I'm trying not to. What's that called—projection? But it's hard to avoid because there are some crazy strong similarities."

"So…you've been in Logan's shoes. If you were Logan, what would you do?"

Seth sat back in the seat and stared through the windshield for a moment. "He ran—that was smart. Well, as far as not getting locked up right away. Probably means he's in more trouble if the cops catch him."

"So he's running from the cops—but he got a look at Longstreet. So is he trying to keep himself safe, or avenge Blake? And is he really on the run? Or does Longstreet have him?"

"I don't know."

Teag nodded. "That spell trap at his house was probably specific to Logan—either Longstreet wanted to know if he came back, or maybe intended to trap him inside…until someone came to get him. My vote is that Longstreet doesn't have him, since the spell on the house was still active."

"He didn't have a dorm room on campus, and if he thinks he's being chased by the cops or a killer, I can't imagine that he'd try to bunk with a friend," Seth mused.

"Do you think he's got any idea there's a supernatural aspect?"

Seth looked down at his hands, overwhelmed by the memories. "I knew something really strange had happened because Jesse and I had gone looking for ghosts—and got more than we bargained for. When I came to, I found his body." He closed his eyes as his voice caught in his throat.

"If Blake just agreed to walk off with a stranger, maybe Logan thought the man had a gun, or that he made threats. Most people aren't open to the idea that the supernatural could be real, so they don't even consider the possibility," he continued.

"Blake's ghost was worried about Logan. So either Longstreet intended to come after him, or maybe Logan was gunning for Longstreet," Teag theorized. "What did you do once you got out of the hospital?"

"I left town, and then searched everything I could online about magic and monsters," Seth replied. "But by that time, it had been months after Jesse's death. The trail was cold. I can't shake the feeling that Logan is still in town. It's only been a few days."

"I agree—that means we need to find him before either the cops or Longstreet do."

"Or before he stumbles onto Longstreet," Seth pointed out. "Even if he has a gun, he's no match. Longstreet might not want to kill Logan right now—he's the best possibility of producing another generation of sacrifices—but Longstreet isn't going to risk having his cover blown after a century."

"So Logan's probably holed up somewhere, Googling how to kill a witch?"

Seth grimaced. "That's my bet. He might have snuck back on campus, and be hiding somewhere with wifi where he thinks Longstreet won't find him." He paused, thinking. "But even if I hack the university system, just proving he's been online doesn't pinpoint his location."

Teag pulled into the parking lot for a coffee shop. "I've got an idea. You get us drinks—I'll see if we can't bring Logan to us."

By the time Seth returned with their lattes, Teag had his laptop up and was typing furiously. "What's the plan?" Seth asked.

"You ever do much with search engine advertising?" Teag asked. Seth drew a chair around so he could see the screen.

"No. My clients want to know where their systems are vulnerable. The kind of stuff you're talking about would be left to the marketing folks."

Teag nodded. "That's what I figured. But think about it—if Logan is holed up somewhere, doing online searches for anything to do with witches, magic, curses, every one of those search terms is a keyword. So if I put together an ad for Mrs. Teller's services as a root worker and use the words and phrases Logan is likely to search on, he should see the ad...and it should lead him right to Mrs. Teller—who will call us in."

"Nice."

Before long, Teag had the ad assembled, keywords chosen, and targeting complete. "I'm keeping the ad focused on the Charleston ZIP codes, so the net isn't cast too wide. If my hunch is right, that should be enough."

Seth sipped his coffee, but his mind wandered. *Longstreet killed*

Blake early because he knew we were coming after him. Logan has every right to hate us.

"Earth to Seth."

Seth looked up, realizing that Teag must have been calling his name without response.

"You had no way to know Longstreet would move up his sacrifice schedule." Teag must have guessed the direction of Seth's thoughts.

"It was a good bet that he was going to. But the alternative—trying to go after one disciple each year... We figured that would not only take twelve fuckin' years, but it would also give the disciples way too much time to strategize."

"You're doing something no one has tried to do in a century," Teag reminded him. "No one else put the pattern together and made it a personal vendetta. That means uncharted territory."

"It's just...we were able to save the others."

Teag leaned forward and met his gaze. "You were in the Army. Did every mission turn out as planned? Were there casualties?"

Seth looked away. "Yeah."

"You're going up against serial killers with a century of experience," Teag pressed, pitching his voice low. "You and Evan, two mortals without any strong magic of your own. And you've won—so far. You're not only threatening the immortality gig for all of the disciples, but killing them as well. Witches and supernatural beings can grow a mighty big ego over the centuries. You and Evan aren't just a threat—you've humiliated them. They're going to fight back."

"I wanted to save the other descendants."

"And you have. Logan would be on the next cycle and his child after him. All those deaths going forward won't happen—because of you and Evan."

"It doesn't make Logan's loss any less painful."

Teag sighed. "No. It doesn't. Or for you, losing Jesse. But it does mean that they didn't die in vain."

Seth looked away. He nodded, because he didn't trust his voice to speak, and pretended to finish the last of his coffee, although he knew the cup was already empty. "While we wait to see if the ad works, let's go look at those other places Longstreet owned. Maybe we'll figure out where he's doing his killing."

"Where first?"

"Let's start at the beginning and work forward," Seth replied. "And hope he doesn't have any surprises waiting for us."

～

"THIS IS APPARENTLY WHAT'S LEFT OF LONGSTREET'S FAMILY PLANTATION," Teag said as he and Seth got out of the car in the parking lot of a large, modern apartment complex.

"According to the deeds, it's been several things over the years," Seth replied, turning to take in the new, three-story condos. "From what I found online, the condos cover everything except some cypress swamp in the very back, which was separated out in another parcel. Probably protected wetland."

"Any family cemeteries? Slave cemeteries?" Teag asked. "That kind of thing comes up a lot when old farms or plantations get re-used. Sometimes the graves are moved, and in other cases, they just fence them in and put up a marker."

"None that I know of. And leaving the graves and just building around them? Lovely—not," Seth said. "Reminds me of the hotel I stayed in that backed up to a cemetery. I slept fine, but when I read the comments, a lot of people complained about cold spots, drafts, voices, and that the 'cleaning staff' kept moving their things."

Teag laughed. "Yeah, I think about that every time I see advertise-ments for haunted hotels—and we've got quite a few here in Charles-ton. I'm not sure people know what they're getting into when they book a room."

A walk around the complex turned up nothing of interest. Seth sighed as he climbed back into the car. "Well, that was a bust."

"The day is young. We've still got six more places to go," Teag replied, and Seth appreciated his friend's effort at being upbeat.

"I hope Evan and Cassidy have found out something useful over at the St. Expeditus Society," Seth said as they pulled out of the lot and headed for the next address on his list.

"Cassidy may not be a hacker, but she knows how to research old school. And Father Anne will make sure the Society steps up with its full resources. If it's there, they'll find it."

"Explain to me again how your magic helps you with computers? I thought it wove spells into cloth?" Seth was desperate to think about anything except the curse that separated him from Evan and the fact that time was running out.

"Weaver magic also helps me weave data into information—so it enhances whatever natural ability I have and makes me a pretty good hacker," Teag replied.

Seth snorted. "I've worked with you. 'Pretty good' is an under-statement."

Teag's cheeks colored at the praise. "You're not too shabby yourself."

Seth shrugged off the compliment. "Mine is old fashioned grunt work—no magic involved. I learned a few rote spells—useful things like opening a lock, summoning ghosts, throwing a stream of fire. They come in handy, but because it's a memorized spell, that's all there is, so I can't make adjustments on the fly the way I guess you can when you actually have magic yourself."

"What you can do—and the way you do it—is valuable. Most magic is the simple kind—the hard, complicated stuff is dangerous, and it takes a lot out of you," Teag replied.

They headed farther out of town, following the directions to the next property on Seth's list. "I guess we were right about Longstreet avoiding Charleston proper," Teag remarked. "If he stayed this far beyond the city limits, it's no wonder he didn't rub elbows with the supernatural community."

The GPS took them down an overgrown lane to a long-deserted farmhouse. At the end of the road, a clapboard house looked ready to cave in on itself, with a porch overhang that had already collapsed. Only a few shards of glass remained in the windows, which looked to Seth like empty eye sockets.

"He's obviously not living here," Seth observed. "Longstreet owned the place right after the turn of the last century, probably bought it not long after Gremory's death. It passed through several hands after he sold it, and the last owner went bankrupt twenty years ago. A holding company finally bought it for future development. Looks like it's sat empty since then. Let's have a look around."

He pulled a shotgun from beneath the seat and racked a shell into the chamber as soon as he was out of the car. Teag grabbed a long staff out of the back, and Seth noted the runes carved into the wood and the braided string wrapped around one end.

"Magic or martial arts?" Seth asked, curious.

"A little of both. I've done competitive mixed martial arts, although we've been too busy lately for me to compete. Now I just train. And the braided string and the runes help me pack a little more power into the punch. I'll take any advantage in a fight."

They walked around the old farmhouse, alert for traps and watchful for snakes in the high grass. The back of the house looked even worse than the front, and from the way the doorways were off plumb, Seth bet that the frame or the foundation was likely to go at any time.

"Considering how recently Blake Miller was killed, it doesn't look like it happened here," Teag said as they finished circling the house.

"I doubt Longstreet held him prisoner in there, either," Seth agreed. "The slightest struggle and I think the whole place would come down."

"Yeah, I agree." Teag turned, looking out over the land around the house. "We might not be near anyone, but there's also not much cover. Seems like a pretty exposed place to do dark magic blood rituals."

"It was the first property Longstreet bought after the disciples scattered," Seth replied, staring at the old house as if he could will it to give up its secrets. "I wondered if buying a farm was his way of reclaiming a little of his family's plantation heritage."

"Lots of landowners went into the Civil War rich and came out destitute," Teag observed. "It might have made them bitter, but they didn't run off and become dark warlocks."

"As far as you know." Seth arched an eyebrow, and Teag had to chuckle.

"The old families of witches in Charleston came out of the war sitting pretty," Teag replied as they walked back to the car. "Some of them sold weapons to both sides, or supported blockade runners, or just used their magic and foresight to make a killing in commodities. Most of them have been in Charleston since the beginning, so for them, the war was just the 'current unpleasantness.'"

The next house, a two-story home in Summerville, was now a busy restaurant near the refurbished downtown.

"That's it?" Teag asked, standing across the street from Summer Bistro, which looked like it catered to the shoppers and tourists.

"Longstreet lived here in the thirties and forties. Ran a shop of some kind, but we're not sure what. Evan's looking into that."

"Looks a little busy for mass murder," Teag remarked.

"And I'm thinking that if it was haunted, the restaurant wouldn't have lasted long," Seth said. "Not much to see here."

"I take it you had better luck with the other disciples' old properties?"

Seth shrugged. "Either their homes or what was left of the places they worked ended up being spots they went back to time and again. This guy keeps switching up the pattern."

Longstreet's next two former homes offered no additional clues. One had been torn down to make room for a gas station, and the other now housed an ice cream shop.

"What a bust," Seth said, resting against the hood of Teag's car. "I'm sorry to have wasted your time."

Teag shrugged. "Ruling things out is as essential as ruling them in. We know where Longstreet isn't, which should help us narrow down where he is."

Seth appreciated Teag's support, but it didn't ease the tension he felt, aware that he and Evan were in a race against time. Whether it was the curse or his imagination, Seth felt an uncomfortable tightness in his chest, and a drain on his energy, as if he had the flu, which seemed to be getting worse.

"You're feeling the curse, aren't you?"

Seth looked up sharply, surprised. "Good guess, or something your magic told you?"

"A little of both. I made the woven bracelets you two are wearing, remember? The ones you bought each other for your birthdays? They carry my protection spells. So especially when we're near each other, I can pick up on the weaving's energy, and right now I can tell it's fighting against dark magic."

Seth nodded, and Teag came to sit on the car next to him. "Yeah. I feel the curse—and it's getting stronger."

"Do you want to go back?"

"Hell, no. It was bad enough when I thought the curse might separate Evan and me by keeping us from living together, being a couple. But now that I know it's going to kill us, there's no time to waste. That's why I'm really having a hard time with coming up dry from where we've been today—we need to find answers, and soon."

"I'm betting you didn't solve the other killings in a day."

"Except for the first one, when I met Evan, we haven't been working against a deadline." Seth looked out over the cozy downtown that housed the ice cream shop. "I'm so happy for you and Anthony, getting engaged, planning a future. I want that with Evan. But we've both agreed that we can't just walk away from the witch-disciples until it's finished. And I'm so afraid something will happen, and we won't get the chance."

Now that he'd put his fear into words, Seth wasn't sure whether he felt better or worse. At least Teag understood the dangers of their life.

"You and Evan are in this together," Teag replied. "That's an added danger, but it also means you both understand what's going on. Anthony supports what I do with the Alliance. He realizes that it's important, even if he doesn't have magic of his own. But except for a few times when he's been dragged in out of necessity, Anthony isn't part of our battles. That leaves him on the outside, worrying and not being able to help. So...different kind of stress, but still stress."

"Crazy life, huh?"

"Definitely." Teag patted the hood of the car and pushed off. "Ready to go have a look at that last address?"

Seth headed for the passenger seat. "Let's at least rule it out, so we can move on to something new. Onward!"

Half an hour later, they were outside Longstreet's most recent property, a large modern house off a rural highway. An elaborate wrought-iron gate blocked the lane, and a decorative metal security fence topped with arrow-sharp tips surrounded the property.

"It's warded," Teag said as they walked toward the gate. "Hell, there are runes and sigils worked into the wrought iron, and lots of magic on top of that. That alone tells me he didn't leave anything worth guarding at his other homes."

"What now?" Seth asked. "I'm guessing it's not worth it trying to break the warding?"

Teag shook his head. "Not without a true emergency—and even then, there's no guarantee. I know how solid the protections are that Rowan and some of our other friends have put on our houses and the shop. They aren't intended to be easily undone."

"Dead end?" Seth asked, feeling despair rise. "I thought we'd find...something." A glint of sunlight off metal caught his eye in the thicket across the road. "Hold on. Maybe we did."

He crossed the road and walked a few feet into the scrubby tangle of saplings and bushes. A cheap surveillance camera on a pole pointed at the gate to Longstreet's mansion. Teag trailed behind him, watching for trouble.

Seth looked at the improvised set-up and then bent to give the camera a good look at him. "Find me," he mouthed since the camera didn't pick up audio. Then he gestured for Teag to join him back at the car.

"What do you think that's about?" Teag asked.

"Too jerry-rigged to be either Longstreet or law enforcement. Maybe Logan. I hope it's Logan's doing, trying to keep an eye on the place. Not sure what he plans to do if he does spot Longstreet," Seth replied. "If he is getting the feed from his doorbell cam and now this one, he's had a good look at me. With luck, when we find him, he'll hear me out."

Teag's phone rang, and he pulled it from his pocket, then read the new text message. "You might get that chance sooner than you think. Mrs. Teller says Logan just made an appointment to talk to her from the ad we placed. She's meeting him at the coffee shop across from the City Market at six-thirty."

Seth glanced at the time. "Let's go. If we don't hit traffic, we can be there in time to join them."

~

TEAG MADE GOOD TIME, AND THEY PARKED IN THE LOT ACROSS FROM THE City Market, on the opposite side from the coffee shop. "How do you want to play this?" he asked Seth.

"I guess we start by introducing ourselves and trying to get Logan to trust us."

"You think that will work?"

"Probably not, but it's worth a shot."

The City Market was empty now, and the lull in foot traffic reflected the dinner hour. A *"Sorry We're Closed"* sign hung in the door of the coffee shop when they arrived, and inside, Seth could see chairs upended onto tables while a man mopped the floor. He came to the door and opened it a crack when they knocked.

"We're Teag and Seth—looking for Mrs. Teller," Teag said. The man opened the door to let them in, then locked it behind them.

"They're in the back. She said you'd be along."

Seth and Teag made their way toward a nook at the far end of the store with a booth that was out of sight of the cafe windows. Mrs. Teller and a younger woman sat on one side, and Logan Miller sat on the other.

Logan's eyes widened when he saw them approach, and he jumped to his feet, his expression frightened and a look of betrayal in his eyes.

"Sit down, boy," Mrs. Teller drawled. "They don't mean you any harm. They're friends of mine, and they can help you."

"You're the ones who went to my house this morning. And then you showed up on my camera—"

"We know Michael Longstreet killed your brother. We intend to stop him from killing you and anyone else, ever again. But first, we need to get you somewhere safe," Seth replied.

Logan Miller was in his mid-twenties, with brown hair and scruff that came in red. From Logan's rumpled appearance and the smell of sweat and dirt, Seth guessed the man had been living rough.

"Safe? There's nowhere safe until Longstreet is stopped."

Teag shot a glance over his shoulder at the man up front with the mop. "Keep it down, if you don't want the cops showing up."

"Damian, the owner, is a friend of mine—and a good client," Mrs. Teller replied. "He's keeping an eye out. We're safe here." She gestured toward the younger woman beside her. "This is Niella, my daughter. She's a first-rate root woman herself."

Mrs. Teller looked from Logan to Seth and Teag. "You said you wanted to know how to protect yourself from evil," she told Logan. "I can vouch for Teag here, and for Seth as well. And I can give you charms and amulets. But if you want to handle the problem permanently..."

"My partner and I came to Charleston to stop Longstreet before he killed again," Seth said. "But we didn't get here in time."

Logan stared at him, and astonishment turned to fury. "You knew that he was going to kill my brother?"

Seth nodded.

"Then why the hell didn't you call the police? Why didn't you warn us?"

"Michael Longstreet is a century-old witch who has killed members of your family every twelve years to keep his own immortality," Seth replied. "The police wouldn't have believed us. And you probably wouldn't have, either."

"My brother is dead!"

"So is mine." Seth met Logan's accusing gaze. "One of Longstreet's witch-buddies killed my brother when it should have been me. That's how I got into the witch hunting business."

"Witches?" Logan looked like he was about to explode. "How is that even possible?"

"It's a long story, best told when we're somewhere we can better protect you. You're the witness who can connect Longstreet to Blake's murder. He's not going to want you on the loose," Seth answered.

"You're serious."

"One hundred percent," Teag said.

Logan looked torn between swinging a punch and running for the door.

"Please don't leave," Seth said. "At least, hear us out. You must have suspected that something wasn't quite 'normal' about Blake's disappearance to contact Mrs. Teller."

Logan seemed to deflate and sat down heavily on his side of the booth. Teag and Seth brought up chairs. Up front, Damian kept mopping, but now that Seth watched, he saw the shop owner glancing out the window, on guard.

"Everything was fine when Blake and I went into the café," Logan said. "He hadn't told me anything about going anywhere without me, and we had plans for the rest of the day. Blake waited at the table while I went up for coffee—it was my turn to 'fetch' and his to hold the table. I waited in the line. By the time I was heading back to the table, this stranger had come up, and I saw him say something to Blake, and then Blake just left with him."

"Do you think the man had a gun?" Teag asked.

Logan shook his head. "I didn't see one. His hands were by his sides—I remember that. I called after Blake, but he didn't stop. He had a weird look on his face—kinda glazed. I thought maybe the man drugged him, but there wasn't time. I ran after him, but when I got through the crowd, they were in a van pulling away."

"How did you know it was Longstreet?" Seth asked.

"I chased the van—got the license plate," Logan replied. "And I have a friend at the DMV who did me a favor and looked up the owner. But by that time, it had been several hours since Blake disappeared. The cops wouldn't take a missing person's report until he'd been gone twenty-four hours, and then when I told them what happened, they didn't believe he'd left against his will."

"Why didn't you go home?" That had been one piece of the puzzle Seth hadn't been able to figure out.

"I thought the guy at the café looked familiar," Logan replied. "Then I realized that I'd seen him taking 'walks' near our house for several days before Blake was grabbed. We've lived in that house all our lives, and we know the people who live in the neighborhood—this guy stuck out in my mind because I didn't recognize him. But at the time, I figured maybe he was visiting family."

"So you realized he'd been stalking Blake?" Teag asked.

Logan nodded. "And since I knew he saw me, I was afraid he'd come back."

"He did. And he set a magical trapline around your house. We think it would have either knocked you out or kept you inside. We neutralized it long enough to get to your door and ring the bell, but we both felt it," Seth told him.

"How is that even possible?"

"You went out to Longstreet's house, didn't you?" Teag asked without answering.

"Yeah, but I couldn't get in. There's a fence, and it was impossible to climb."

"Not impossible—warded," Teag said. "The opposite kind of spell to what we found at your house. He had protective spells to keep out anyone with bad intent—in this case, you."

Logan turned his attention back to Seth. "You said that you knew he was going to come after Blake. How?"

"Someone in your family died nine years ago suddenly and unexpectedly," Seth replied. "An older man."

Logan frowned. "Our father."

"And twelve years before that?"

Logan thought for a moment. "His older brother, my uncle. How—?"

"Every twelve years, Longstreet has killed one of your relatives—the oldest male in the direct family line. It's been going on for a century because one of your ancestors killed his witch master. That's how I was able to find your family and figure out who would be next."

"But it hasn't been twelve years," Logan protested. "It's only been nine."

"My partner and I started coming after the dark witches, and some of them figured out that they'd be next. I think Longstreet moved up his agenda to keep us from stopping him."

Logan came out of his seat at that, with a right hook that caught Seth on the chin and rocked his chair backward. Teag lunged forward and grabbed Logan, wrapping both arms around him to pin him and taking them to the floor. Logan fought to get free.

"That's enough!" Mrs. Teller snapped.

Seth rubbed his chin, feeling like he owed Logan that. Teag jerked Logan to his feet and pushed him back into the booth, keeping a hand clamped on the man's shoulder to yank him back if necessary.

"Blake could have had three more years, is that what you're saying?" Logan was panting with exertion, his eyes wide with anger and pain.

"Maybe he would have. But then he would have died just like the other men in your family— like you will, if we don't stop Longstreet," Seth answered. "We've stopped two other witches—and we intend to do it again, with or without your help."

"That won't bring Blake back."

"Get your head out of your ass," Teag snarled. "We're trying to save your life, and find your brother's killer. Are you going to help us or not?"

Teag's phone went off, and he glanced down, looking surprised at the ringtone. "Alicia?" He gave Seth a look that made it clear he hadn't expected to hear from the medium.

"Put me on video. I need to speak to Logan."

"How did you know Logan was with us?" Seth asked.

"Blake told me."

Logan shook his head and started to stand. "Oh, no. Oh, hell no. You don't get to put words in Blake's mouth—"

"You're about to be killed by a Zamboni." Alicia's voice sounded like it had when she'd channeled Blake before, and while Seth hadn't known her long, he felt a chill go down his spine, certain that the ghost was speaking through her.

"Blake?" The Deadpool quote seemed random, but obviously, it had meant something between the brothers.

"You used to have a red plastic rocking horse when you were little. You named him 'Clifford' after that dog in the books," Alicia continued. "You had a teddy rabbit named Boingo, and you accidentally left him behind at that hotel in Myrtle Beach with the big starfish in the pool."

Logan looked stunned. The anger vanished, replaced by grief. The devastated expression on his face was far too familiar to Seth, who had seen the same heartbreak in the mirror after Jesse's death.

"How—?"

"It's me, sport." Alicia's voice had a rueful note. "And I don't have much time. I borrowed the 'suit' to make an appearance, but I can't stay long," Blake/Alicia added. "These people are the good guys. Help them if you can, but let them protect you."

"I let you down." Logan sounded utterly broken, and tears streaked his face.

"Never. The guy mojo'd me, and I couldn't fight it. I was screaming in my head the whole time he was walking me out of that café," Blake/Alicia replied. "I'd have never left you alone if I had a say about it."

"I miss you." Logan choked on a sob.

"Miss you, too, squirt. But I *do not* want you coming over to this side any time soon, got that? You're gonna find a nice guy and settle down, adopt some kids, and kick off when you're ninety from a heart attack when you're in the middle of sweaty sex—"

"Blake!"

Alicia's pained smile mirrored Logan's grief. "I want you to live to a ripe and horny old age, so you can't let this asshole kill you, got that? I'll be waiting when you get here—and in the meantime, I'll haunt your ass to keep you company. But don't go being stupid and getting yourself killed. Please."

Logan nodded miserably. "Okay. But...can you stick around for a little while? Unless you can go somewhere better?"

"Don't worry. I want to see this guy get what he deserves," Blake/Alicia assured Logan. "And make sure you're safe."

"Will I get to talk to you again?" Logan looked young and lost.

"If I don't overstay my welcome and she lets me talk through her again. So save the mushy goodbyes. I'll be back." Blake said that last sentence in the Terminator's heavy Austrian accent, and Logan had to chuckle through his tears.

Abruptly, Alicia's entire manner changed, and she sagged in her chair. "Sorry to just barge in like that, but Blake's ghost showed up and begged me to call you right then." She sounded exhausted.

"You did good," Teag assured her. "Perfect timing. Thank you."

"I'm going to crash now." The video call went dark, and Teag put his phone away.

Logan moved to wipe his face with his sleeve, and Mrs. Teller shoved a napkin into his hand with a look of grandmotherly reproof. Logan blew his nose and cleared his throat.

"Now what?" Emotion choked Logan's scratchy voice, but the stubborn determination in his blue eyes gave Seth hope the young man would get through this.

"Now we get you to somewhere truly safe, and figure out how to stop Longstreet," Seth replied.

"Safe? You just said the guy was a witch. Where do I go to be 'safe' from that?"

Teag and Seth shared a glance. "A friend of ours runs a place—"

"We've got trouble!" Damian bellowed from the front of the café. Seth moved to stand behind a half-wall where he could see out into the street. A figure in a dark sweatshirt with the hood shadowing his face stood framed in the big plate glass window.

"Shit," Teag muttered.

"We're secure in here, for the moment, but we can't stay here long," Seth said.

"Good thing you don't have to." Mrs. Teller looked up with a satisfied smirk. "I called Rowan right after I called you. She's on her way. You two take him—Niella, Damian, and I will keep them busy up front."

"Are you crazy?" Logan protested. "You can't shoot someone in downtown Charleston!"

"Who said anything about shooting anyone?" Mrs. Teller said in a reproving tone. "We'll work a crossing on him, and he won't be going after anyone while he loses his lunch and dinner—both ways." Her smile promised retribution.

"What about Rowan?" Teag asked as he and Seth rose.

"Just got a text from her," Niella replied. "She's pulling up now. Get Logan over to Father Anne's, and we'll handle the mop-up. I let her know you're coming."

"What—?" Logan protested as Seth grabbed his arm and pulled him out of his seat.

"C'mon. We've gotta go." He turned back to Mrs. Teller and Niella. "Thank you."

"You're welcome. By the way—nice ad. Got some new business from it," Mrs. Teller added with a grin. "Now move!"

"Alley's under construction—you're going to have to run to the corner to get in the car," Damian yelled over his shoulder.

Seth and Teag headed for the café's back door with Logan hustled between them. "Keep your head down, and don't touch anything," Teag ordered.

"You're kidding. He's kidding—right?" Logan asked, swiveling to look at Seth.

"Nope. We've got this. Just duck."

Teag reached into his backpack and pulled out a woven rope net with weighted corners, and a narrow coil of silvery metal. Seth hadn't brought his gun, so he readied his best rote spells in his mind, and figured he'd improvise. "Ready?" Teag asked.

"Ready." Seth echoed.

Logan definitely did not look ready, but he set his jaw and gripped the table knife he had taken from the booth.

Only three buildings separated the café from the cross-street. The opposite side of the alley was torn up along the edge of the roadway, probably utility work, Seth thought. They sprinted toward the waiting black sedan, keeping Logan in the middle. Seth saw Rowan standing next to the car, facing to the side, arm extended, battling someone— perhaps the man from the window.

"We've got trouble!" Seth called out, spotting a man racing toward them from the opposite direction.

"Keep running!" Teag grabbed Logan's arm and tugged him toward the corner.

"Get to the car—I'll slow him down," Seth shouted. Without waiting for confirmation, Seth pivoted and brought up his right hand, repeating a spell and channeling all his will into the words. Dozens of small stones rose from the worksite, hovered in the air, and then pelted the man, driving him back.

Their attacker shoved his left hand into the front pocket of his hoodie, and a green light flared around him, as a blast of energy barreled toward Seth, knocking him off his feet and sending him tumbling. Seth scrambled up as the stranger drew closer, and called up the words to another rote spell, this time sending a streak of fire that hit their pursuer in the chest, igniting his sweatshirt.

Again the green light flashed, and the flames extinguished. Then Teag was beside Seth, and the silver coil flashed in Teag's left hand, snapping out and cutting into the attacker's forearm, forcing him to withdraw his hand from his pocket. Something tumbled to the ground, and the man looked about wildly, searching for what he'd lost.

"He's got a relic," Teag shouted. "Don't let him find it!"

Seth could feel the effects of the curse, making him even more drained than usual when he used rote magic, but he didn't dare stop now. He sent another hail of rocks at their attacker, forcing his attention away from his search. Teag threw the woven net with practiced accuracy, and it hit the mark, landing on the stranger's head and tangling him in its mesh. Except instead of fighting to get free, as Seth expected, the man shuddered and sank to his knees.

"What did you do?" Seth yelled as Teag ran toward the attacker.

"Wove magic into the net." Teag reached the tangled man, touched the net, and spoke a word. Their attacker dropped face-forward onto the cobblestones, out cold.

"Come on, help me get him to the car." Seth grabbed one arm, and Teag grabbed the other, and they ran as fast as they could carry the dead weight between them. Logan waited where Teag had left him, obviously unwilling to run closer to Rowan without backup.

"What about the thing he dropped?" Seth glanced over his shoulder down the alley.

"I'll text Mrs. Teller. They'll find it. I'm curious about that myself," Teag replied.

"Get in the car!" Seth yelled to Logan as Rowan stepped out of sight around the corner. The sedan's door opened, and Logan dove inside.

Seth and Teag reached the car a few seconds later, and dragged their prisoner inside and onto the floor, making sure to keep the net from dislodging. Rowan jumped into the passenger seat, and the driver roared away.

"Did you just...kidnap that man?" Logan stammered.

"The one who was trying to kill us? Yep." Seth replied.

Logan gently nudged the man with the toe of his sneaker, but the prisoner didn't respond. "Is he dead?"

Teag shook his head. "Just out cold." He looked to Rowan. "What about the guy you were fighting off?"

"Ran away," she said. "I think he might have just been the distraction. He didn't look like he felt too well—I think Mrs. Teller's jinx was working. But he dropped an item of power that I picked up, and I want to take a better look at it."

"What are you going to do with him?" Logan sounded equally horrified and curious.

"Get some answers," Seth replied, anger heating his tone. "He had something in his pocket that made him glow on his first couple of salvos, and when I hit him a second time, he dropped it."

"You think they had some kind of amulets to increase their power?" Despite the danger, Teag's eyes glinted with the adrenaline of the fight.

"Yeah, so the question is—where did it come from, and who sold the pieces to them?" Seth answered.

"Did you miss the part where we just kidnapped that man?" Logan turned to look through the rear window, panicky.

"Did you notice he was trying to kill us?" Teag countered. "This isn't the first time we've been attacked—but I damn sure want to make it the last."

"Oh, God." Logan clasped his hands between his knees and sat with his back rigid, like a character in a heist movie gone wrong.

"Relax," Rowan told him. "We're not going to kill him—but the Coven will want to know what the fucking hell he thought he was about, and where he got whatever he was using."

"Coven? Wait, you're a witch? I thought you told me a witch killed Blake."1

Seth laid a hand on Logan's shoulder to calm him, and Logan shook it off. "Tell me what the hell is going on," he demanded.

"Longstreet is a bad witch. I'm a good witch. No munchkins were harmed in the making of this escape," Rowan deadpanned. "Magic is like any other weapon—whether it's good or bad depends on what you do with it. Longstreet—the man who killed your brother—uses it for his own gain, at the expense of others. My coven—and the rest of the sanctioned covens in the city—abide by a set of ethical precepts. That guy," she added, with a glance at the unconscious man on the floor, "is meddling where he shouldn't, with power that isn't his. Which makes it our business."

"Okay," Logan said quietly, with an expression that said it was anything but. "Where are you taking me? Us?"

"To the St. Expeditus Society's safe house," Seth replied. "You don't have any magic, so that makes you a sitting duck for Longstreet to eliminate since you can tie him to Blake's disappearance if not directly to his murder."

"The police didn't believe me," Logan said.

"We're not the police," Teag reminded him. "They don't understand supernatural crimes, and they aren't prepared to deal with practitioners gone wrong. We are."

Logan let out a breath and fell back against his seat. "Sure. Why not? None of this makes any sense."

"Are you sure about that?" Seth asked, inclining his head to make eye contact. "You followed that ad to Mrs. Teller because your gut told you that Blake's disappearance wasn't normal. Something made you think 'supernatural' instead of wondering whether your brother might owe money to the wrong people or have a drug dealer on his tail."

Logan shook his head. "Blake wasn't like that. At all. That's why I knew it had to be something else."

"Blake sounds like he was a good guy." Seth couldn't keep the sadness out of his voice. Logan gave him an appraising glance.

"He was the best." Logan fell silent for a moment. "You said your brother got killed, too."

"Yeah. Jesse. He was awesome. He deserved better."

"I'm sorry."

"Sorry about Blake, too." Seth made eye contact. "We'll stop Longstreet, and avenge Blake. But you heard what your brother said— he wants you safe."

"I want to fight."

"And you can—from the safe house," Rowan chimed in. "Think of it as covert operations. Like being an analyst for the CIA—only in this case, the witchy side."

"In Charleston? How is all this going on, and no one knows?" Logan still had a deer-in-the-headlights look.

"Oh, some people know. People like us. And the rest don't want to know, so when they run into something that's our kind of weird, they talk themselves out of it," Teag replied. "So...welcome to the club. It's not the kind of club anyone wants to join—you get here more out of necessity."

"I'll do whatever I can to help. For Blake." Logan looked rattled, but the idea of being able to lend a hand and make a difference seemed to steady him. Seth remembered those early days, after Jesse's death, when nothing made sense and all he had was pain. He'd gone running headlong into danger and been incredibly lucky to find mentors like Milo and Toby to keep him from getting killed on his first hunt. Seth silently promised to do everything he could to pay that forward with Logan.

Seth felt the prickle of strong magic as they drove through the gate at the entrance to the St. Expeditus compound. His spirits rose as he saw the RV and his Hayabusa safely parked off to one side.

"The trailer doesn't look like it got damaged," he said, relief clear in his voice.

"Is that yours?" Logan craned his neck for a look.

"Yeah. I inherited it when the disciple killed my parents and burned down our house after Jesse died. Evan and I live in the RV, so we can track the disciples to each of their cities."

Logan's eyes narrowed in thought as he gave Seth a long, appraising stare. "So you really do this for a living? Hunt the killers?"

Seth shrugged. "Not exactly 'for a living.' I'm a computer security consultant, and Evan is a graphic designer. That's our living. The rest is...a fucked-up sort of quest."

Logan gave a bitter laugh. "Aren't all quests? I mean, I love reading fantasy, but it's all 'you killed my father, prepare to die.' That's kinda the whole hero's journey thing."

"Except the hero part of the journey sucks," Seth said quietly, and

Teag nodded. "The best part is sitting in the tavern with your friends, swapping tales. Those stories tend to gloss over the really bad stuff. And personally, I'd like to read a few where the damsel rescues herself, and the hero ends up with his sidekick."

That got a grin from Logan. "Yeah, me too."

Seth saw Rowan's amused smile before she sobered. "I'm hoping that Logan can work with Beck. Beck might have been sent away from his family fairly young, but he still knows a lot about the other old families and how supernatural high society works in this city."

"Beck is a witch, too?"

Seth had helped Teag and Cassidy deal with problems caused by Beck's renegade cousins. He wasn't sure how much to say, so he let Teag answer.

"Not anymore. Beck was the heir of one of the old, powerful witch dynasties, and he gave up his magic to stop a vengeful demon. Damn near died doing it. Now he's just a regular guy who knows a lot about witchy stuff."

That answer seemed to satisfy Logan, but Seth had to hold back a snort at how much it left out. *Ah well. Beck'll tell him the rest if he wants to.*

"Okay." Logan sounded tentative. "What kind of stuff are we analyzing?"

Rowan looked pleased with Logan's acceptance. "Old manuscripts, for one thing, to find a way to break the curse on Seth and Evan."

Logan's head swiveled. "You're cursed?"

Seth grimaced. "Yeah. Don't worry—it's not catching." He didn't want to explain the cockblock curse to someone he'd just met.

"And once we put Longstreet away, Seth and Evan have a number of other disciples to hunt—you and Beck would be part of their intel team," Rowan added.

Logan's genuine smile eased the strain of grief in his features. "That sounds like it could be exciting."

"It would be amazingly helpful. I can't guarantee 'exciting,' but in my book, excitement is overrated and ends with someone getting a concussion." Seth was pleased to hear Logan perk up.

Having a purpose and feeling like he was making a difference would go a long way to helping Logan deal with his grief. If he hit it off with Beck and the others at the compound, he would be safe and among people who understood. Seth couldn't think of a better way to help him move forward.

"I'll get out here with Logan and make introductions," Rowan said as the driver stopped the car in front of a large, white house. "He can take you back to Cassidy's, or wherever you're staying."

"Cassidy's house is fine," Teag said. "And thanks again for the rescue."

Rowan grinned. "Anytime. That's what friends are for."

"Didn't you forget something?" Seth pointed to the still-unconscious man in the backseat.

"Oh, if we must," Rowan replied, rolling her eyes.

"Permit me." The driver, who was built like a nightclub bouncer, got out and manhandled their attacker as if he were a child.

"I'll be right back," he said, carrying the man none-too-gently to the house.

Rowan's phone buzzed, and she looked up when she had checked the screen. "Mrs. Teller and Niella found the item our 'friend' had in his pocket, and she said they'll bring it out tomorrow. She sent me a picture, and confirmed that it's magically active." She turned her phone to show them an odd amulet in a shape Seth had never seen before.

"Another power-booster?" Teag asked.

"That's my bet," Rowan replied. "What I really want to know is, who's their dealer?"

"Wake your new guest up and ask him," Seth said. "And be sure to let us know what you find out. My money is that Longstreet's tangled up in this somehow."

"Oh, we'll get to the bottom of it. You can be sure of that," Rowan promised.

The driver returned, and minutes later Seth and Teag were headed back to downtown Charleston. It had been a long day, and all Seth wanted was the one thing he couldn't have—a long slow evening of lovemaking with Evan before falling asleep tangled up with each other.

"We'll figure it out," Teag said after a while as if he could guess the cause of Seth's worried expression.

Seth gave a curt nod. "I'm sure we will," sounding more confident than he felt.

When he got back to the house, Cassidy and Kell were in the kitchen, working on their laptops and nursing cups of hot chocolate. The aroma of warm cocoa and nutmeg smelled good enough to lift Seth's spirits, especially when he saw Evan at the dining room table with his computer.

"Welcome back!" Cassidy greeted them. "There's plenty of hot cocoa and all the fixings, so grab a cup for yourselves."

Seth poured a cup of the rich mixture and went to sit with Evan. It wasn't the first time they had spent a day apart, but always before Seth had the homecoming to look forward to, taking Evan in his arms, kissing him senseless, and then later exploring each other's bodies in the dark.

Now he felt touch-starved, since the best he could do was blow an air kiss. He leaned close to Evan's neck, not touching, and breathed in the scent of him—shampoo, aftershave, and something uniquely Evan. His cock hardened, not having gotten the memo about the curse.

"Missed you," he growled. The want in Evan's eyes made him even harder.

"Missed you, too." Evan chanced brushing against Seth with his shoulder. They both lurched apart, as if they had touched a live wire.

"I'm sorry," Evan replied, looking miserable. "It's getting worse."

"How do you feel?" Seth pulled up a chair, getting as close as he dared.

"Like I'm fighting off a bad cold," Evan admitted. "I took some ibuprofen. It helped, a little. For now." They both knew what he meant. The symptoms were going to get worse until they were incapacitated. Before they died.

"I'm not going to let Longstreet beat us," Seth replied, knowing that Evan needed to hear that. "We didn't exactly find what we were looking for—but we might have happened on some things that are just as important."

He recapped his day, then listened intently, sipping his hot chocolate, while Evan did the same for him.

"I have the feeling that all this ties together in an important way, and we've actually got more pieces of the puzzle than we realize, but damned if I can put them together yet." Evan finished the last gulp of his drink. Seth thought he detected a whiff of Bailey's and Jameson and didn't begrudge Evan one bit. He was a little jealous he hadn't thought of it himself.

Evan yawned and rubbed his eyes. He looked tired, and dark smudges beneath his eyes told Seth all he needed to know about how worried Evan was about the curse and their ability to stop Longstreet. Seth also knew that if he mentioned Evan needed to rest, his boyfriend would argue the point, and insist on staying up out of a sense of duty and desperation.

Seth wanted to break the curse—and destroy Longstreet. But if his days—hours—with Evan were numbered, then he wasn't ready to let go without coming as close to making love as they could, at least one more time.

"I'm beat. Let's turn in. I'll get up early with you."

Evan drew a breath to protest, but he must have seen something in Seth's eyes that made him change his mind. "Sure. I just wish—"

"Yeah. Me, too."

They said goodnight to the others and headed to their room. Seth closed the door behind them, and Evan fell backward on the bed, arms splayed wide, knees bent at the end of the mattress, legs apart. He looked so sexy, so completely fuckable, and Seth's stiff cock ached with desire.

"Let's get naked and make love," Seth said, his voice low and husky.

Evan raised his head off the mattress. "Are you kidding? We'll spontaneously combust—and not in a good way."

"I've got an idea. Trust me?"

Evan looked at him with a gaze full of longing and love. "Always."

They stripped quickly, and Seth's breath caught when he saw Evan sitting naked on the bed, one leg out straight, and his other knee bent, far enough apart to give Seth a glorious view of Evan's satisfying package.

"God, you're beautiful," Seth said, feeling like he had that first night together when everything was new and unknown between them.

"So are you." Evan looked down, adorably shy, with long lashes and cheeks pinked with desire.

"Lie down on your side, facing the middle." He and Evan were equals, and aside from some fun role play, neither of them tried to dominate the other. But tonight, the tone of command in Seth's voice sent a shiver through Evan. Evan moved to comply, and Seth stretched out across from him.

"If we can't touch, we can at least come together," Seth said. It wasn't exactly "making love," but tonight, robbed of the ability to do more by the curse, all the other terms for the act seemed crass and trivial. "Go ahead. Touch yourself."

Seth reached down, taking himself in hand. It had only been a few days since they'd really made love, but knowing that they couldn't made the ache feel like it had been weeks. Evan did the same, and watching made Seth even harder than before.

"Look at me while you do it," Seth said, keeping his voice low so they wouldn't be overheard, which just made the moment more intimate. "Do you see my hand, stroking my cock? I'm thinking about fucking you. Right now, I'm thinking about how warm your mouth is, how good it is sliding down my shaft, how your tongue feels when you flick it across the head, or through my slit. How I love to see you lap up my pre-come. How your lips look when you've sucked my cock."

Evan groaned, and one glance told Seth his boyfriend was hard as steel and dripping.

"Tell me," Seth said, squeezing the base of his prick so this didn't end too quickly. "Tell me what you're thinking."

"I'm thinking of what it feels like when you open up my ass to fuck me," Evan said, sounding unsure. He raised his gaze to meet Seth's and seemed to find what he needed. "How you rim me with your finger, or your tongue, getting me soft and open. How good it feels when you push a finger inside, and it burns a little, that feeling that tells me I'm gonna get fucked real good."

"Uh." A grunt was all Seth could manage, lost in Evan's voice, the images his words painted, and the sensation of his palm against the sensitive skin of his cock.

"And then, when your finger hits my spot, and all I can feel is fire and hunger." Evan's tone grew bolder, perhaps because he could see the effect his words had on Seth. "And then you slip in another, and it's not enough. Because I want to be filled. So I wriggle a little, to get you to give me three and stretch me good because what I really want is that thick, hard cock of yours balls-deep in my ass."

"Fuck, Evan."

"Yeah, that's what I like," Evan answered with an impish grin. "I love it when you fuck me like you can't hold back, like you're so horny you use my hole to get off, and you pound into me. I love feeling you lose control, knowing I made you go crazy for my ass. I like to feel your fingers dig into my hip, or my shoulder, holding on so you can go faster and harder, knowing there'll be marks."

"God, Evan—" Seth was so close, his balls felt ready to explode. He fucked into the channel of his hand, pretending it was Evan, but although he knew it would do the job, his palm was a poor substitute for the real thing.

"And then, when you come, and I can feel you fill up my ass, and I watch your face, and I realize that I did that to you, I gave you that. And you pull out, and I can feel your come running out of me, down my leg, making me yours—"

Seth came, barely biting back a shout. Ropes of hot spend shot from his cock, landing on the sheets between them. Evan's hips bucked forward, bowing his spine, head thrown back in ecstasy, eyes wide and mouth open, gasping for air as his release fountained over his fist.

For a moment, they lay still, shattered by the force of their climaxes, separate but still together.

"I didn't even get to the part where I fuck you," Evan said, sounding a little sad.

"I love you," Seth whispered.

"I love you, too." Evan's gaze rose to meet his, asking all the questions he'd never put into words. Seth hoped Evan could read all the promises he couldn't speak in his own eyes.

Please don't let this be the last time.

"We should get cleaned up," Seth managed because staring into his lover's eyes was breaking his heart. "And clean up the bed so our host won't have to. I'll go get a cloth. Um…two cloths, maybe." Just in case the curse counted spunk as "touching."

Aftercare was one of Seth's favorite things when he could lavish Evan with attention, gently wiping him clean in the most intimate places, allowing Evan to return the favor. It was a ritual, practical and yet carnally sacred, a binding of sorts between lovers.

He forced himself to leave the bed. The air smelled of sweat and sex. Jerking off together had scratched one itch, but for the first time since he and Evan were together, Seth felt lonely after sex.

That was the real reason why he'd hated hook-ups and one-night stands. Sure, it was exciting upfront, hunting for a partner, anticipating the deed, doing it quick and dirty.

And then…leaving alone.

Waking up alone.

For Seth, that emptiness leeched all the pleasure out of the memory and left him feeling worse. Until he met Evan, and everything changed. Evan hadn't left—even though all Seth could offer was danger and a clusterfuck of a life on a crazy quest they might not survive. Evan stayed, had his back, trusted him. Loved him. And in return, Seth loved Evan harder and deeper than he ever thought he could care for anyone.

Now, Longstreet wanted to take that away from them. *Fuck Longstreet.*

Seth came back with two warm, wet washcloths. He dropped one onto Evan's bare thigh so that their fingers didn't accidentally brush. Evan made a slow, utterly pornographic display of wiping himself up, and Seth watched, breath fast and shallow, like he was seeing a peep show.

"I want to beat this curse," Evan said. Any shyness had fled, and the determination in the set of Evan's jaw and the glint in his eye showed Seth the stubbornness he'd come to expect from his partner.

"We're going to finish Longstreet, and then the rest of those fuckers, and we're going to live a long, happy life filled with awesome sex."

Despite everything, Seth had to chuckle. "After this dry spell, don't expect to get out of bed for a month." That made Evan smile, as Seth had intended. Anything to not see despair in his lover's eyes.

We're going to get through this. And for all the grief he's caused us, I intend to push Longstreet through that fucking rift myself.

7

EVAN

"The good news is, we've traced the heritage of the touch-me-not spell cast on you and Seth," Rowan said.

"What's the bad news?" Evan looked up from the old registry books he'd been combing through at the St. Expeditus safe house. He got up for a fresh cup of coffee, a necessary indulgence to fight off the fatigue of the curse. If he didn't have much time left, Evan was damn sure he was going to stay awake for as much of it as he could.

"We still can't lift it." Rowan grimaced, a sign of shared frustration, although her consequences for hitting a dead-end weren't nearly as literal as Evan's. "But for what it's worth—and it might turn out to be worth something important—it did give us a little more insight into Michael Longstreet."

Evan drained his coffee in one long pull, set his cup on the side-board, and came back to the long table where he, Logan, Beck, and an ever-changing set of St. Expeditus Society members had spent much of the day combing through old documents kept by the supernatural community, about the business dealings of its members.

He and Logan bonded over their shared shock at the details the old documents revealed. Beck didn't seem surprised, but then, he'd grown up in that strata of society, even if he'd renounced all ties.

"Cheer me up. Tell us what you found." Evan did his best not to dwell on what the curse had taken from him, or what lay ahead. That focus kept him functioning but hadn't raised his spirits. Last night, Seth had insisted on sleeping on the couch, after an accidental collision in bed had them both scrambling clear in pain. Waking up alone plunged Evan's mood deeper into darkness.

"You said that Longstreet's family had been wealthy and then lost everything in the Civil War," Rowan said, looking at Evan.

He nodded. "That's right. Seth and I found the location of his family's old plantation."

"The touch-me-not curse was favored among wealthy witch families as a way to keep their children from making unapproved matches," Rowan replied. "So if Mama or Daddy didn't like the suitor, a curse made sure nobody eloped—or ended up unexpectedly pregnant."

"Wow. Controlling much?" Evan muttered.

"Over time, its use fell out of favor," Rowan added. "It came to be considered archaic, overstepping, especially when the 'children' were actually adults." She shrugged. "I guess it goes to show that witchy families have a lot of the same problems with teenagers as everyone else."

"I wouldn't be so sure that the curse fell into disuse, although I believe they gave lip service to the idea," Beck spoke up. "The older generations never really gave up on a preference for arranged marriages to further the family fortunes and strengthen the magic. I saw how some of my cousins were married off. The old men worried about consent about as much as they liked gay heirs to the inheritance," he added, with a flinch that gave Evan to suggest Beck spoke from experience.

"I don't doubt that you're right," Rowan agreed. "People who are discouraged about the rate of progress in normal life would despair over how slowly things change in supernatural society."

"How does that tell us anything about Longstreet?" Evan pressed.

Rowan met his gaze. "Because that kind of curse—and the wealth that fostered those types of concerns—was still above the station of Albert Mosby's family, even with their relative prosperity." She used

Longstreet's original name. "They were well-off by general standards, but not in the league of the old families, even before the War."

"Aspirational curses?" Beck asked, raising an eyebrow. "Seriously?"

"It makes sense, in a twisted sort of way," Evan replied. "There's usually a love-hate relationship going on when someone envies the wealthy. On one hand, they hate the snobbery and pretense, and on the other, they want to have just as much money so that they can be snobby and pretentious, too."

"He's right," Logan agreed. "It reminds me of high school bitchiness, but I guess some things never change."

Beck's expression mingled interest and sadness. From what little Evan had heard about the man, he'd come from wealth and power and given up both voluntarily. That he'd taken up residence in a safe house compound suggested that others hadn't been much at peace with his decision. That gave Evan grudging respect for Beck.

"There are different versions of the curse," Rowan continued. "That's pretty common. It's like folksongs or old poems—the details change over the years, and certain performers make changes that suit their own styles. Spells work much the same way."

"Really?" Evan couldn't help being intrigued. He and Seth had learned rote magic from other hunters, but he'd never had the chance to work with a witch who was an ally. He hoped he lived long enough to put what he learned to good use.

"Oh, witchcraft has its divas, to be sure." Rowan laughed. "Some of them just can't help but make everything dramatic. Others like to add little flourishes, and a few have 'signatures' of sorts in the way they craft their spells. That helps us trace a curse like this back over time—almost like leaving fingerprints."

"And?" Logan looked curious, despite his earlier apprehension. Then again, Evan thought, Logan had been sneaking glances at Beck Pendlewood all day.

Evan couldn't fault him—Beck was a handsome man. Early thirties, thick chestnut hair, toned body, and high cheekbones. He looked like he'd walked off the cover of a fashion magazine, even dressed in a T-shirt and artfully ripped jeans. Logan didn't break any mirrors, either.

Maybe the two fugitives would find each other, which would defi-nitely improve their experience being in witchy WITSEC. Evan wished them well.

His phone vibrated, and he glanced down. *Thinking of you. Wish I was there. Love you.*

Evan's lips quirked in a sad half-smile, and he texted a reply under the table, trying not to be conspicuous. *Miss you. Love you.* He sighed. Seth and he had started sexting when even the slightest touch— through clothing and padding—made contact unbearable. *At least the curse doesn't prohibit digital connection,* he thought. Those little stolen moments were keeping him sane.

"—there are enough signature flourishes for us to trace a particular version of the spell through the hands of the most notable practition-ers," Rowan replied to Logan's question, jarring Evan out of his thoughts. "One of whom was Lucius Pendlewood, back in the 1930s, and Sinclair Etheridge, in the 1940s."

Beck sat up like he'd been poked. "What were they doing with a guy like Longstreet?" He must have realized how that sounded because his cheeks colored, and he looked chagrined. "Sorry, that really came out wrong. Then again, there's no good way to say it. If we're right, Longstreet's prior identities all involved not just sacri-ficing people to keep his immortality—bad enough—but maybe having a hand in the underground relic trade. So he's shady as fuck, doesn't run in the same society circles, and isn't a particularly strong witch on his own. Why would Lucius and Sinclair have bothered with him?"

"At least in the early days, after Longstreet relocated to Charleston to follow the deputy he was stalking, he probably tried to ingratiate himself to the old families," Rowan mused. "Favors given and received. It wouldn't be the first time a powerful witch strung along a lesser warlock and then didn't keep his end of the bargain."

To Evan, it sounded like witchy drama only differed from its non-magical counterpart in being a lot more dangerous. *Having magic—like money—doesn't automatically make anyone a better person. Just able to do a lot more damage when they go bad.*

"What does that matter?" Evan felt his temper grow short—like his time. They might be turning up fascinating tidbits of trivia, but nothing yet that would bring down Longstreet or save him and Seth.

"We had a look at the relic the man who attacked Seth and Logan was using to amplify his power." Rowan had a glint of compassion in her eyes that suggested she understood Evan's impatience. "It's old and well-crafted. Not something that would be left lying around, or picked up at a flea market, so to speak."

Are there witchy flea markets? Evan couldn't help wondering. His mind conjured up an image of Diagon Alley sidewalk sales, and the absurdity made him smile, just a bit.

"So how did he get it?" Logan asked. He looked a little panicked, probably reliving the chase. Beck shifted closer, and Evan averted his eyes before he could see whether Beck laid a comforting hand on the other man's arm. Evan hungered for Seth's touch so bad it made his teeth ache. He didn't want to be jealous, but he mourned his enforced isolation.

"The man's name is Jon Fuller," Rowan replied. "He's a witch of minor power and minimal training—just enough to be dangerous. He runs with a group of witchlings who call themselves the Shadow Coven, but they're more of a street gang, if the truth be told."

Beck laughed, but his humor had a note of self-recrimination in it. "Witchy West Side Story? What you're really talking about is white-collar crime versus street crime. The Pendlewoods and the Etheridges founded two of the oldest covens in Charleston, and I wouldn't hold either family up as a paragon of virtue." His bitter tone suggested to Evan that Beck was still coming to terms with his tainted heritage. Logan's compassionate glance confirmed the instant attraction Evan had suspected between the two.

Rowan didn't take offense. "You're right. But most coven members don't have your...unique...perspective."

"Lucky them," Beck muttered.

"Fuller was unconscious from the mojo we laid on him last night, so all we know is based on the ID in his wallet," Rowan continued. "Want to come watch the questioning?"

"You guys aren't going to...torture him or mind-meld him...are you?" Logan paled.

Rowan shook her head. "No. I told you we're the good guys." She shrugged. "I won't rule out smacking him around a little, but definitely stopping short of Force choking. Boleskine House Conventions forbid it."

"What kind of conventions?" Logan asked, looking simultaneously scared and intrigued.

"Think of it as the witch version of the Geneva Conventions," Rowan replied. "Rules for warfare and the treatment of prisoners."

"If Fuller isn't helpful, you don't have to do the smacking," Evan said. "I'll be happy to step in. After all, he came after Seth. Maybe you could step out for coffee and give me a minute or two alone with him?" The others chuckled, then sobered when they realized he wasn't kidding.

Rowan gave him an appraising look. "Maybe. If it comes to that. I'll keep it in mind. Come with me."

They followed Rowan deeper into the Society's safe house, to the back right quarter, which had been reinforced with spells as well as steel bars. "This is for when we have supernatural folks who can't be released but aren't willing to stay voluntarily," Rowan said.

"Witch jail?" Logan asked, looking nervous.

"Pretty much. We can't give our kind over to the regular police. So we park them here—where they can't do any harm—until we figure out what to do next," Rowan replied.

Evan's first thought was that it all seemed high-handed. Then he reminded himself that he and Seth—and the other hunters—took it upon themselves to be judge, jury, and executioner when it came to the witch-disciples and the monsters. So maybe the differences were more a matter of skill and degree between himself and the witches. That insight was uncomfortable, but he couldn't deny the truth of it.

The gray room looked like all the interrogation chambers Evan had seen on TV. Rowan ushered them into the viewing area, with a one-way mirrored window that Evan could sense without touching had been augmented with magic.

"We can send magic through in an emergency. Those in the room can't send it out," Rowan replied, guessing his thoughts as he studied the glass.

Logan looked completely freaked out. Beck stood close enough to bump shoulders. Evan's gut twisted in grief and envy, missing Seth.

"Father Anne will be doing the questioning," Rowan said. "She'll wear an earpiece, so if we have questions we want her to ask, I can let her know," she pointed to a microphone on the recording console.

Two guards brought in the man Seth and Teag had fought in the alley. Jon Fuller was probably five foot eight and one-fifty, manacled at the wrists and ankles with what was doubtless spelled silver.

Evan had found himself expecting Fuller to look like a bad biker or a Hogwarts reject from Rowan's description as a "gang" member. Instead, he resembled the kind of local tough guy Evan saw at every roadside bar. Evan figured Fuller was probably about his age—mid-twenties—but at the moment, he looked younger, flipping back and forth between fear and swagger.

"I don't know who you are, but this is kidnapping. I demand to be released." Fuller's salvo would have been more convincing if his voice hadn't risen in panic.

"You attacked three men in an alley. We want to know why," Father Anne asked, her tone cold and flat.

"Not me. Musta grabbed the wrong guy," Fuller replied with a smirk, but the cockiness didn't reach his eyes.

"Nope. We've got witnesses. So...who put you up to it?"

Fuller was twitchy as fuck, gaze darting all over the room, jaw clenching. "I can't tell you. Whatever you're gonna do to me, they'll do worse."

"Or we can give you safe passage to somewhere they won't find you, where you could start over—with supervision, until you prove good intentions," Father Anne offered.

"Look Father, it don't work that way." Fuller's tongue darted out, moistening dry lips.

"Are you afraid of the other gang members, or whoever's running relics and spells to you?"

Fuller looked up sharply. "How—?" Realizing what he'd nearly said, he clamped his mouth shut.

"I don't work for the old families or the established covens. And right now, I'm not working for God, either," Father Anne replied, and

MORGAN BRICE

with her Doc Martens and tats, she didn't look like someone to cross. "Your gang wanted attention. You've got it. And you're also getting played by your arms dealer."

"I don't know what you're talking about." Fuller looked away, looking tough and terrified.

"You and the other witchy gangs think you're poking the bear," Father Anne said. "You figure if you're a big enough pain in the ass, the old families and powerful covens will notice you and make a place at the table. And the truth is, you shouldn't have been left out on your own—but this is the wrong way to get invited inside. The person who's supplying the relics and spells to you and your friends has his own agenda—and you're just redshirts."

Evan glanced at Logan. He saw what he figured was an expression similar to his own on the other man's face—torn between sympathizing with Fuller's goal and faulting his methods. Beck still stood protectively close to Logan, but his attention remained riveted on the prisoner, with a look on his face Evan couldn't decipher.

"We'll give you asylum," Father Anne said. "Because we both know you can't go back. You didn't finish the job, and no matter what you tell your gang, they'll figure you flipped on them once we brought you here."

"Fuck you." Fuller's voice lacked venom, and Evan figured the other man had probably come to the same, unenviable, conclusion.

"Why did they want the men you attacked?" Father Anne asked, switching directions.

Fuller stared at her in silence for a few minutes, then sagged. "I don't exactly know."

"How about telling me what you do know, even if it's not 'exact'?"

Fuller licked his lips again and looked like he wanted to bolt. The silver chains and locked door made that impossible. He finally let out a long breath. "I'm not very high up. Just a soldier. I've got just enough magic to be too weird for the mundanes, and not enough to count with the witches. But Colin, our leader, doesn't think it's fair we can't be part of the 'real' witches. And Mikey, his second-in-command, has an old grudge against the big-deal witches. Something about how when bad things happened to his family, none of them would help."

"How does this have anything to do with the men you attacked?" Father Anne prodded. But Evan saw the way her gaze cut to the window, where Rowan watched. If Longstreet was pissed after a century that he hadn't been invited to sit with the "cool kids," Mikey sounded like he was on the same path.

"Don't know. I get orders, not explanations," Fuller responded. "But I overheard some of the lieutenants talking. Something about how when the shake-up happens, we'll get our due. And getting those charms to help us do more with our magic, that's just the beginning."

"How?"

Fuller bit his lip as if he were arguing with himself over how much to say. "If we do good, the dealer says he will introduce us to his boss, who can make us live forever."

Evan caught his breath. He knew first-hand what happened to those who met Longstreet's "boss." That wasn't the kind of immortality anyone wanted, being consumed by an angry witch-ghost trapped in a pocket of space and time. His fists clenched at the deception Longstreet used to lure his accomplices, who he'd be quick to abandon or kill to save his own neck.

"Do you know why the dealer wanted the men you attacked?" Father Anne asked again.

Fuller shook his head. "Just that they had to be alive when I brought them in, and that they had some magic, so I'd need the relic." He slumped. "I lost it. They'll kill me just for that."

"Are there other relics?"

Fuller nodded. His earlier bravado was gone, and he looked like a beaten dog. "Yeah. They do different things, but all of them turn up the volume on our magic."

"Had you used a relic before?" Father Anne had gone from hardass to confidante, offering a slight smile of encouragement.

"There was this other guy the dealer said we needed to tail. Said his boss wanted to see the guy. I was supposed to follow him and report back on where he was. The charm they gave me made my magic stronger, at least for a little while. I can give someone a jolt when I touch them, knock them out."

"Shit. I've seen him before." Logan stared at the prisoner, eyes wide. "He kept showing up places we went. I figured it was just a coincidence. I mean, you live in a neighborhood, you run into the same people. That son of a bitch was tracking us!" He looked like he might go through the window to get a piece of Fuller.

Beck laid a hand on Logan's shoulder. "Easy."

Logan glared at him but didn't shake free. "He helped the guy who killed Blake."

Beck nodded. "And he's chained up. He's never going home. Let it play out."

Logan finally dropped his head, and his body relaxed. Beck squeezed his shoulder. Evan looked away.

"Did you notice any other effects from the relic?" Father Anne asked the prisoner.

Fuller licked his lips nervously. "I didn't like it. When I carried it, sometimes I'd have blackouts. I'd wake up places I didn't remember going to, with blood on my hands, and I'd have bad dreams about things I might have done."

That sounds even worse than I expected, Evan thought.

"What happens now?" Fuller asked.

"You'll go before the Tribunal for using magic as a weapon, relic misuse, probably other charges," Father Anne replied. "I'll make a note of your cooperation, and any additional help—like names, locations, that sort of thing—will certainly be considered when it comes to determining your punishment. Then you'll be relocated to a safe, magic-limited area until the problem here is handled, and you've served your time."

Fuller didn't look happy, but Evan figured the other man knew he was getting a better deal than he'd get from his gang. He didn't say anything else when the guards came for him, and he shuffled out, looking tired and defeated.

Evan shook his head. "First the curse, now Longstreet sends goons to rough us up? Why not just kill us?"

"Because you've been protected," Father Anne said, as she came through the doorway into the viewing area. "He didn't count on you having connections with the Alliance. If you'd shown up entirely on your own...it might have gone very differently."

Evan swallowed hard since he hadn't thought things had exactly gone swimmingly. But it could certainly have been worse.

"We've still got a few hours before I promised Cassidy I'd drop you off at Trifles and Folly," Rowan said. "Go get some food in the kitchen, and I'll make sure there's fresh coffee in the conference room."

"I think we've got a better idea of which businesses Longstreet and his past identities used," Beck said as they followed Rowan down the hall. He and Logan walked together, leaving Evan up front with Rowan, and Father Anne behind them. "Up until the fifties, he was a lawyer. After that, he was one kind of 'business consultant' or another," Beck continued. "My bet is that he was using magic or relics to fix his clients' problems."

"That's possible," Rowan replied. "He'd be using limited magic, nothing that was likely to draw attention from the established players."

"I've been looking at the Tribunal reports from years ago, for anything that might link back to Longstreet," Evan said. "I've got a list of possibilities I need to research more. Maybe this isn't the first time Longstreet's provoked trouble. I wouldn't be surprised if he's stirred the pot all along."

"A couple of the relics have links to Chalmers Etheridge, who was a notable collector of occult objects," Rowan said, ushering them into a tidy kitchen. Bags of snacks, fresh fruit, and a vegetable tray filled the table. A fresh pot of coffee sat ready, as well as cans of soda.

"Eat up, boys," Rowan said.

"Chalmers Etheridge is dead." Beck continued the conversation as they all helped themselves to food. "My cousins killed him, looking for the demon box so they could kill me."

Evan filed that piece of information away for later. "I'm thinking about what Fuller said about their dealer—probably the middle man between the gangs and Longstreet—telling them that the big boss could make them live forever." He frowned. "I doubt Longstreet wants to hand out immortality like that."

"What do you think he intends?" Logan asked.

"I have a theory, but I want to do a little more checking first," Evan replied. "And I think I'm going to bring Brent Lawson and Ben Nolan in on some PI stuff."

They ate quickly, and Evan was surprised at how hungry he was. His appetite had been off, and he'd attributed it to the curse, as well as his mood. The coffee helped, and so did Rowan's touch, when she added healing energy and eased the curse's hold once more.

"It's getting harder to do, isn't it?" he asked when she removed her hand from his arm. Beck and Logan looked on, worried. Father Anne just looked pissed, and Evan knew that she'd take a piece of Longstreet if she ever caught up to him, just on account of the curse.

"I'm sorry," Rowan replied. "But, yes. The curse is tightening. We need to find Longstreet—the sooner, the better.

Evan forced himself to function, even though he felt like he was working through an awful cold or a bout of the flu. His head had a non-stop, dull ache; he knew he was running a low-grade fever. His ribs were sore. Even his eyes hurt. Coffee soured in his stomach, but it kept him awake and working. As the saying went, he'd sleep when he was dead.

When they finished eating, Father Anne and Rowan excused themselves. Evan pulled out his phone. "Go ahead," he told Logan and Beck. I want to make a couple of calls, and then I'll be right in."

Beck's worried gaze lingered. Evan managed a wan smile. "I'm okay enough to make it back to the conference room," he assured his new friend. Beck didn't look convinced, but he left Evan to his calls.

Finally alone, Evan reacted to the latest texts from Seth. He didn't how, when, or where Seth had managed to snap a few dick pics, but there they were, in all their glory.

Nice. I think the profile's a bit better than the full-frontal, he texted back. *Wish I could taste test.* He sighed, feeling their enforced celibacy in his heart as well as his balls. Evan swore he would never take casual touches for granted again, not when he desperately missed the warmth of Seth's hand and the brush of his lips.

Evan hesitated, then deleted the photos. If he didn't survive, no one going through his phone needed to see them. Then he found Brent Lawson's contact info and placed the call.

"Hey, Evan! How are things going?"

Despite everything, hearing his friend's voice cheered Evan, at least a little. "Not as well as I'd like. I wondered if you could team up with Ben Nolan up in Cape May and chase down some gumshoe stuff for us. I'm looking for a pattern of missing persons with unusual circumstances in Charleston, and people who went missing and were found dead—with odd damage to the bodies."

"That's really specific," Brent said. "Is everything okay?"

"We're going after the next disciple in Charleston, and it's tougher than usual. I think he's responsible for more disappearances that just the descendants of the posse, but I need proof—and I'm still working on the 'why.' And there's a bit of a rush for this."

"Okay," Brent agreed. "I'll call Ben, and we'll dig in. We might even figure out some of the why once we find out who went missing and whether they were linked to any of the other people. What period?"

"Start with the last twenty years and ignore the men in the Miller family who went missing—they're the deputy's descendants."

"Gotcha. When do you need it?"

Yesterday. "As soon as possible. The disciple put a curse on Seth and me, and time's running out."

"Fuck. Let me get started. I'll call back tonight with whatever we've found so far. Have you talked to Travis about this curse stuff?"

"I think Seth gave him a call early on. I was pretty banged up in the car wreck, so I don't remember a lot from the first days."

"I'll have him call if he needs more info. Hang in there, Evan. We're gonna do right by you and Seth."

Evan resolved to hang on to borrowed hope for as long as he could. He had so many reasons to want to live—a future with Seth, a chance for a normal life of peace and quiet when they were done with their quest, and friends who had their backs, even in crazy situations.

There were times in the past when Evan had been close to giving up. When he'd been kicked out of his home and church right after high school, sent into the world with nothing but a backpack and the money he'd been able to save from summer jobs. And later, when a relationship turned abusive and he'd run for his life from his ex. But each time, Evan had mustered the will to go on, although it had been a near thing, sometimes.

But now, with a life filled with Seth, friends, and a purpose, Evan had more reasons than ever to find a way to survive. The stubbornness his father had always considered a flaw turned out, once again, to be an asset.

Fuck Longstreet. I'm going to survive just for spite.

They went through another few pots of coffee, and stacks of old books and ledgers. Logan and Beck huddled over their tomes, often bending their heads together to confer on a passage or odd language. Evan had to admit they made a cute couple and hoped for both their sakes that the attraction sparked into something more. He didn't know either man well, but he thought both of them seemed lost and lonely.

When his phone buzzed a few hours later, Evan thought it might be Seth, or perhaps an update from Brent or Travis. Instead, it was a number he didn't recognize.

"Hello, Evan? It's Emily, the intern from the Historical Archive. Mrs. Morrissey said you were in a hurry, so I wanted to call with what I've found so far."

"Hi, Emily. Do you mind if I put you on speaker?"

Logan and Beck looked up.

"That's fine," Emily replied.

"What do you have?" Evan found himself crossing his fingers under the table.

"It took some digging because the names you gave me must have been real introverts, or they just didn't like the spotlight, but I did turn up some connections," she reported. "Basically, I put together a spreadsheet, and I can email it to you if that's okay."

Okay? You're a frickin' angel. "Yes, that's definitely okay," Evan replied.

"I turned up the business and professional licenses and office rental deeds under the names you gave me," Emily replied. "So all of their license and certification renewals, their LLC filings, that sort of thing. And in the process, I also found out that those men all used the same attorney and accountant. Or at least, the same firm—it's a long stretch of time, so the individual people would have changed, of course."

Evan wasn't so sure about that if Longstreet had found other long-lived people to help him hide his immortality. "You're right—that is weird. Is that information—the names of those people—also in the report?"

"Sure is," she answered. "I'm still going to keep looking—I'm not through everything yet—but I thought you'd rather have it in chunks rather than wait."

"You thought right. I can't tell you how much I appreciate this." Evan gave her his email address. "Thank you from the bottom of my heart."

She laughed. "Wow. I'm glad something I did means so much to someone. Usually, research is a thankless task."

"Not this time." Evan resolved to see if he could find a way to do something nice for her in return. He figured Cassidy would know what might work. "And if you do find anything else, please let me know."

"Absolutely!" Emily sounded so chipper; she made Evan believe things might work out.

He ended the call just as his laptop pinged with the new file she sent.

"If you don't mind forwarding a copy to us, we can go over it and see if anything jumps out," Beck offered. "I often end up knowing more than I think I know because I'll see a name or detail that pulls up a memory I didn't think was important."

"Thanks." Evan felt worn ragged, but he gulped down the last of his cold coffee, waiting for the caffeine to hit with a burst of energy.

Beck cleared his throat. "I, uh, know a little about curses, having been under one myself. You don't know me, and you don't have a reason to trust me. But if I can help in any way, I'm here for you."

"Me, too." Logan jumped in.

Evan managed a tired smile. "Thank you. I appreciate it. We've been under tight deadlines before with the disciples, but usually because they were going to kill the victim, not because we were going to drop dead. Or, whatever it is that's going to happen."

"If the theory is right that Longstreet is provoking a confrontation, he sure seems to be making it hard to find him," Logan observed.

"I was thinking the same thing," Beck said. "And that might mean we've missed something that's under our noses. I want to go back over everything—plus Emily's information. There's got to be a link between the missing people, the witch gangs, the relics, and the data we've got on Longstreet and all his prior selves. If he's expecting you and Seth to stage a showdown, then he must believe you can find—or have already found—that information."

"Or he thinks we're smarter than we are."

Logan rolled his eyes. "I don't think so. We can figure this out—and beat this son of a bitch. I'm not letting him get away with killing Blake —and I have no intention of letting him kill you and Seth, either." Evan saw fire in the man's eyes, and the certainty of Logan's conviction heartened him.

Beck reached over and took Logan's hand. Logan hesitated for a second, then interlaced their fingers. "We are not going to let you die," Beck said, his voice low and quiet. "So that's enough of that."

"Okay," Evan said, nodding. "You're right."

Rowan came to the door. "Are you ready to head out, Evan? I promised Cassidy I'd take you over to Trifles and Folly."

Evan looked at Logan and Beck, unsure.

"Go," Beck said with a wave of his hand. "We'll let you know if we find something, or need to cross-reference. It'll help for you to get a change of scenery."

Evan thanked them again and headed out with Rowan. He gave her the condensed version of their discoveries on the way back to town.

"So we've found a lot of information, but we're missing the thing to tie it together, the 'a-ha' moment," he concluded.

"That can happen when you're racing the clock. I know this is easier said than done, but if there's any way to give yourself a mental break—take a nap, play with Cassidy's dog, watch a movie—sometimes your brain serves up the answer after it's had a chance to change the subject."

Evan bit back mentioning the reality of impending death. *Rowan knows that. And she's right. It's just hard to think of anything else.*

"I'll try," he promised.

"Father Clemons has his contact at the Sinistram tracking those relics," she added. "There may be something that gives us a clue to where they came from and how they're being moved. And once this is over, I want to talk more with you and Seth about this 'rote magic' of yours."

"It's not real magic," Evan replied.

"Actually, it is."

He turned to look at her, dumbfounded. "It is?"

Rowan nodded. "You've got latent power. Not strong enough to register on ability tests, probably less than the members of the witch gangs. But it's still magic, still real."

"Wow," Evan said, surprised and oddly happy at the thought. "I hope we have the chance to figure it out."

Rowan gave him an encouraging smile. "Hang in there. Good people are working on it."

Evan felt self-conscious as Rowan put her four-way blinkers on and double-parked in front of Trifles and Folly to walk him to the door just a sidewalk's width away, like a small child.

"I know it's only four feet," she said quietly. "But a lot can happen in unwarded space in four feet."

Evan stepped to the door, and felt a tingle of magic flow over him, like at the Society's compound and Cassidy's house. *If—when we're through with this, I need to learn how to strengthen the wards on our truck and RV.*

"Talk to you soon," Rowan promised, heading back to her car.

Trifles and Folly was located in an old block of storefronts on King Street, with gilded letters on the big front windows, large, decorative carriage-style lanterns on either side of the store, and a black fabric awning. The window display held a tasteful collection of antique china, vintage costume jewelry, and bric-a-brac.

The bell over the door rang as Evan entered. Bells were an old form of protective magic, warding off evil as well as notifying everyone of a new visitor. He stopped and looked around, taking in the shop, trying to square it with his mental picture.

Inside, a wooden floor and dark wooden display cases gave the shop an old-world feel. The cases held expensive jewelry made from gold, silver, and gemstones. Shelves along the walls showcased antique silver tea and coffee sets, an elaborate Russian samovar, large china serving plates, old clocks, and other beautiful and expensive pieces.

Cassidy and a woman Evan didn't recognize looked up when he entered. Cassidy's broad smile made Evan feel at home.

"Evan! Wow—is it already that time?" Cassidy checked her phone and shook her head. "The day has flown." She gestured toward her companion, whom Evan guessed was the assistant Teag had mentioned.

"This is Maggie, our utterly invaluable right-hand woman!" Cassidy said proudly. Maggie grinned. Her gray hair, streaked with magenta, was in a trendy cut, and her clothing was a quirky boho mix that looked good on her.

"You must be Evan. Teag and Cassidy have told me all about you and Seth. I'm glad to finally meet you!" Maggie's friendly, open manner put Evan at ease.

"We've been pretty busy, but I think I can steal a minute or two to show you where everything is." Cassidy slipped out from behind the counter and waved for Evan to follow her into the next room, which held a table and chairs and a galley kitchen.

"We've got good wifi, so you can set up here," Cassidy offered. "There's a fresh pot of coffee, sweet tea, and some snacks in the refrigerator, homemade cookies from Maggie on the counter, and the bathroom is that way," she added, pointing. "We'll close up on time, but it's been busy, and I don't want to leave Maggie with everything."

"That's perfectly all right," Evan said. "I can entertain myself—and I've got a lot of data to search through." He patted his backpack. "Rowan sent the relics and amulets taken from the gang members in the attacks. She was hoping your magic would be able to make something of them."

Cassidy regarded his backpack like it had become a snake. "Okay. Let's do that after we close up—in case it knocks me for a loop."

Evan used the restroom, poured himself some tea, grabbed a couple of snickerdoodle cookies, and then settled down at the table with his computer. The old store felt oddly comfortable, although Evan had never visited before. He chalked that up to the protective wardings. A glimpse of all the intriguing pieces for sale up front tugged at his curiosity, but he figured that was best saved for after the shop closed and the regular people went home.

Given Cassidy's ability with touch magic and her Alliance connections, Evan felt certain all the inventory had been screened for haunts or bad juju. He wondered how that process worked and vowed to ask Cassidy about it later. Evan couldn't help feeling excited to see Cassidy use her gift on the relics he'd brought.

How did the store find the pieces it sold? Evan's imagination supplied several possibilities—estate sales, private owners, auctions—even yard sales. That made him think more about where Longstreet sourced the black-market relics and objects he supplied as weapons to the gangs.

Evan wasn't the hacker that Seth was, but he'd learned a lot from his partner. He and the others had been focused on researching the background of Longstreet and his connections. Maybe Evan could flip things and look at how Longstreet acquired the pieces, and how they got from him to guys like Fuller and his gang.

That meant logging into the Darke Web, an "underground" internet protected by ensorcelled encryption used by members of the supernatural community. While some areas of the Darke Web served legitimate purposes—connecting researchers and people with magical abilities who had questions only their peers would understand—there were plenty of other, shadier sites that attracted a seedy and criminal clientele.

Seth had shown him how to navigate this hidden online world, with special browsers and layers of magicked security. Like going to the cheatin' side of town, no one here used real names, and no one was who they claimed to be.

"A wretched hive of scum and villainy," Evan muttered to himself.

Items posted for sale on the sites here were guaranteed to be stolen, haunted, cursed, or maybe all of the above. Evan logged into the Darke Web equivalent of eBay, but none of the supposedly magical items looked legit. That left Crowleyslist, named for the famed English dark magician. Just going on that site always made Evan want to smudge with sage and take a supernatural Silkwood shower—maybe at the same time. Everything listed was real—and bad news.

Need a Hand of Glory? Take your pick. Bits and pieces of people, birds, animals, and sea creatures for various spells? Available dried, pickled, flash-frozen, vacuum-packed, and, for a premium, custom-shipped in dry ice. Evan felt certain that nothing on Crowleyslist was responsibly or sustainably sourced—or even slightly legal.

The amulets offered for sale looked authentic—and terrifying. Evan could almost feel the dark power and malice through the connection and hoped it was merely his imagination. Just in case, he stopped, went to the cupboards for supplies he felt sure Cassidy would keep on hand, then set down a salt ring around his chair, and burned a bundle of sage on the table next to him.

Mummified remains, misappropriated antiquities, medallions carved with dark magic runes and sigils "guaranteed" to wreak all kinds of harm...all bought and sold with Bitcoin, keeping both parties anonymous.

Evan's mind spun. How did these sites get away with the illegal trade? But he knew the answer. Layers of secrets and lies, anonymous servers, payoffs, and blackmail, and a willingness to vanish from one place and pop up in another.

He scanned the objects, looking for ones that amplified power, or seemed similar to those they'd recovered from the gang. Evan frowned as he noted a seller's name that looked familiar in a listing. Ryan. He flipped back to the other listings he'd noted. All from "Ryan."

On a whim, he searched the site for "Ryan." Two pages of results made him stare at the screen and let out a low whistle.

One page of listings showcased a dozen malicious objects of power. The other page, labeled "Ryan's Mart," listed people for sale, described in language that accentuated what would be most attractive to a super-natural buyer. Minor or latent magical talent. Blood type. Health record—including a note about whether any conditions were communicable through blood, raw meat, or uncooked organs. Whether they'd been reported missing, been added to the federal database of missing persons, or had a criminal record which might make them—or their fingerprints—identifiable to authorities.

The site's name sounded vaguely familiar. He did a search on the regular web and felt bile rise in his throat. "Ryan's Slave Mart" had been the precursor of the Charleston Slave Market, one of the largest and busiest human auctions in the world, before the Civil War.

Evan's stomach pitched as he realized what he was looking at. Human trafficking—of a very specific kind. "Ryan" supplied humans to supernatural and magical creatures for use in rituals, as blood slaves, servants, Renfields, sacrifices—and food.

"Oh, God." He ran for the bathroom and puked his guts up, partly from the curse, partly at the implications of what he found.

A knock on the door roused him. "Evan? Are you okay?" Cassidy asked.

Evan wiped his mouth. "Yeah. Sorta. I found something important. I'll be right out." He cupped his hands under the faucet and rinsed his mouth, then flushed away the evidence. When he came out, Seth and Teag had joined Cassidy in the break room, which meant Maggie was still up front.

"Evan?" Seth asked, worried. Evan could see the tension in Seth's body as he strained against instinct to hug Evan.

"I think I know what Longstreet's been up to," Evan said, unable to keep his loathing out of his voice. "He's selling dark magic relics—and those people who've gone missing? He's selling them, too."

The others stared at him in stunned horror. "How sure are you?" Teag asked when he finally found his voice.

"Pretty damn sure." Evan brought up his search results, and the others gasped and cursed as they read the damning evidence.

Teag glanced to Cassidy. "We've got to alert Sorren. He and Donnelly are not going to take this well."

Cassidy snorted. "Ya think? This is going to go very badly."

"What do you mean?" Seth asked as he looked from one person to another.

Cassidy chuckled. "Archibald Donnelly is a necromancer. And you know about Sorren. Sorren and Donnelly were among a number of the witches and immortal creatures in Charleston—and the South—that did not support the Confederacy. Some of those 'amazing strokes of luck' that turned the tide of the war were subtle magics or supernatural meddling. Both Sorren and Donnelly have very strong feelings on the subject. So if Longstreet might have gotten any leniency before—not that he deserved any—that likelihood now is zilch."

Evan gave a curt nod. "Good." A commotion in the front of the store made everyone turn as the bells above the entranceway jangled wildly, and the door slammed open.

"Where is she? Where is Cassidy Kincaide?" a man demanded.

"Now just a minute!" Maggie protested. "You can't go back there."

Cassidy and the others rushed toward the shop just as the stranger reached the doorway to the break room. Evan saw them all brace for a fight. Instead, they stared in surprise as the newcomer dropped to his knees.

"Sanctuary!" he pleaded. "I claim sanctuary!"

8

SETH

CASSIDY TOOK A STEP CLOSER TO THE STRANGE MAN, STAYING WELL OUT OF his reach. "I'm Cassidy Kincaide. Who are you?"

"Ian Taylor. My older brother, Curtis, is the leader of the Shadow Coven. I will tell you everything you want to know, but please, save my brother. They're going to get slaughtered."

Seth took a half-step to the side to get a better look. Ian appeared to be in his early twenties, with long dark hair and sharp-edged features. His gaze darted around the room, on alert for threats, reminding Seth of a feral cat.

"Can we give him sanctuary?" Maggie asked, standing in the doorway behind Ian, broom in hand and raised to give the man a good thwack if needed.

Cassidy thought for a moment, then nodded. "Actually, I think we can. From magical pursuers, if not human law enforcement. Sorren is part owner of Trifles and Folly, we're heavily warded, and Sorren has declared the city—and certainly the shop—to be under his protection. So anyone who attacks the store magically isn't just going to draw the ire of the Alliance. Sorren will consider it an attack on his person and his honor."

"They'd have to be fuckin' stupid," Evan murmured. Seth nodded, agreeing wholeheartedly. Sorren might be on their side, but he was still a scary-as-hell vampire.

Teag stepped up beside Cassidy. "Okay, Ian. How about having a seat at the table and telling us what's going on?"

Maggie lowered her broom, then went to shut and lock the front door, since it was almost closing time. She popped her head back into the break room. "I thought I'd go over to your house and help Kell get dinner for a crowd. I've got a feeling there's gonna be a gathering."

Cassidy gave a tired smile and nodded. "Thank you, Maggie. That would be wonderful."

"Oh, and there are some rough characters out on the front sidewalk. Bet they're looking for this guy," Maggie's normally friendly tone cooled, and her eyes narrowed as she glared at Ian, obviously not ready to forgive him for bursting in so dramatically.

"Please, don't hand me over to them," Ian begged. "They followed me here. I might be betraying the Shadow Coven, but I'm not betraying my brother. I don't want him to get killed."

"Nobody is handing anyone over," Cassidy replied. "I know Rowan will want to hear what Ian has to say—and I'm betting that when she shows up, the folks outside will make themselves scarce."

Seth took the temporary lull as a chance to study their new informant a little more closely. He'd never run into a witch gang before, but they didn't really fit the look he expected from TV. Nothing about Ian had a criminal vibe. He wore a dark denim jacket over black jeans and fashionable-but-not-overly-expensive sneakers. A few tats peeked from the collar of his T-shirt and the cuffs of his jacket, but that sort of thing wasn't even edgy these days. Seth sniffed the air, but couldn't pick up any hint of weed or alcohol—not even regular cigarettes. As gang members went, Ian seemed understated.

"Can I, uh, have a drink of water? Please?" Ian asked after they sat in silence for several minutes. Teag went to oblige, careful to set the glass down and remove his hand before Ian reached for the water so they did not touch, making it clear that while they were willing to hear Ian out, no one extended their trust.

Evan sidled up beside Seth, close but not touching. Seth caught a whiff of his scent—shampoo, soap, and sweat—and his body reacted, even though his mind remembered the curse.

"How're you feeling?" he asked, turning his full attention on his boyfriend. One glance answered his question. Evan looked peaked, a bit too pale, with dark smudges beneath his eyes.

"Crappy. Probably the same way you are."

Seth nodded. "Yeah. Ribs?"

"Better than they were. Rowan did another 'booster,' but it didn't seem to help as much this time."

"Maybe we've caught a couple of breaks," Seth replied, keeping his voice low. "This could be what we need to get to Longstreet."

"Hope so," Evan replied, looking miserable. "Because the curse sucks."

Everything in Seth wanted to wrap his arms around Evan and pull him close, giving comfort and support. Knowing that Evan was hurting and there was nothing he could do about it made Seth's heart ache.

"Just a little longer," Seth said. "Hang in there."

"I will. I promise. You, too."

Seth managed a smile. "I will. Promise."

"Those boys just lit out of here," Maggie reported from the front room. "Must mean either the cops or Rowan are here."

A knock at the back door sounded. Teag moved cautiously to answer and stepped aside to let Rowan in.

"They're gone," she told Maggie. "You can get to your car without a problem."

Maggie grabbed her shawl and purse. "That works for me. I'll see you folks later." She hustled out the back door, and Teag went with her, returning a moment later after he'd made sure she reached her car safely.

Rowan crossed to stand in front of Ian, who had taken a seat at the table. She gave him a look from head to toe. "I've seen you around," Rowan said. "Why are you here?"

"My brother, Curtis, is the leader of the Shadow Coven," Ian repeated. "Bad stuff is happening, and I don't want my brother—or my friends—to get killed. I tried to reason with Curtis. He's in over his head, and he knows it, but he's convinced there's no way out except to go along with what's in motion and hope for a lucky break. I don't believe in luck, and I'm pretty sure we've been owned."

"Explain." Rowan's cold tone made it clear that she wasn't about to go easy on Ian.

Ian took a long breath and let it out. "My friends and me, we don't have training, or money, or come from the big witch families. But we've got some magic—maybe not a lot, but enough to do things. All we wanted was a chance to learn how to use the magic right, make the most of it. Be real witches."

He leveled an accusing glare at Rowan. "But there's no place for folks like us. It's like a fuckin' country club. If you don't have the right name or the money to play, you don't get in. So we had to come up with our own way."

Ian looked to each of them in turn, pointedly looking away from Rowan. "I can't speak for the other gangs. I only know that when Curtis and Ronnie started the Shadow Coven, we wanted to pool our knowledge about how to work magic, do spells, and harness the little bit of power we had."

He blew out another breath. "If you want to learn from a *bruja* or a root worker or a houngan, they'll teach you. But if you're looking for straight-up witchcraft? Might as well try to get into one of those fancy Ivy League schools."

Seth thought he saw Rowan wince and suspected that she recognized some truth in Ian's words.

"So we did what we could with what we had. If someone found a spell book, we all used it. Anything we learned, we taught each other. We made protective amulets, and got tats to keep away evil spirits, and learned how to use our magic without blowing ourselves up. Trial and error. It was a family. And then it all went wrong."

Cassidy moved to sit across from Ian at the table. "Tell us," she urged. "How did it go wrong?" She pushed the box with Maggie's cookies toward him, and Ian munched one, giving her a grateful half-smile.

"Curtis and Ronnie, they didn't mean for us to make trouble. We just thought we'd be stronger together, watching each other's backs, since we didn't belong anywhere else." Ian washed down the cookie with a gulp of water. "Then Ronnie disappeared. Couldn't find him anywhere. He had a record, so we didn't expect the police to try too hard, but we all knew he didn't skip out on us. We never found him."

Evan exchanged a look with Seth, and Seth knew they both came to the same conclusion, given Evan's latest research.

"Mikey Conroy made sense to take Ronnie's place—he was good in a fight, had a little more magic than most, and knew how to use it. But he wasn't content to just learn. He wanted to get access. Break down the gates, knock down the doors, and get our due as part of the witch community in Charleston. He held a grudge because his mother died from a spell gone wrong, and she couldn't get a 'real' witch to help her." Ian's voice held a bitter edge.

"I tried to be a balance, keep Curtis from going too far. But he started listening to Mikey more than me. Mikey wanted to stir up trouble, let the old families know we deserved a piece of the action. Mikey knew people. He had contacts. He started sharing spells he said he 'found' in old books, and weird bits of junk he said would make spells work better, help us do magic longer, boost the signal. I didn't trust him, but hey—I'm just the bossman's little brother. No one listened."

"What happened?" Teag prompted. Seth glanced at Rowan, whose body language said she was on alert, but she seemed fine with others taking the lead in questioning Ian, probably figuring he'd clam up for her.

"At first, everything worked just the way Mikey said it would. I figured maybe I'd freaked out too much, you know?" Ian twisted the hem of his jacket nervously. "And then a couple more of the guys went missing. Left all their stuff. Just—gone. We all got scared. Mikey said he'd heard the old families were hunting us, and that we'd better be ready to defend ourselves."

"That's not true," Rowan refuted.

"Can you prove it?" Ian shot back. He returned his attention to the others, ignoring Rowan again.

"I wondered where Mikey was getting all the stuff. So I followed him," Ian went on. "He met up with this guy at an old abandoned farm. Place was a real dump. I didn't get a good look at the guy, but Mikey came away with more of the weird charms."

Was that Longstreet? Or a middleman? Seth wondered. Surely Longstreet wouldn't put himself at risk dealing with someone he likely considered a street tough.

"Did he realize you'd tailed him?" Cassidy asked.

Ian shook his head. "Pretty sure not, or he would have busted my chops."

Seth thought Ian's protectiveness of his brother seemed to be a one-way street since Curtis seemed willing to let his second-in-command push Ian around, but he stayed quiet, letting the others do the talking.

"Curtis, he's a good guy," Ian went on. "He's trying to run the coven to keep everyone safe, and then bad stuff started to happen, witchy stuff, like we were under attack. That just made people listen more to Mikey, about defending themselves. And then you two showed up."

He looked right at Seth and Evan.

"Us?" Seth couldn't keep the surprise from his voice. "We didn't come here for your gang."

Ian shrugged. "Mikey said his dealer told him you two were bad news. Witch hunters. That you'd gone on some kind of sick road trip, killing witches to add notches on your guns or something."

"Aw for fuck's sake—" Seth protested. Evan leveled a look at him, and Seth eased up. "We came to Charleston to find the dark warlock who killed Blake Miller—part of a bad coven whose members killed my brother and tried to kill Evan."

That tidbit made Ian pause. "Huh. That's interesting." He cocked his head and looked at them, taking their measure. "I mean, you guys don't look like Van Helsing. And you're not dressed in flannel like those guys on TV."

"Did Mikey send Jon Fuller to hurt Seth and Teag?" Evan had been quiet until now, but everyone turned to look at him when he spoke up. Seth saw anger glint in Evan's eyes and knew that Evan took the attack personally.

"Fuller's an asshole," Ian spat. "Keeps sucking up to Mikey, like he'll ever be more than a grunt. Mikey likes that, though, and he used

Fuller to do jobs for him. He wasn't the only one Mikey sent after you guys. Guess none of them were any good, since you're still here. Except this time, Fuller didn't come back."

"He's alive and safe," Rowan said. Ian's head swiveled sharply to look at her, but her expression gave nothing away. "He was also willing to tell us everything he knew—in exchange for protection."

"Yeah, he'll need it. Mikey doesn't like snitches. Which means I can't go back. I gave up everything to come here, hoping that I could get the folks with the big-deal magic to stop a war and save my brother."

"What war?" Cassidy asked, gaze sharp.

"Mikey's been poking at the big covens any place he could find a weakness. Hexes. Curses for bad luck and bad health. Little magics in the right places to cause 'accidents' no one would blame on witchy stuff. Mikey called it 'being nibbled to death by ants.'"

Rowan's expression sobered. "Well, that explains a lot." She turned to Cassidy and the others. "We've only got his word for the cause, but there have been a series of incidents that could be explained by this. Nothing that seemed like an attack, but damage was done."

"I told Curtis he needed to throw Mikey out. Or that he and I needed to leave the coven and get out of town. Curtis didn't like the new stuff Mikey was doing or the charms that hurt people. But he was afraid that if he gave up the control he had left, it would get worse. Our friends in the coven would get hurt. Mikey didn't care about that —he had an agenda."

"Or someone gave him one," Seth muttered.

"Go back to the 'war,'" Cassidy prompted. "What did you mean?"

Ian chewed on his lip, as if unsure what to say. Then he rubbed a hand across his mouth and dove in. "Mikey told the coven that the charms and stuff could be used as weapons. He took Curtis and me along on a ride to pick up this latest batch—which Mikey said were the strongest yet. We didn't actually meet the bossman. He stayed in the background, with a hat that kept us from seeing his face. But I saw his hand. He had a big gold ring with a hella huge ruby. Like a mobster from one of those movies."

Seth looked to Evan. "Amulet," they said in unison.

Seth turned to the others. "Want to bet the ring is Longstreet's focal point? The others had necklaces, but it could be a ring, right?"

Rowan nodded slowly. "Yes. Anything worn on his person."

Seth returned his attention to Ian. "Who does Mikey want to go to war with? The old families? The established covens? The other witch gangs?"

"I don't think it matters to him," Ian replied, looking miserable. "Everybody. Anyone in his way. He's the kind of guy who spouts off, saying things like 'anarchy is freedom.' Like having any rules or order means he's being oppressed."

Rowan rolled her eyes. "Yeah. We've met that kind before. They don't like any rules until they're in charge to do the oppressing."

"If your brother wants to lead a gang, he needs to grow a pair," Seth said. "Where's his spine?"

Seth wasn't prepared for the pain in Ian's eyes. "That's just it—this isn't like Curtis. He's always been a fighter, but he protected the people who couldn't protect themselves. He didn't start the Shadow Coven to burn down the powers that be. He did it so a bunch of us who got born with crap-magic could learn and practice and be safe." Ian swallowed hard. "I think Mikey did something to him."

"Is that possible?" Evan asked the others. "Could Mikey have put a whammy on Curtis to get him to go along with things?" Seth felt certain Evan remembered just how much a hex bag or spelled chit could bend a person to the maker's will, after their own dire experiences.

"Or did Longstreet give Mikey a spell to use on Curtis so Longstreet could in turn use Mikey to do his dirty work—undercutting the established magical community that snubbed him?" Seth asked.

"Shit," Teag muttered. "That sounds way too plausible."

"It does, doesn't it?" Rowan replied. She turned her attention back to Ian. "You've got a legitimate gripe against the way magic is handled here in Charleston. I certainly don't control the covens or the old families, but along with some of our colleagues, I've got a degree of influence to make changes. It won't fix everything at once, or bring you into the inner circles or undo centuries of elitist magic. But it shouldn't have come to this for us to create a safe place for fledglings to learn. I can help make that happen."

Cassidy licked her lips. "You know, I should have brought this up a long time ago, but we've been a little crazed lately. Travis Dominick runs what he calls his Night Vigil, and my cousin Simon has his Skeleton Crew—they're informal networks of untrained, mostly low-power people with magical talent who work together to learn and help protect the community. We could do the same thing here in Charleston."

Rowan chuckled. "Oh, the South of Broad squad is going to have a conniption, but there's no covenant against it. And if we spin it right, as a way to end the gang problem, they might not fight it. Especially if Sorren and Donnelly throw their weight behind the idea."

"You know they will." Cassidy grinned at Teag. "I guess our fellow-ship just got a little bigger."

Ian looked on with disbelief. "You mean it?"

Rowan nodded. "Yes. But to get to that point, we need to stop the man who's pulling the strings behind the scenes. I can keep you safe—and I need you to go over your story one more time, for my research friends who might pick up on important details we didn't notice."

Seth knew she intended to take Ian to the St. Expeditus safe house. Ian looked concerned, but he'd burned his bridges in coming to them.

"Okay," he said, looking young and lost without his defiance. "Just please, I've got to save Curtis."

"We'll do our best, now that we know what's going on," Teag told him. "Give Rowan the information on where to find Curtis and which of the other gang members aren't willingly siding with Mikey. We'll take it from there."

Rowan and Ian left, with Rowan's promise to call later with what-ever new information she could provide. Everyone else let out a collec-tive sigh of relief that the situation had ended peacefully.

"I was just about to take a look at those relics before we were inter-rupted," Cassidy said, looking to Evan. She poured herself a glass of sweet tea and took a seat at the table. Evan opened his backpack and carefully withdrew three items, each wrapped in what Rowan had called "magic-dampening" cloth. They had come from the recent attacks, at the coffee shop where they met Logan, and in front of the Historical Archive.

"You two haven't seen me do this before, so let me tell you what to expect," she said with a glance to Seth and Evan. "I'm a psychometric. That means I can read the history and magic of objects by touching them. That's especially true for items that have a strong emotional resonance. I see what the object was present to 'witness,'" she added. "So it can be hit-or-miss."

"Do you think it's a good idea to touch the relics?" Teag asked, sitting next to Cassidy. Seth had the feeling they'd done this kind of thing many times before.

"Probably not. Never is. When has that stopped us?" Cassidy replied with a smile that didn't quite reach her eyes.

"Why don't you try it through the cloth, and see if that keeps you from getting the full wallop?" Teag looked nervous. Seth figured Teag had seen things go wrong a time or two.

"We can try. I don't know if I'll be able to get enough, but it's worth a shot. I'd rather not get knocked on my ass," she said.

Cassidy reached for the first piece. The outline through the thin cloth showed an item in an "X" shape. She closed her eyes as her fingers touched the surface.

A sudden intake of breath startled them. "Oh. Wow." Cassidy's eyes flew open, pupils blown wide, and her face flushed.

"Cassidy?" Teag bent closer. Cassidy didn't respond, and Seth couldn't help thinking she looked like someone caught up in the thrill of a roller coaster's steepest descent.

She began to fidget. Her heels tapped against the floor, then the fingers of her free hand drummed against the table, and finally, her whole body bounced in her chair.

"Cassidy!" Teag grabbed a wooden pencil and poked the cloth-wrapped item out from under her hand, breaking her contact with it.

"Whoa." Cassidy came around with an all-over shudder. "That was like grabbing a high voltage wire. The power surge was intense."

"Are you okay?" Teag looked at her worriedly, obviously doing his own appraisal.

She hesitated for a moment, then nodded. "Yeah. I think so. But I really wouldn't want to be connected to that for any length of time. It could get...addictive."

"Would it make your magic more powerful?" Seth asked, eyeing the amulet like it might bite.

"That's my guess," Cassidy replied.

"We can do the others later, if you want," Teag offered.

Cassidy shook her head. "No. Do it now. I know what to expect, and there's more I want to find out."

This time, she let her hand hover over the shrouded relic, instead of touching it. "Even this close, I can feel it," she told them. "It's like drinking a latte and a Red Bull and taking NoDoze all at once, only for your magic instead of to stay awake. It's a rush. But..." she frowned as if she were trying to put what she felt into words.

"There's an edge of darkness, like a shadow off in the distance. I'm not sure what that means. Let me try the third one."

Cautiously, Teag used the pencil to remove the second talisman and push the last relic in front of her.

Once again, Cassidy stretched out her hand above the piece, close but not touching. This time, her entire body went rigid, and her outstretched hand tightened like a claw. Breath came in short, shallow pants, and her eyes widened in panic.

"Cassidy!" Teag tried to shove the relic away, but it would not budge. He jumped up from the table, sending his chair to the floor with a crash, and ran into the office, coming back with a worn duffel bag. Teag thrust his hand into the bag and pulled out a silvery mesh net, which he tossed to land on Cassidy's hand and the amulet.

"Seth—pull Cassidy's chair back while I try to push the relic into the net," Teag said, getting into position with the pencil. "Go!"

Cassidy's chair screeched across the floor as Seth yanked her backward. Teag shoved at the relic, trying to move it from beneath her hand and keep it inside the net. Cassidy screamed in pain.

Evan pulled out a small bottle from the pocket of his jacket and squirted a stream of holy water onto the relic, then tossed a handful of salt, as Teag pulled at the silver net. The cloth-wrapped object came loose, Cassidy slumped in her chair, and Teag scooped up the dangerous amulet in the net and rushed into the office with it.

Seth and Evan knelt next to Cassidy. She had lost the frightening stiffness from moments before but now was limp, with her chin on her chest and arms slack by her sides.

"Cassidy? Can you hear me?" Seth coaxed. He looked to Evan and saw his own fear in his partner's eyes. "What do we do?"

"She's breathing," Evan said. He touched her neck, feeling for a pulse. "Got a heartbeat. Damn, her skin's cold."

"Come on, Cassidy. Wake up," Seth pleaded. He didn't know whether the malicious amulet had merely drained her, or put some worse spell in place.

"Let me through, please." Teag appeared, minus the net or relic, and had a glass of sweet tea in his hand and a long, narrow piece of handwoven cloth in the other. He draped the cloth around her neck like a scarf and spoke a word of power. Cassidy's eyes fluttered, and she took a deep breath.

Seth and Evan both reached out, in unison, to steady her so she didn't fall. Cassidy opened her eyes and raised her head. "What happened?"

"Drink this." Teag pushed the glass into her hand and helped her guide it to her lips so she didn't spill. When she finished, he set the glass aside and reached into his pocket for a large, polished onyx disk, and he put it between her hands, wrapping her fingers around it, and his hands around hers.

"Evan—can you please light that sage bundle and walk a circuit of the room?" Teag asked. Evan hurried to oblige.

"What can I do?" Seth asked, worried.

"You're doing it," Teag replied. "Keep your hand on her shoulder. She's drawing energy from us to help expel the dark magic. The onyx and the spelled cloth will help," he added, with a nod toward the woven fabric draped around her neck.

Seth watched nervously as Cassidy's shaking stopped, and color came back to her face. She took another deep, shuddering breath.

"That was…not good," she said, sounding strained.

"Is it gone?" Teag looked her over like a doctor, checking her pupils and pulse, and then touching the woven scarf with an expression that made Seth wonder if the other man could somehow "read" the magic that had been transmitted.

"Yeah. But I'm glad y'all were here with me. I don't know if I could have gotten away from it by myself."

Evan refilled her tea and brought the glass to her. Cassidy gulped the drink down like it was the elixir of life. Seth found the super-sweet beverage to be an acquired taste, since it wasn't something he'd grown up with in Indiana, but he figured all that sugar would be perfect for replenishing energy after a drain.

"Are you up to doing a debrief?" Teag asked. He brought her a couple of cookies from the box on the table, and Cassidy ate them gratefully.

"Yeah. Wow. I hate to imagine how those affected the people Longstreet sold them to," she said, shaking her head.

"The people Mikey gave them to," Seth added.

She nodded. "The first one was a rush. I felt—more. All my senses, my magic, my energy—more of all of it. But I can see where it could be like a drug. Because why would you want to be 'less' when you gave the relic up?"

"And if you get addicted to a relic, you're vulnerable to the person who controls it," Teag finished.

"Yep. I doubt the gang member who 'lost' it gave that piece up voluntarily." She looked toward the second amulet, which still lay on the table. Seth and Evan moved closer, wanting to hear everything she had to say.

"The second piece was also an amplifier. I definitely felt like my magic was turned up too high," she continued. "But I could see the darkness on it like a shadow. I think that the first piece probably would have burned out the user, given enough time. The second piece felt seductive like it wanted me to hold on as tightly as I could."

She frowned. "That second piece would have tried to make me use my magic in bad ways."

"Lured you to the dark side?" Teag joked, but Seth could see his concern.

"For real."

"What about the third one?" Seth couldn't contain his curiosity. "Your reaction scared the crap out of me."

"Scared me, too," Cassidy admitted. "The third one had parts of both of the other two. It amplified my magic. And it made me want to do things with it that I shouldn't. But I swear I could feel *someone* else, like it was a connection through the magic."

"Longstreet?" Evan asked, alarmed.

"That's my guess," Teag replied, and Cassidy nodded.

"Do you think he could hear everything we've said near it?" Evan looked ready to throw up.

Cassidy thought about it and shook her head. "Doubtful. It would drain a lot of magic to just leave a link like that open, and Longstreet might be immortal, but he's not all-powerful. Of course, even though I didn't touch the relic, my magic must have made the connection."

"Just imagine what it would have been like if it hadn't been wrapped in magic-dampening, spelled cloth," Teag added. "Or if you'd picked it up and made full contact."

Cassidy shivered. "Honestly? I don't know if we could have broken the link until he let me go. I'm not sure I could have fought it. And a person who didn't have as much training and experience using their magic? I'm pretty sure Longstreet could actually control someone through the link if the person couldn't defend themselves."

"That's the relic Jon Fuller was carrying when he tried to attack Logan and Seth and me," Teag said. "I thought he was just trying to avoid responsibility when he told Father Anne about how it affected him, but now I think he might have been telling the truth—as much of it as he could remember."

"Where is it?" Cassidy looked around, a little panicky.

"I put it in the lead box, in the safe," Teag assured her. "We'll let Sorren deal with it. The other two pieces should also get locked up, since they're dangerous, too."

"It's scary to think Longstreet has been dealing these amulets like weapons," Seth said. "Who knows how many are out there and what they do?"

Evan bit his lip, thinking. "Longstreet only had a dozen or so items on Crowleyslist. I don't think he'd want a lot of them in play at one time. They probably all require some input of magic from him, and I would expect that he'd keep a link to them, to make sure the person he sold it to was doing what he wanted. So that's a drain on his power, and even if he just got an early refill with Blake Miller's sacrifice, Longstreet's magic must have limits."

"We hope," Seth replied.

"All magic has limits," Teag said. "He's a witch, not a god. Evan's right—he won't want too many of these active at one time. Plus, there's probably a kill-switch built in, because Longstreet isn't going to take a chance that someone might get more powerful than he is. Which means it's unlikely that there's an army of relic-controlled witchlings out there, gunning for us."

"I don't think Longstreet ever expected us to connect with you and Cassidy—and the Alliance." Seth leaned against the table, and Evan brought a chair up, sitting as close as he dared. "He probably figured that we'd be easy to kill, and working with you folks threw a monkey wrench into his plans."

"Happy to oblige," Teag said with a grin.

"Think about it," Evan added, "if Longstreet's managed to fly under the Alliance's radar all this time, he probably also figures that once we're dead, things go back to normal. He doesn't know—or at least, he didn't until the connection with Cassidy through the relic—that you're onto his arms dealing and trafficking."

"We didn't realize the disappearances were really trafficking until your awesome research," Cassidy said. "But it ties a lot of things together. The people who've gone missing from the Shadow Coven gang—and probably other witch gangs as well. The attacks on more powerful witches by the low-powered gangs. And the sacrifice cycle with the Miller family."

"Fuck," Teag muttered. "Longstreet's probably been doing all three for the last century, right under the Alliance's nose."

"And practically right in front of the old families and established covens, which would have also shut him down if they'd known," Evan pointed out. "I've got Travis, Ben, and Brent all working angles, and Emily at the Historical Archive thought she'd have more tomorrow. Plus whatever else Logan and Beck figure out."

Whatever else Evan meant to say was forgotten as he gasped and clutched at his chest, knees buckling. Seth moved instinctively to grab Evan, but Teag blocked him from touching his boyfriend and making it worse. Belatedly, Seth realized his mistake and stepped back.

"Evan? What's wrong?" Seth knelt so he could see Evan's face, even if he couldn't touch him.

"I don't know. I just felt like something knocked the starch out of me." Evan looked even paler, and a sheen of sweat covered his forehead.

The curse. Seth had been feeling the effects more strongly all day, but he hadn't wanted to mention it to Evan, fearing that he'd either worry his partner or plant the thought in Evan's head, causing sympathetic symptoms. Maybe they'd both been keeping their pain a secret.

"Let's get him back to my house," Cassidy said. She bustled around the back rooms, turning off lights, putting the tea in the fridge, and fitting Evan's computer and cords in its case.

"The cars are in the alley behind the store." Teag helped Evan to his feet, and Evan stood, but he needed support far more than Seth expected, deepening his worry about the curse's effects on top of the injuries from the accident.

"I'll be okay." Evan met his gaze as if he could read Seth's thoughts and guess his concern.

"I know you will," Seth replied with a bravado he didn't feel. They were running out of time, and Longstreet had the upper hand. Sure, they had figured out his plans, but would they have enough time to stop what he'd already put in motion?

TEAG HELPED EVAN UP THE STEPS TO CASSIDY'S FRONT PORCH AND GOT him to the couch in the parlor. Seth hung back, feeling useless, unable to assist his boyfriend or comfort him with touch.

"Get comfortable, and we'll bring in some hot tea," Teag told Evan, with a jerk of his head to get Seth to join him in the kitchen. Evan nodded, looking like he felt shitty, and sank into the couch, wiped out.

"It's hitting him hard," Seth said quietly, making no effort to hide his worry.

"Curses don't always settle the same on people," Teag replied. "Sorta the way medicine doesn't work exactly the same, depending on the patient."

"I can't lose him." Seth met Teag's gaze, and something in the other man's eyes told Seth that Teag understood, perhaps too well.

"We're not out of time. Not yet," Teag said. "I'm going to check in with Travis and see if Brent and Ben found anything. Why don't you give Milo and Toby a call? They might have a lead—and you know they'll whip your ass if they have to find this out second-hand."

Translation: If we go down in flames. If the curse kills us.

Seth blew out a defeated breath and nodded. He'd known he should have called his surrogate fathers sooner, but Milo's heart trouble had Toby worried to distraction. Seth hadn't wanted to add to their stress. And to be fair, the other two men had gone on a hunt that took them up in the mountains with really lousy cell phone signal.

But Teag was right. Toby and Milo were a resource—they'd both been hunting a long time. More than that, they were family.

"Okay," Seth said. "I'll call them. It's just...we need a break on this, and soon." He didn't try to hide the emotion in his voice. He knew he didn't need to—Teag had him figured out.

Teag clapped a hand on his shoulder. "Go make your call, and I'll see what I can find out. Maybe Evan'll feel better once he sleeps a bit."

Seth walked down the hallway to the back of the house so he didn't wake Evan. He heard Teag step out onto the porch. Seth mustered his courage, hit Toby's number on speed dial, and listened to it ring.

"Hello, Seth. We were just wondering what you and Evan had gotten up to. How's it going in Charleston?"

Seth blinked hard, trying to keep his composure, as the feelings he had tried to contain washed over him.

"So far, we're not winning this one, Toby. We were in a car accident and came out mostly okay, but Longstreet put a curse on us, and we're running out of time and...Evan. Oh, God."

Toby was silent long enough that Seth thought perhaps the call had dropped. "Give that to me again, son. How bad was the accident?"

"I got knocked around a bit, Evan bruised ribs and got a minor concussion. But when we were in the hospital, we felt dark magic sweep over us. Longstreet knew we were vulnerable, and he put a touch-me-not curse on us. Cassidy's witch friends can't break it. It only ends when we kill Longstreet—or he kills us."

"Then you've got a warlock to kill."

"He's stayed a step ahead of us, Toby. We've got everyone working on it. Cassidy has a network of people with abilities here that you wouldn't believe. But we're all coming up aces and eights." Seth pinched the bridge of his nose, willing himself not to cry, but tears slipped down his cheeks anyhow, and he felt certain he wasn't fooling Toby, not with how rough his voice had gotten.

"Seems to me, Longstreet wouldn't be trying so hard if he didn't think you were a real threat," Toby replied. "If he figures he's got you beat, he'll get cocky and overplay his hand. That's your chance."

"Evan's not doing well," Seth confided, dropping his voice. "The curse is hitting him harder than me. Maybe because he was hurt worse from the accident. Maybe just...because we're different. He's fading. And I can't do this without him, Toby."

Toby drew in a ragged breath. "Yeah. I know what you mean. Milo's given me a wild ride, lately, with all the heart trouble. I told him that I was too stubborn to let go, so he better not dare try to leave." Another pause. "He's still with me."

"Glad to hear it."

"Sounds like this hunt of yours went off the rails."

"That's...an understatement. Everything we thought we knew about the witch-disciples, the ritual—it was all wrong." Seth gave Toby the shortest recap he could manage, wrapping up with Cassidy reading the relics' magic.

"All right. That's a lot. But no one said it was gonna be easy. So you've got to fight—for Evan, and for Jesse. You can't let this son of a bitch beat you."

Toby's rough pep talk fanned the flicker of Seth's resolve back to a flame. "I'm not going to give up. I'm just stuck."

"Do it old school," Toby advised. "Make a list of what you know.

Make another list of what you need to find out. Work the process. Sometimes, hunting is just applied shoe leather."

"Any suggestion on how to buy ourselves some more time with the curse?"

"Maybe. I ran into a guy who knew a lot about German witches. He claimed that there were symbols you could draw on your skin that would blunt a witch's power to hex you. It's a long shot, but I can text you a picture of the markings—it might help, and it can't hurt."

"Anything, Toby. I'll take it."

"Give me a little bit to find those notes, and I'll send it on as quick as I can. Sounds like you've run through all the things that won't work to break the curse, but there might be some other tricks to slow it down. Let me put out the word, and I'll send you what I get."

"Thanks, Toby. I'm kinda at wit's end here."

"I figured that out, son. Let me go do what I said, and we'll just work this until we find the right angle. You don't get to give up, you hear me?"

Seth forced a tired chuckle. "Loud and clear. Give our best to Milo, will you?"

"That old fart is taking a nap. *Another* nap," Toby groused, but Seth heard the fondness in his voice. "I'll tell him you asked after him."

"Thanks, Toby. For everything."

"Humph. None of that, now. This is all gonna turn out okay. Mark my words. Just hang in there."

"Will do." Seth ended the call. He leaned back against the wall, letting his head thunk lightly, closing his eyes. Talking to Toby had helped his spirit, even if it didn't fix what was wrong. And maybe the hex symbol would buy them some time. Right now, Seth would take whatever he could get.

Seth glanced into the parlor long enough to make sure Evan was still sleeping. He could see Teag through the window, pacing on the porch as he talked on his phone. Seth hoped Teag was making more headway than he was.

He heard a phone buzz, but the sound was muted. A quick search led to Evan's pockets, and Seth fished out his boyfriend's phone, showing a recent, missed message from a Charleston area number. He glanced at Evan, who had slept through the whole thing. Moving back to the hallway, Seth unlocked Evan's phone and returned the call.

"Evan?" A woman answered.

"This is Seth, Evan's partner. He's resting. You called?"

"Hi, Seth. I'm Emily—a research intern at the Historical Archive. I wanted to let Evan know that I found a few more things on those people he'd asked me to check on. I emailed him a report. The short version is, all of the people on his list might or might not have known each other, but they knew a lot of the same people, and they bought commercial real estate from each other more than once. Weird, huh?"

Not really, Seth thought. Not when the "people" were aliases for the same immortal man, Longstreet's many personas over the past century.

"Do any of them still own those businesses?" He and Evan had tracked down Longstreet's old homes, but Evan had gone the next step to look at his business affairs.

"Oddly enough, yes," Emily replied. "There's a farm that passed through several owners, but it recently was acquired by a holding company, and a little digging turned up Michael Longstreet as the principal. The same thing is true of a warehouse near the docks. There were a lot of leases and rentals, but it never actually left the holding company's control."

She paused to take a breath. "Oh—and the weirdest one was this piece of swampland. It was part of a bigger property that got sold to build condos, but this little corner got separated out. I thought it might have been for wetlands conservation, but there wasn't any environmental lien or government paperwork. Guess who owns it?"

"Same holding company?"

"Got it in one! It's all in the report, but I figured Evan might want a head's up."

"Thank you, Emily. I know this was an odd request, but everything you've found is very important."

Seth headed into the living room, feeling a surge of excitement and hope for the first time in a while. Teag came in from the porch a moment later.

"I think we've found something," they said, nearly at the same time.

"You, first," Seth said. "Anything on the curse?"

"Travis found a potion that won't lift it, but it's supposed to stave off the worst of the effects, at least for a while," Teag reported. "He emailed me the ingredients."

"Toby is sending me some German hex designs that are supposed to do the same thing. We'll need to draw them on our skin. It's worth a shot," Seth replied.

"Travis tracked the pictures of the relics Cassidy just read to a couple of collectors known for dealing in dodgy magical and occult objects," Teag went on. "Guys like Chalmers Etheridge, who had the money to buy what they wanted, and connections to secret, shady auctions where people of particular tastes bid on things that are completely illegal."

"Like what Evan found on Crowleyslist."

"Yeah, only offline. If you're rich and twisted and know the right people, you can get invited to these parties that double as private sales functions," Teag replied.

"Sounds like what happens when you cross a Tupperware get-together with Eyes Wide Shut."

"And now I have to bleach my brain," Teag groaned. "But yes. Sort of. Travis checked in with Erik Mitchell—the guy who used to chase down art fraud who's in Cape May, remember him?"

Seth hadn't met Erik personally, but they'd talked on the phone about cases, and Erik's boyfriend Ben Nolan was working the private investigator angle with Travis's hunting partner, Brent Lawson. Small world. "Yeah, I remember."

"According to Erik, there have been several notable occult collections that have gone missing. He was pretty sure the relics you showed him came from a guy who liked to collect items that were reputed to be cursed or haunted. Total skeptic, apparently—he thought it was all a big joke, like they were movie props. It didn't end well for him. But Ben did some digging, and it seems that the unlucky collector knew people who knew Longstreet."

"Bingo," Seth muttered under his breath.

"Ben and Brent also found a web of connections between Longstreet and some very unsavory people on the dark side of the magical community," Teag continued. "People whose names come up when the discussion turns to stolen artifacts...and supernatural human trafficking. And get this—when they started looking into the people who've gone missing lately, ruling out ones that could be easily explained, about ninety-five percent had a connection to one of the witch gangs, which probably means latent magic."

"And the others?"

"There was something about them that would be appealing to certain supernaturals. Rare blood types, traits like different colored eyes, that sort of thing," Teag replied. "It confirms the trafficking angle." He paused. "Something else Brent pointed out. About fifty years ago, Longstreet stopped being a lawyer and became a fixer."

"What the hell does that mean?"

"I asked Brent the same thing. It means that instead of trying to work within the system—even by exploiting loopholes and technicalities—Longstreet moved outside of the system, to make problems go away through whatever means necessary."

"Sounds like the Mob."

Teag shrugged. "You're not far off. Longstreet decided he was above the law, and only results mattered. That tracks with supplying spells and relics, using magic to control pawns, and becoming a supplier to powerful supernaturals."

They walked into the kitchen, and Teag poured them both glasses of sweet tea. "Maybe it makes sense, in a way, if Longstreet's family lost their wealth in the Civil War," he mused as they sat at the table. "Even though Longstreet wouldn't have been born at the time of the war, the bitterness over what people lost lasted a long, long time. His family didn't have a problem owning slaves, and all that entailed."

"So he fell back on the old family business? Buying and selling people and trading influence."

Teag nodded. "Exactly. And at the same time, he creates problems for the high society folks—magical and human—who looked down on his family and hung the small plantation owners out to dry after the war."

"This is great background, but how does it help us find and catch this bastard?" Seth asked. "I don't want to build a case against him, I want to kill him."

"One thing at a time. I'm going to run out to get the ingredients for the elixir Travis mentioned. And when I get back, we can draw that hex sign on you and Evan. That should help."

Their phones buzzed almost at the same time. Seth saw an incoming message from Toby, and saw that the attached photo was of a circle with a complex design in the middle, oddly like the decorations he'd seen on the sides of barns—also referred to as hex signs.

"It's Rowan," Teag said, as he answered his call with a terse greeting. He listened for a few minutes, then thanked her and hung up. "Ian got a call that one of the Shadow Coven members has gone missing. Dylan Wade. Ian says the guy is in his early twenties and had a middling level of power—enough to be useful if someone wanted to leech off him."

"Shit."

"On the plus side—Logan and Beck looked at those commercial properties that Emily found. Turns out that one of them not only got sold to Longstreet's holding company, but it's now a private airstrip."

"Son of a bitch." Seth met Teag's gaze, knowing they both understood the significance. "That's how he gets the kidnapped people out, and the relics in."

Teag nodded. "That's my thought. Of course, small boats are also a possibility, but planes are faster."

"If Longstreet's grabbed another person to sell, he's not going to want to hold on to him for long. We need to get eyes on that airstrip, as well as on his house."

"Agreed. Let's get you and Evan fixed up, and we'll take it from there," Teag replied.

While Teag went on his supply run, Seth tried to recreate the hex sign Toby sent to him. It took several tries, but Seth was finally able to reproduce the sign accurately with pen and paper. When it came to magic, details mattered. Teag came back just as Seth leaned back from his practice drawings, ready to draw for real.

"Do you need my help with that?" Teag asked, setting his bag of ingredients on the counter.

"I can ink it on my left arm—that way I can still use my right hand. But I'll need you to do Evan."

"Sure thing. Get yours done, and by then I'll have this concoction together. No guarantees about how it tastes—"

"I don't care, as long as it works." Seth took up the pen again, biting his lip in concentration as he reproduced the hex sign on his left inner forearm. As Teag mixed up the potion, Seth caught a whiff of an odd collection of ingredients and wondered just how bad it would be to swallow. Not that he'd object. He just didn't want to bring it back up.

"All right. That's ready. Teach me to draw that sign, we'll get Evan fixed up, then you can both drink this slop, and we'll go deal with Longstreet."

Seth walked over and stood behind the couch. Teag moved to sit beside Evan, who woke looking adorably disoriented. His confusion cleared when he saw Seth. "What's up?"

"We think we found a couple of things to buy you and Seth some more time from the curse," Teag explained. "I need to draw something on your arm, and then there's a mixture for you to drink."

Evan sat up, still groggy. "You're not going to draw a dick, are you? I fell asleep in fifth-grade algebra with my arm straight out on top of my desk, and Stevie Clark drew a dick on it with permanent marker."

Teag chuckled. "No dicks. I promise."

Seth showed his own arm with its new design. "It's just waterproof marker. But that should last as long as we need it to."

Evan held out his arm to Teag. "Go ahead. I always wondered if I'd ever get any ink."

Seth fought a stab of sadness as Teag began the drawing. He wasn't jealous—Teag had his own man—but it hurt that he couldn't touch Evan or be the one to give him this protection.

"Babe, if you want to get real ink, just tell me. We'll pick something together."

Evan's eyes lit up at that, the first happy expression Seth had seen since the curse took over. Seth's heart ached at not being able to touch

Evan, and his cock didn't understand at all. He figured it was some sort of penance that ever since he'd had to sleep on the couch to keep both of them safe, he'd had the best sex dreams of his life. He promised himself they'd make up for lost time once Longstreet was dead.

Teag took the marker to the kitchen and came back with two glasses partially filled with what looked like swamp water. He handed one to each of the other men. "Raise a toast, gentlemen. To Michael Longstreet's complete and utter destruction."

9

EVAN

Seth and Evan didn't dare clink their glasses. Instead, they lifted their drinks in salute, then pounded them back like cheap tequila.

"Oh fuck, that's awful," Seth sputtered.

It required all of Evan's concentration not to puke.

"Feel any different?" Teag asked, looking anxious.

Only a few minutes had passed, but Evan thought he could feel a difference. "Maybe it's just wishful thinking, but yeah—I feel better. Less achy, a little more energy. Not back to normal, but it's an improvement."

Seth nodded. "Me too. Not one hundred percent, but closer."

Teag smiled. "Good." He looked to Seth and Evan in turn. "I'd like to go check out that airstrip, while it's light. Whoever is coming in isn't going to file a flight plan, but if we know the lay of the land and if we're there when the plane comes in, it might be our best shot at Longstreet."

Seth frowned. "Why do you think he'll be there? Wouldn't he send a minion?"

"Maybe. Then we nab the middleman," Teag said. "But the guy they grabbed, Dylan, wasn't a nobody. He belonged to the Shadow Coven. And if Mikey is working with Longstreet, like we think, then he probably knows our people are safeguarding Ian. Convenient that Ian got the phone call, isn't it?" His smile showed his teeth.

"Mighty convenient," Seth agreed. "I wondered about that myself. And we've figured Longstreet wanted to provoke a confrontation with us. He knows the time is running down on the curse. I think he's getting off on forcing our timing to fight him because he wants to kill Evan and me in person for screwing up the system. This is starting to look like an engraved invitation."

"Then we need to go." Evan pushed up from the couch, stronger than he'd been earlier, but he couldn't hide that he almost fell back on his ass.

"Let Teag and me handle this," Seth said, meeting Evan's gaze. "Longstreet wants a fight. He knows we're hurting. That already puts the odds in his favor. If he sees a way to use the curse against us, he will. I can't protect you and fight him."

Evan wanted to argue. Every fiber in his being wanted to be shoulder to shoulder with Seth on that airstrip. Win or lose, together. He opened his mouth to protest, and then shut it again, shoulders sagging. "You're right. I'd slow you down."

"Oh, babe." Seth took a half step closer to Evan and reached out his hand before he caught himself. "I'm not worried about that. But Longstreet knows we're together. His choice of curse wasn't accidental. And if he hurt you, to put me off my game—"

Evan could see the turmoil in Seth's eyes and knew the request hadn't been made easily. As much as he wanted to do this Butch-and-Sundance-style, he knew Seth had a point.

"Then drop me off at the St. Expeditus compound." Evan raised his chin. "I'm not going to sit here and be useless. At least I can see what Logan and Beck have come up with and help them research."

"We can drop him off and then double back," Teag replied. "I want to pick up some special equipment from the Society anyhow. And we need to let Cassidy and Sorren know the plan. Let me gather a few weapons we keep stashed here, and I'll be ready to go." With that, he headed into another part of the house.

Evan stared at Seth and licked his lips nervously. "I'm scared," he confided, his voice just above a whisper. "I'm afraid that something will happen, and you'll need me, and I won't be with you."

"I always need you." Seth's open expression let Evan know just how true the words were. "But I wouldn't let you go into a fight with a broken leg or a big bloody wound, and that's what this curse is for you. I'll fight better knowing you're safe. I have every intention of coming back for you."

Evan swallowed hard and nodded. "You'd better."

Teag showed up just then, with a worn duffel bag bulging with its contents. "Ready?"

The ride to the St. Expeditus compound was quiet. Seth rode up front with Teag, and Evan rode in the back. Evan fought the urge to tangle his fingers in Seth's hair, and hated that the curse denied them even a kiss before going off to confront Longstreet. He tried to keep his thoughts from drifting to all the ways this could go badly and mostly failed. That just fueled his rage toward Longstreet—for the curse, the murders, the kidnappings, all of it.

When they reached the compound, Seth got out of the car to see him to the door. Evan thought it was like an awkward date where no one went in for the kiss.

"Stay safe," Seth said, and the look in his eyes said everything he couldn't express with his touch.

"You, too. Come back to me in one piece. Preferably without the curse." Evan knew Seth would take his bravado for what it was.

"I'll do my very best. After all, you've got your bucket list of road trips, and I don't want to miss it." Seth managed a cocky smile, which Evan figured was a cover for his fear, just as Evan's had been.

Evan stayed on the porch, watching Teag's car until the taillights faded, before coming inside.

"Evan. Glad you're here. We've got a problem." Beck Pendlewood met him at the door. Beck's hair, usually carefully styled, looked as if he'd been running his hands through it. Evan had figured Beck to be the unflappable sort, but he was definitely on edge, worried…and scared.

"What's wrong?" Evan put down his backpack on a table near the door.

"Logan. He's gone."

If Evan had any doubt that a spark had flared between Logan and Beck, one look at Beck's face settled that issue.

"Gone where?"

"After Longstreet."

Shit. Evan looked around, hoping to see Father Anne or any of the other members of the Society he'd met during his other visits. This section of the big house seemed to be empty, save for the two of them.

He grabbed Beck by the wrist and drew him to the couch, then sat next to him. "Tell me."

"We were comparing the spreadsheet Emily sent over with what we'd found. Something didn't seem right. Then we noticed that when the original Mosby plantation land was sold off to make condos, a parcel was held back that was in the cypress swamp." Beck pushed his fingers through his hair, making his dark mane even more unruly.

"That's not so unusual—wetlands and all—but we couldn't find any record that there'd been any official reason to separate the parcel. Which made us wonder, why bother?"

He shook his head. "I should have paid closer attention. Logan wouldn't leave it alone. He looked for Google Earth photos, topographical maps, anything he could find. And he turned up a pre-Civil War map that showed both the Mosby plantation and the swamp. According to the map, there was a small island in that part of the swamp. And from an old notation in one of the documents, there was a fishing cabin on the island."

Evan's head snapped up. "A cabin. In the swamp. Blake's ghost said he could hear frogs and birds."

"What?"

Evan remembered Beck hadn't been with them when Alicia made contact with Blake's ghost. He filled Beck in, and the other man's eyes widened. "We told Logan about it after he'd had an experience of his own with Alicia channeling Blake."

"Fuck. That's why Logan went nuts. He started talking about finding the cabin and burning it down, that it might be Longstreet's base, or where Blake died. I told him we needed to wait to get a crew together, that it was too dangerous without some magical back-up."

He rolled his eyes. "Technically, I'm not supposed to leave the compound at all, ever—and neither is Logan. That's the whole WITSEC thing."

"You think Logan went anyway?"

"Yeah. If we weren't on the compound, I'd be afraid someone snatched him, but that's not a risk here. Which means he left on his own. One of the jeeps is missing, and a canoe." Beck swore under his breath. "He told me he was going to take a nap—said he had a headache. I heard him go upstairs, and I didn't notice he was missing for an hour. When I went up to his room, he was gone. That was just a few minutes before you got here."

"Did that put the compound on lockdown?"

"Not really. We knew he hadn't been kidnapped. That narrowed down the possibilities. Father Anne called Rowan, who's on her way after she picks up Cassidy. We're going after him."

"I'm coming, too."

Beck stared at him. "I thought you weren't doing well with the curse."

Evan shrugged. "Teag and Seth worked some magic to boost us for a while." He pushed up his sleeve to show Beck the hex mark. "And if they're right about Longstreet going to the airstrip, we shouldn't have to worry about him being at the cabin."

"I hope you're right."

Evan frowned, thinking. "This could work out. The witch-disciples we fought before had a preference for caves and tunnels to work their rituals. But a cabin in a cypress swamp would do just as well—nice and private. The cabin might also be his anchor since it's on his original family property. Destroy the anchor, and we weaken Longstreet. That gives Seth and Teag a better chance."

Father Anne walked in and raised an eyebrow when she saw Evan there. "Come to join the party?"

"Wouldn't miss it for the world. Seth and Teag are going after Longstreet at that private airstrip. Teag said he was calling Cassidy and Sorren to let them know."

"Looks like it's going to be an interesting night," Father Anne observed.

They headed out in two cars, with Rowan and Cassidy in her RAV4, and Father Anne driving Beck and Evan in one of the Society's Jeeps. Each vehicle had a canoe tied atop it. Evan figured he and Beck were companions in misery, both worried about the men they loved.

"So...you and Logan?" Evan asked because the silence made his own thoughts too loud.

Beck looked up from where he'd been toying with the zipper of his jacket. The uncertain smile made him look boyish and softened his cover model good looks. "It's very new. Who knows where it'll go? But...yeah. Being in Protection isn't so bad. Beats being kidnapped and shot at. I like working with the Society. I feel like I'm making a contribution, helping the cause. But finding someone to be exiled with? That's not something I dared to think might be possible."

"Just because a connection happens fast, don't think it's not real. Seth and I went on the run together after four days."

Beck gave him a look. "Seriously?"

Evan nodded. "Yep. I just knew it was right." He paused. "Logan seems like an okay guy."

Beck's smile widened. "He's got a big heart—and brass balls. So different from the kind of people I grew up with. They had money, power, magic—and too much was never enough. Logan's down-to-earth. I'm just sorry he had to lose his brother for us to meet."

"When Seth lost Jesse, he started this whole hunt-the-witch-disciple quest, and it was essentially an absolution-and-suicide road trip," Evan replied. "Toby and Milo, the older hunters who taught him, they're sorta like surrogate fathers—told me that they were worried about him until we met because he didn't have anything to live for except vengeance. Maybe you and Logan can save each other; you know what I mean?"

Beck's smile grew sad. "Yeah, unfortunately I do. And—I think you're right. We could be good for each other. I was in hiding even before the Society gave me sanctuary, trying to stay one step ahead of my cousins. I didn't dare get close to anyone, even as a friend. They could have been used against me. Or been paid to turn me in. Logan hasn't been running for nearly as long, so he's not quite as...*damaged*...

as I am. But it's going to take him a long time to get over Blake's death, even if we do kill Longstreet. We've both got scars, I guess."

Evan bumped his shoulder in solidarity. "Scars aren't the end of the world. And in this crazy hunting life, it's good to have someone who understands what it's all about. I hope it works out for you and Logan."

"Thanks. I hope you and Seth break the curse and burn that fucker Longstreet to the ground."

It was late afternoon by the time they reached the old Mosby land. They ignored the new luxury condos and drove to the far end of the parking lot, where marshland gave way to the cypress swamp.

"Look there!" Beck said, pointing to an identical Jeep parked as far away from other cars as possible.

"That's one of our vehicles. Logan's here," Father Anne agreed.

Evan's phone rang, and he reached for it, hoping Seth had news. Instead, he recognized the Myrtle Beach area code. "Simon. What's up?"

"I just had a vision that knocked me on my ass," their friend said. "I have no idea what it means, but you and Seth are the only ones we know who have something big going down. I saw a small airplane—a two-person private plane—land in a field, and then there were zombies and gunfire and blood."

"Fuck," Evan muttered. "We figured out that Longstreet owns a private airstrip. Seth and Teag are headed out there to stop a deal from going down."

"I wish my visions were more helpful," Simon replied. "I don't know who's doing the shooting or bleeding. But if nothing else, take it as a warning to be extra careful."

"Will do," Evan promised, thanking Simon before ending the call. He immediately called Seth. The call went straight to voicemail.

Shit. "Seth—Simon had a vision. The airfield may be a trap. Please, be careful. Love you." Just to be safe, Evan texted the information as well, with more details. He hung up and let his hand drop back to his lap, even more worried than before.

"We'd better get moving if we want to find Logan before it gets dark," Father Anne urged. "I, for one, don't want to be paddling around the swamp at night."

They went around the fence at the end of the parking lot and put the canoes in the water. Evan and Cassidy had the coordinates of the cabin, and Evan prayed the directions were correct.

He hoped they could retrieve Logan without a fight, but in case any of Longstreet's associates were nearby, the group came prepared. Cassidy had her wand and something that looked like an antique walking stick. Rowan's magic was the only weapon she needed. Father Anne carried a wicked-looking knife in a sheath on her belt, as well as a length of heavy silver chain, and a shotgun in a holster on her back. Evan had his rote spells, and both he and Beck carried shotguns with salt and iron rounds. Evan suspected that Cassidy and Father Anne also probably had a few surprises he didn't know about. Despite their weapons, Evan's nerves threatened to get the best of him.

"You up to this?" Father Anne gave him an assessing once-over.

"Absolutely," Evan lied. He felt better than he had before Seth and Teag had intervened, but that left a lot to be desired. Since he couldn't go with Seth, Evan was not about to be left behind when it came to rescuing Logan. "I'm ready."

Two canoes, room for six people, which left a space for Logan on the return trip. Evan hoped that no one noticed them launching the canoes and called the cops. The area didn't have signs forbidding boat access, but Evan suspected the owners wouldn't be pleased.

Logan had more than an hour's head start, enough for him to get to the island well ahead of them. He'd said he intended to burn the cabin, but Evan didn't see flames. Did that mean Logan had second thoughts, or had he been captured?

Evan's gaze flicked to Beck, whose jaw was set in a hard line. He figured Beck had come up with all the same questions. Simon's vision suggested that Seth and Teag were walking into a trap. Had that happened to Logan, too?

They angled the canoes through the narrow channels of open water as they maneuvered through the marshland, toward the cypress swamp. The late afternoon sun cast a warm glow on the tall grasses and reflected off the water. Once they reached the cypress swamp, the shadow of the trees gave a twilight feel.

Evan couldn't help staring at the trees, which were so different from what he had ever seen. Tall, straight trunks rose from stilt-like roots, and the cypress bark turned the water black. Knobby 'knees' jutted from the roots on the shoreline and in the shallows, making the cypress seem like something from an alien world. He picked up a rotten egg smell and knew it was sulfur and methane from rotting vegetation.

The dip of their paddles seemed loud in the near-silence of the swamp. The noise and distractions of the city might have belonged to another world. As Evan concentrated, he heard the harrumph of frogs, the buzz of insects, and the chirps of the birds that lived in the wetland.

Birds and frogs. Blake's ghost hadn't known where he'd been killed, but his description fit this place perfectly. Evan desperately hoped that they would be in time to keep Logan from joining his brother.

"I can see the island," Father Anne whispered, just loud enough for them to hear.

"And there's a canoe, just like ours," Evan murmured.

Rowan and Cassidy signaled for them to stop before they reached the rickety dock. Father Anne brought their canoe up alongside. "Can you get a read on it?" she asked.

Rowan's eyes were shut in concentration. A few seconds later, she opened them. "There's someone in the cabin. I only pick up one person, but the island's energy is...wrong."

"After what happened with those relics, I think I'm going to be most effective staying here in the water as the lookout," Cassidy said. "That resonance is so dark, it'll come right up through the soles of my boots."

"What kind of energy?" Evan pressed. "Magic? Ghosts? Some kind of Hellmouth?"

"Ghosts—definitely," Cassidy replied. "I don't know whether the place has always been 'bad,' or whether Longstreet made it bad. But so much dark magic has been done there that it's nearly overwhelming."

"Are there any other creatures? Things we need to blast?" Beck had his shotgun on his lap and looked ready to use it.

Cassidy and Rowan shook their heads. "Not that are showing up to our magic," Rowan replied. "That doesn't necessarily mean there's nothing wrong—just nothing we can pick up."

"Lovely," Evan muttered.

"Let's get Logan and get out of here," Beck said. "And for the record—I'm totally in favor of burning the place to the ground."

Cassidy maneuvered her canoe to the dock, where Rowan got out. Evan was surprised that the weathered boards held a person's weight. The old structure canted to one side, and several of the posts looked rotted.

"Step lightly," Rowan told the others, picking her way to firm ground. Cassidy paddled far enough away for the second canoe to pull up.

They drew the craft alongside of the dock, and Beck tossed a rope to secure the boat. One person crossed at a time, just in case. Father Anne saluted Cassidy, who paddled far enough away to have a view of the swamp in both directions.

"We're losing the light. We need to move," Rowan said. She and Father Anne took point, with Evan and Beck coming up behind with the shotguns.

Close up, the cabin looked like something from a horror movie. If it was as old as the dock, it had been built better, since it had survived more than a century of storms. Blackened wood siding covered the frame, with a steeply pitched tin roof. The front had a single window and a door with heavy shutters pinned open to expose the wavy old glass.

Cue the scary music, Evan thought, racking his shotgun, just in case. Beck did the same. The sound echoed.

Birds rose at the noise, and the flurry of wings made Evan jump. The frogs went silent. It felt to Evan like the swamp held its breath.

"Logan?" Beck called out.

Evan saw a flash of light inside the cabin, there and gone fast enough that he thought he might have imagined it.

Logan?" Beck took a step closer.

Rowan threw her arm out to block him. "Wait. There's a spell." She pulled a small bag of charms and powders from her backpack and dropped it on the ground, then crushed it with her foot as she murmured an incantation.

"Father Anne, set down a salt path wide enough for us to walk on right here," she instructed, holding out her hands a few feet apart as a guide. The priest grabbed a canister of salt from her bag and did as Rowan asked.

"Stay on the salt path," Rowan told them. "There's a trap spell around the cabin to keep people in. I'll stay here to keep the path open and watch for trouble."

"What if we need someone with magic, once we get in there?" Beck asked.

"I can do a little magic." Evan found himself speaking up. "Let's go."

Evan led the way, followed by Father Anne and Beck. Once they crossed the magical perimeter, the sulfur smell grew worse, along with the sickly-sweet scent of decomposition.

"Logan!" Beck called again.

"Beck?" Logan's muffled voice came from inside the cabin. "Stay back—I can't get out!"

Father Anne set down a thick salt line by the door, then spoke a banishment, and splashed the door with holy water from a flask in her bag.

The door swung open slowly, untouched. Logan stood framed in the opening, wild-eyed and disheveled, but unharmed.

"Oh, my God. I didn't think I'd ever get out!"

Beck rushed forward and folded Logan into his arms. "You should have waited for us before you came out here." Logan stepped outside, and Beck passed him a shotgun from their bag.

"What's in there?" Father Anne asked as she and Evan moved up to the doorway.

Logan paled. "Blood. Lots of it. A heavy table. Magic stuff. Bones." He dug into his pocket and pulled out a man's watch. "I found this. It belonged to Blake. It's got his name on the back." Logan's voice held, but now that Evan could see him up close, the red eyes and blotchy skin told him Logan had taken the discovery hard.

"I was going to burn the place down, but fortunately I realized that I couldn't leave," he added.

"Glad you figured that out first," Beck said, looking shaken. He pulled Logan in for a tight hug as if he would never let go, and Logan held on for dear life.

Evan and Father Anne headed inside, sweeping the interior with their flashlights. The cabin might have been built to be a fishing outpost, but it had long ago been converted into Longstreet's sacrifice chamber.

Bile rose in Evan's throat as old memories crowded to the fore, recalling when he had been the intended victim stretched out for the kill. A sturdy table served as the altar, likely darkened by years of bloodshed. Guttered pillar candles formed a ring around the table. Sigils and runes had been chalked onto the rough boards of the cabin's walls. A pile of bones lay to one side, human and animal.

Three cans of gasoline sat next to the table, Logan's contribution.

"A forensics team could probably solve a lot of cold cases with what's in here," Evan said quietly.

"Can you imagine trying to ask for a search warrant?" Father Anne replied. "As soon as the media caught wind, all the headlines would be screaming about Satanic cults. Longstreet's smart enough not to leave anything that would tie him to the deaths. Logan's right. We need to burn the whole thing."

Evan nodded. "Do you see anything that could be Longstreet's anchor? If we destroy the anchor, we make him weaker—and that helps Seth and Teag."

They made a slow check of the cabin's meager contents, but there was no sign of anything like the objects the other witch-disciples had used to anchor their magic.

"I think the anchor is the cabin," Evan said. "It's on his family's old plantation. The whole place feels…wrong. It's his link to the past he thinks was stolen from him."

"I agree," Father Anne replied. "Let's torch the place and get out of here."

Father Anne tested that they could still get out, and Evan sloshed gasoline over everything, splashing it high onto the wooden walls for good measure. He and Father Anne backed out of the old cabin. The smell of gas made a noxious mix with the heavy scent of the swamp.

"Head's up!" Cassidy called out, just before Evan lit the gasoline. "Incoming!"

"What the fuck are those things?" Logan stared at the horrors crawling out of the black water. Half-decomposed corpses, dressed in sodden rags, hauled themselves from their soggy grave to defend their killer's charnel house.

"They're target practice," Beck snarled and blasted the nearest creature with his shotgun.

Evan ran to join the line, deciding that they should wait to blow up the cabin until they could get off the fucking island. He leveled his shotgun and hit his mark, dropping the zombie in its tracks.

Father Anne pulled a sawed-off from a sling across her back and opened fire. Even with four of them firing, more of the unholy monsters kept climbing from the swamp. Rowan chanted, raising an iridescent curtain of magic on one side of the cabin that seemed to work like an electric fence, zapping the zombies and sending them back into the water. It didn't stop the creatures from trying again, but it kept the monsters from flanking their little group.

"Evan, watch out!" Logan shouted. Evan turned to see one of the swamp zombies close enough he could count the teeth remaining in its bony jaw.

Training overcame fear, and Evan shouted the rote spell Seth had drilled him to learn. A streak of fire lanced from his outstretched palm, sending the ragged skeleton up in flames.

Evan stared as a gust of force swept half a dozen of the creatures off the island and sent them tumbling into the swamp. Cassidy sat in her canoe several yards offshore, with her wand leveled at the waterline. She alternated blasts from her wand with a stream of fire from the walking stick, sweeping the beach and torching the zombies that remained.

Rowan's curtain of light sizzled like a bug-zapper, adding the stench of burned hair and dirty rags to the night air.

"We've got to burn the place and get off the island!" Evan shouted. "Can you plow the road to get us to the dock?"

His companions nodded grimly, laying down blast after blast with the shotguns to clear the way. Evan ran back toward the cabin, only to find the door sealed once more.

"Fuck." He used his elbow to shatter the glass of the single window, then wheeled as he heard a rustle close by.

"Evan! Behind you!" Beck shouted.

The zombie lurched at Evan, and he shoved it away, sending it crashing through the broken window and into the cabin. He mustered his will and infused his rote spell with all his intention—for their escape, for Seth's safety, for the end of the curse, and Longstreet's destruction. Power flowed through him, stronger than he had ever channeled before, loosing a torrent of flame from his palm that incinerated the zombie and lit up the gas-soaked interior.

"Get out of there!" Father Anne's voice had an edge of panic.

Evan's rote magic lacked range. He knew he was too close, but they'd come to do this, and by damn, he'd get it done. He ran, feeling the drain of the curse and the exhaustion that came with calling the spells.

The cabin went up in a fireball behind him, with a blast that threw him to the ground. Evan cried out as the impact jarred bruised ribs. He could feel the heat like a blistering wave. *I might not make it.*

Strong hands grabbed him and yanked him to his feet, half-carrying, half-dragging him toward the dock.

"Next time," Beck grated, "run first, then shoot fire."

Cassidy paddled her canoe toward the dock to pick up Rowan and Logan. Father Anne had already gotten into their boat and called to Logan to cross the bridge.

Just as Logan stepped from the land to the dock, a skeletal hand grabbed his ankle, yanking his legs out from under him.

Cassidy raised her walking stick, but hesitated, unable to send a blast of fire without hitting Logan or setting the dock aflame. Evan tried to gather the energy for one more rote spell and nearly blacked out with the effort.

"Logan!" Beck eased Evan to the ground and raised his shotgun, but the angle was wrong, and Evan knew that Beck couldn't hit the zombie without shooting Logan as well.

Evan watched helplessly as Logan kicked and tried to blast the zombie with his shotgun, but he couldn't fire the gun and hold on to the dock. Evan felt sure that getting pulled into the water would mean certain death. Logan grabbed at the dock, and the rotted wood snapped with a loud crack, coming loose in his hands and sending him sliding toward the water. Beck edged forward, but Evan knew they didn't dare risk more weight on the rickety structure, which left Logan on his own against the zombie.

Behind them, the cabin burned like an inferno, a ball of fire belching dark smoke. Sweat poured down Evan's back, even at the water's edge. But in seconds, the temperature dropped until Evan could see his breath cloud in front of him.

"Oh my God." Beck gasped, as Evan struggled to his feet.

A gray figure grabbed Logan's wrist, yanking him free. Logan kicked the zombie in the skull, as more ghosts swarmed the zombie, forcing it back into the swamp. All over the island, the spirits of Longstreet's victims held the zombies at bay, keeping them from blocking the dock.

Logan stared up at his translucent rescuer, and Evan gasped, since the resemblance between the two brothers was undeniable.

"Blake?" Logan's voice held a mix of wonder and grief.

Evan watched as Blake Miller gave his brother a reassuring smile, then lifted his left hand to the side of his head in the "call me" gesture, and vanished.

Rowan dragged Logan to his feet and hustled him toward the canoes. Beck practically scooped Evan into his arms and hurried them down the dock, which creaked and swayed under their combined weight. A board broke under Beck's foot, and he barely caught himself before they tumbled, but he staggered forward, regaining his balance, and lowered Evan into the canoe before climbing in himself.

"What's to keep those things from coming after us in the water?" Beck asked Father Anne as they pushed away from the dock.

The cabin exploded, sending a plume of flame skyward and showering them with burning embers and chunks of wood. Evan lifted his arm to protect his head and saw the zombies fall to the ground at the same instant. The ghosts vanished seconds later.

"Apparently, Longstreet's magic doesn't extend to the whole swamp," Father Anne replied, as she and Beck put their backs into paddling. Cassidy, Rowan, and Logan's canoe glided back toward the edge of the swamp, where the orange glow of sunset dispelled the gloom. While they had been on the island, Cassidy had fastened Logan's borrowed canoe behind hers, towing it back to shore.

"With the cabin gone, he's lost his anchor—and the focus of his protection spell. There's nothing to protect, so no zombies. Blake and any other ghosts can rest in peace."

Evan reached for a paddle, but his ribs forced a groan. Beck looked over his shoulder at him.

"We've got this. You did good back there. Let us do the heavy lifting now."

Evan wanted to argue, but his body had other plans. His ribs felt like they were on fire, his head throbbed, and every muscle ached with exhaustion. *I might have pushed myself too far.* Using rote spells took a lot out of him on a good day. He hadn't had any good days since the accident and the curse. Evan knew he'd been running on borrowed time, with Rowan's spells, the hex sign on his arm, and Travis's potion. He didn't have reserves left.

He feared they might get back to the condo parking lot only to find the police waiting for them. Surely people had noticed the cabin's fireball and called authorities. But when they reached the lot, it was dark. Sirens screamed in the distance, and a helicopter flew overhead, but no one at the condos seemed to take notice.

"Come on," Beck said, helping Evan out of the canoe. Rowan was already securing one canoe atop Cassidy's RAV4, and Father Anne flipped their craft effortlessly and got it settled on the Jeep's rack, then did the same with Logan's canoe and the Jeep he had driven.

Beck got Evan to the Jeep, then turned to pull Logan into a hard kiss and a fierce hug. "Don't ever scare me like that again." His voice sounded choked with emotion.

"I'm sorry," Logan said. "I fucked up."

"Get in! We've got to go!" Father Anne started the Jeep, and they buckled up, with Evan in the front, Beck and Logan in the back. Rowan drove the Jeep that Logan had used, which left Cassidy in her RAV4. None of them turned on their headlights until they were back on the main road, headed for Charleston.

"Why didn't you tell me?" Beck demanded. "I would have gone with you."

"I should have," Logan admitted. "It was stupid. I just felt like... like I needed to do it myself. For Blake."

"You almost joined him." No one could mistake the hurt, angry, possessive tone in Beck's voice for anything platonic. He kept his arm around Logan, and his hand gripped Logan's shoulder tightly enough to bruise.

"I thought I was going to," Logan said quietly. "And that's when I realized how much I'd screwed up. I brought the gas to torch the cabin and couldn't get out. I was afraid Longstreet would come back before you found me... If you came looking."

"Of course I came looking!" Beck growled. "You scared the shit out of me. I thought...I thought you were gone for good."

Logan leaned against him, wrapping his arms around Beck's waist. "I realized, once I got there, that Blake would have ripped me a new one for doing it. And as much as I wanted to see him again, avenge him, I was afraid you and I would never get to know each other."

Beck pressed a kiss to Logan's lips. "I'm glad you're here."

Once they had their reunion, Father Anne cleared her throat. "So... that ghost back there—"

"Blake saved me." Logan sounded teary. "I couldn't hold on. That thing had my leg, and I thought it was going to pull me under. And then Blake was there, pulling me loose."

"That gesture he made, right before he vanished?" Beck asked.

Logan gave a sad chuckle. "Deadpool's 'call me.' Blake loved Deadpool. He had the T-shirts, all the action figures. We watched those movies over and over, and we used to quote the lines and do the gestures like a secret language. That was our code for 'see you later.'" A sob choked his voice, and Beck wrapped both arms tightly around him.

Evan tried and failed to reach Seth, and his text to Teag also went unanswered. Now that they were out of danger themselves, his worry about them confronting Longstreet at the airstrip was all that he could think about.

"We need to go back up Seth and Teag," he urged. "They might need our help. I can't reach either of them."

"You and Logan are in no shape for another battle," Father Anne said. "Cassidy told Sorren what was going on. He'll back them up if needed. You need to sit this out."

Evan wanted to argue, but he knew Father Anne was right. He stared at his phone, willing it to ring and assure him that Seth and Teag were safe, but it remained dark and silent.

They arrived at the St. Expeditus compound without incident. Evan hadn't realized he was holding his breath until they drove through the gates without finding a police roadblock waiting for them.

Father Anne parked the Jeep, and Cassidy pulled up beside them. She and Rowan got out and walked over.

"What now?" Cassidy asked.

"They'll have supper ready inside," Father Anne said. "I think we could all use a good meal—and then a debriefing."

"Sounds good to me," Evan said. He let go of the doorframe, took a step toward the safe house, and collapsed.

Dimly, Evan heard voices calling his name. Then beefy arms scooped him up in a bridal carry as if he weighed nothing. He didn't recognize his rescuer, a brawny guy who looked like he ought to be a bouncer, or maybe a pro wrestler. He caught a whiff of food, but felt too exhausted to think about eating. Voices and awareness faded in and out, but pain was a constant.

The bouncer laid him on a couch, and Evan sank into the cushions, hoping he'd pass out all the way so everything would quit hurting.

Rowan sat next to him, but it seemed so hard to concentrate on what she was saying.

"Burned yourself out...curse is moving faster...do what we can. Please...hang on."

Evan thought about how happy Beck was to find Logan alive and well. And how bittersweet Logan's reunion had been with Blake. Seth was counting on him to survive, just like he depended on Seth to keep his promise to return. Evan's stubborn streak had gotten him in a lot of trouble over the years, but now he banked on it as he gathered all his remaining energy and dug in, holding on with everything he had left.

He roused himself enough to see a missed call and message from Seth, and a text about a warehouse, but he was too drained to make sense of them. Just in case the worst happened, he texted Seth, as he struggled to stay conscious.

Fading. I love you.

10

SETH

"SORREN AND DONNELLY ARE ON THEIR WAY TO THE AIRSTRIP." TEAG PUT down his phone and looked at Seth. "Longstreet isn't going to know what hit him."

"Sitting this out feels wrong," Seth replied. "I know it makes sense to let the guys with the big mojo go after him. But—"

"It's your case. You tracked him. Your legwork made all this possible," Teag said, leaning against his car. Teag had hacked into Logan's surveillance camera that was pointed at Longstreet's mansion, and they watched the feed on Teag's tablet from a parking lot a mile away. "And if you hadn't come to Charleston, it might have taken us a lot longer to connect Longstreet with the disappearances and the relic trade."

"It's not like I'm in a hurry to get smacked around," Seth answered. "But handing it off just feels like I'm missing the climax of the movie."

Teag shrugged. "I guess it depends on whether you're worried about getting the job done—or personal vengeance."

"Can't I have a little of both?" Seth rested against the passenger door while Teag sat on the hood. "You're right. It's like when I was in the Army. It's your unit that runs the mission, your unit that makes the kill. Doesn't matter who pulls the trigger. And getting Longstreet is what matters. It's kind of nice not to be getting zapped by dark magic for a change."

Teag's phone rang. "Hey, Travis—what's up?" He put the call on speaker so Seth could hear.

"Got a vision, and it came with a hell of a headache, so it must be important. I was at an airstrip, but it was empty. No people, no planes. Everything looked normal, but empty. And then I was in a parking lot, behind a warehouse with a blue billboard. And people were getting on a plane in the parking lot. I know that doesn't make sense. Visions aren't always literal. I've got no idea what any of that means, but I woke up knowing you needed to hear it. And now I'm going to take some Advil and lie down."

"Thanks, Travis. That actually matters—a lot."

"Good. I'd hate to get this bad of a headache for nothing."

Teag met Seth's gaze. "The rendezvous isn't going to happen at the airstrip. Something changed."

"Or the airstrip isn't where the important action is," Seth countered.

Teag opened up the photos Emily had found of the commercial properties that had belonged to Longstreet's personas over the years. He picked one of a building that had been bought by Longstreet's holding company.

"Look." He passed Seth the phone. The modern-day photo of the boxy warehouse showed a large billboard on top.

"That's got to be it. But what did the vision mean? Should we tell Sorren and Donnelly to go to the warehouse instead?"

Teag was already pulling up directions. "I'll tell them what happened, and say that we're heading for the warehouse and send directions. Sorren can't go anywhere until sundown. They can check out the airstrip, and if nothing's going on, they can meet us at the warehouse."

"In case that really is where the deal is happening, and we need reinforcements?"

"You've got it."

Teag sent the text. Seth watched with interest. "Your immortal vampire boss uses texts?"

Teag chuckled. "Sorren says that vampires who can't adapt don't survive. So, yes. Cell phone, email, text. Internet—but not social media."

"I'd gotten so used to thinking of the witch-disciples as immortal and evil; I hadn't really considered that immortals might also be good."

Teag headed toward the warehouse. "Sorren says he's seen enough death and destruction, and that it's like watching the same movie over and over. So he decided to do what he could to change the script. Donnelly, too."

Seth pulled out his phone to text Evan and saw that Evan had already messaged him and left a voice mail. "Simon called Evan. He had a vision, too. Evan thought it meant the airstrip was a trap—and there might be zombies."

"Well, that lines up with what Travis saw. Only Travis got a bit more of the story, with the warehouse," Teag replied. "So that sounds to me like we're on the right track."

"Interesting." Seth took a moment to text the change of plans to Evan. He noted that the text was received but not read, and wondered what Evan was up to. Seth decided to call, but it went right to voicemail.

"Hey, change of plans. Looks like we're heading for a warehouse, not the airstrip. Just wanted you to know. So…be careful, and I'll see you soon. Love you." He ended the call.

He sighed and let his head fall back. "I really want this curse to be over."

"How are you feeling?"

"Like I've got the flu. Achy. Crummy." He shrugged. "I've been worse, in the Army on a mission. So don't worry—I've got your back."

"I wasn't worried."

They parked a few blocks from the warehouse. The sun was low in the sky, not yet night. "This could be a wild goose chase," Teag said as they sat in the car.

"It could be. But Simon and Travis both got visions. They thought the messages were urgent. We know the curse has an expiration date, and Longstreet wants a fight. So…if it's not today, and the clock is ticking, then when?"

"How do you want to play this?" Teag asked. "South Carolina is a gun-friendly state, but we'd be pushing it—a lot—to go strolling down the street with a duffle full of weapons and a couple of sawed-offs."

"In the past we've used tranq guns, grenades, throwing knives, and fire. Bullets slow down a Renfield, but they don't affect the witch much when he's juiced up." Seth paused. "But we had the advantage of fighting in remote places—not practically downtown."

"This area is pretty quiet after dark. Most of the warehouses are abandoned or for sale. The area is due for a big makeover. And since it's kind of grungy-industrial, there aren't any apartments or houses nearby. Short of blowing up one of the buildings or burning one down, no one is going to notice. If Longstreet chose to set up a hand-off here, I'd bet that even the cops don't come around often," Teag added.

"If we can get his amulet, it'll weaken him," Seth said. "The ring. I'd feel better if we had destroyed the anchor, but we'll work with what we've got."

"Dylan's the wild card," Teag drummed his fingers on the steering wheel. "Ian said he had some powers, but they must not be very strong or he wouldn't be wasting his time with a gang. Longstreet probably has him drugged, or bound with something that limits his magic."

"The last disciple we fought thought he had it fixed so I couldn't use my spells, but I didn't have to speak them or gesture to make the magic work," Seth said. "If Dylan helps us, that's one more on our side."

"He could just run away as soon as we free him," Teag pointed out.

"I wouldn't blame him."

"How much can you carry under your jacket?"

"I've got a couple of knives in wrist sheaths, a machete, plus my Glock in my waistband—with silver bullets, just in case," Seth replied. "My sawed-off will fit in my backpack—and it's got special shells filled with a lead and silver shot plus a mix Rowan said would temporarily weaken magic. And my rote spells, for what they're worth."

"They're worth a lot." Teag raised an eyebrow. "I've got knives, my sawed-off, and my silver whip, plus some tricks of my own." He pulled out a tranq pistol. "I wove binding spells into threads that are part of the fletchings on the darts. The tips deliver a knock-out potion with an anti-magic chaser. I'd rather not get close enough to use my knives."

"You and me both," Seth agreed. He frowned, looking at a few other items Teag had pulled from his bag. "What are those?"

"A bolo with a cord I wove, infused with magic, soaked in salt and colloidal silver. A couple of amulets Cassidy got from Rowan that will temporarily amplify our magic without cursing us or killing us."

"Good features."

"And some specialty items from our friend, Chuck—who used to be with a black-ops government team that dealt with the supernatural."

"C.H.A.R.O.N.?" Seth had heard of the group, always negatively.

"Yeah. Long story. He's on our side now. He always has the best toys." Teag grinned, clearly excited about the tech despite the danger. He pulled out three grenades and a grenade pistol.

"We are never going to explain that away if a cop pats us down."

"Then we're going to have to avoid the cops. The grenades have the same kind of mix as the tranq gun, so if we set them off, we don't want to be in the blast zone, or we'll get de-mojo'd too."

"Chuck sounds like a great guy," Seth replied.

"A little odd, but yeah, he's pretty cool."

Teag and Seth tucked their weapons away beneath jackets or in backpacks, as the last of the sun faded. "Ready?" Teag asked.

"As ready as I'll ever be."

They locked the car and walked toward a site Teag had picked that would give them a protected vantage point to watch the parking lot. Teag unrolled a length of rope around the area where they waited.

"The rope is salted, and I've woven a distraction spell into it," Teag explained. "It won't make us invisible, but it deflects attention else-where unless we do something to stand out, like make noise."

Overhead, the dark sky glowed on the horizon with the lights of the distant city, but the lot where they kept watch had no security lighting, and the surrounding buildings were dark. A waxing moon made it possible to see, but the moonlight didn't penetrate the shadows around the edges of the open area.

The parking lot obviously hadn't been used in a long time. A broken, abandoned dumpster hulked along one side. Refuse lay scattered across the cracked asphalt—cans, bottles, and larger items like dented buckets and old traffic barrels. An empty fifty-five-gallon drum rolled with the wind like a metallic tumbleweed.

Seth and Teag set their phones to silent. Seth checked, but Evan hadn't replied. That worried him, but right now wasn't the time to call again. He reminded himself that Evan was with Cassidy and the others, that he had people looking out for him. None of that eased the knot in his gut.

"Look," Teag murmured. Seth brought his attention back to the parking lot, where a dark SUV with heavily tinted windows rolled up, lights extinguished.

A few minutes later, another dark SUV joined it, entering from the opposite direction. Two men got out of the first car, and Seth figured them to be the buyer and his bodyguard. Seth couldn't make out many details about their features, but the bodyguard wore a T-shirt and jeans, while the other man had a leather jacket on over dark pants.

The passenger door for the front seat of the second vehicle opened, and a brawny man got out. He opened the rear door and held it for a tall, slim man in a suit. The bigger man went to the cargo area and lifted the hatch, then manhandled a slightly built man from the back, whose wrists were bound and ankles were hobbled.

Dylan, the kidnapped witchling.

The big man jerked his uncooperative captive to stand behind the man in the suit, whom Seth figured was Longstreet. Leather Jacket Guy took a step forward, and said something, with his attention focused on the prisoner.

Longstreet answered. Seth couldn't hear what was being said, but it appeared Longstreet's client balked at either the terms or the merchandise.

Teag gave a nod, and Seth slipped from cover, keeping to the shadows, with the tranq pistol in his hand. Unlike Teag, he had no strong magic, making him less likely to draw Longstreet's notice. Once he was in range, Seth squeezed off two shots. The big man holding Dylan clawed at the dart in his neck and raised his gun, then dropped to the ground. A moment later, the second bodyguard staggered and fell backward. Longstreet wheeled and grabbed Dylan before the young man had a chance to run. Seth didn't have a clear shot at the buyer, who jumped back in the first SUV and roared away, leaving his bodyguard behind.

Seth heard the grenade launcher fire and saw Longstreet search the dark sky for a target. Seth picked up a rock and threw it, breaking a window and drawing Longstreet's attention. The grenade clattered to the asphalt and detonated with a flare of light and a muffled boom, filling the air with a cloud of powder that covered Longstreet, Dylan, and the SUV, as well as the downed guard.

Army training kicked in, and Seth had a new position by the time the dust settled. Longstreet gripped the ropes that bound Dylan's wrists behind his back. Seth, from his new vantage point, kept an eye on the SUV, unsure whether Longstreet had a driver who might be inclined to join the fray. He shoved the tranq gun in his bag and pulled his Glock from his waistband, trying to get a good shot at Longstreet without hitting Dylan.

"Seth Tanner...have you come to finish this?" Longstreet called. If the grenade's payload dampened his magic, it didn't dim his bravado. "Come out, come out, it would be a shame to kill this delectable little prize," he taunted, jerking on Dylan's bonds.

Dylan didn't fight, but he also didn't cooperate. Seth wondered if Longstreet had used a hex to keep Dylan pliant and unable to disobey.

Seth couldn't shoot Longstreet without hitting Dylan, and so he hunched down and moved cautiously, staying in the darkest shadows.

He had no idea where Teag was but doubted he'd stayed in their original spot. Longstreet scanned the lot and turned in a slow half-circle, moving Dylan with him as a shield, keeping his back to the SUV.

"That curse must be wearing on you by now, isn't it? Nasty little thing. I'll give you a clean, quick death. You're barely on your feet, much weaker than before. Your partner's light is fading. I can barely feel it through my link. Give up. I've won."

Seth heard the grenade launcher fire again, and windows shattered in Longstreet's SUV, then came a blinding flash of light and a thunderous bang that rocked the vehicle and sent Longstreet and Dylan stumbling.

Dylan, however, seemed to "fall" in a direction opposite Longstreet, which Seth suspected might be as much resistance as the bound witchling could muster. In the seconds Longstreet had been distracted with the flash-bang, Seth had changed position again, and had Longstreet in his sights with the Glock when another bruiser—probably the SUV's driver—lunged from the shadows to grab Seth from behind.

Seth brought his foot up, hard, between the big man's legs, landing a solid connection with his sac. When the driver doubled over, Seth rammed his elbow into the man's nose, and shot the man in the leg, to keep him from coming after them again. He sidestepped the cursing, bleeding goon and dodged, just in time, as Longstreet sent a crackling arc of energy where Seth had been standing seconds before.

He heard an odd whistle in the air, and Longstreet shouted in anger. Seth popped up from his hiding place to see Longstreet attempting to kick loose from the bolo wrapped around his ankles. Seth racked his shotgun and fired, catching Longstreet in the shoulder as the witch-disciple turned at the last instant.

Their attempts might have dampened Longstreet's magic, but they hadn't rendered him helpless. Longstreet ripped the bolo from his ankles and sent another arc of blue-white energy aimed at Teag. Dylan lay on the ground, trying to inchworm away from his captor.

Longstreet pivoted and focused on Seth, stretching out his arm, fist clenched. The big ring on his left hand glowed. Seth gasped and fell to his knees, struggling to breathe, as the curse tightened. He heard the sound of a shotgun loading, then the blast as Teag fired, forcing Longstreet to break his concentration. Between Longstreet's inattention and the borrowed relic's juju, Seth shook off the attack and reached for his gun.

Longstreet used his magic to hurl trash at Teag, raining down bottles, garbage, and loose pieces of asphalt. Teag fired again, and Longstreet had to dodge to avoid the spray of salt and lead.

Longstreet's power flung a rusted, derelict dumpster toward where the blast had originated, and Teag screamed.

Before Longstreet could press his advantage, Seth squeezed off a shot with his Glock, aiming for the dark witch's left hand and his ring, the amulet that helped to connect him to his stolen magic. The bullet blasted two fingers, including the one that held the ring. The witch-disciple howled in pain, blood flowing from where the fingers had been and rounded on Seth.

"It's time to finish this. You've caused me far too much trouble. Your partner's nearly dead. It's your turn now." Once more the curse tightened like jagged barbed wire, cutting into Seth's skin, squeezing his chest, and sending pain coursing through his body, more than his borrowed relic and protective jewelry could counter. Even without his amulet-ring, despite their attempts to dampen his power, what remained of Longstreet's magic was still strong enough to present a lethal challenge.

Seth shoved his hand into his pocket, wrapping his fingers around the relic Teag had given him. He fell, throwing himself to land next to Dylan, as he focused his attention on one of his rote spells.

Seth slapped his hand down on the rope binding Dylan's wrists and spoke a spell which untied the ropes and unlocked the ankle bonds.

"Get out of here!" he rasped, seeing Dylan's frightened eyes go wide. Dylan scrambled away, and Seth wondered if the cuffs had bound him to Longstreet's control.

Where was Teag?

Your partner's nearly dead. Longstreet's taunt rang in Seth's ears and lanced through his heart. Evan was fading. He had trusted Seth to save them, and Seth refused to let him down.

Longstreet strode toward him, ready to end it. Seth knew this was his last chance.

He'd have to pick carefully—the curse had depleted him, and even at his best, the rote magic took a lot out of him. But Seth was willing to risk draining himself to get justice for Blake Miller and all of the others Longstreet had killed or sold over the years, to break the curse and save Evan.

Odds were good that he'd die either way.

Longstreet stumbled and gasped. One minute, he'd been cocky and sure of his victory. Then he staggered, nearly falling, looking as if he'd been sucker-punched. Something had changed, and it threw Longstreet off his game. Seth's hope flared. Had their friends managed to find and destroy Longstreet's anchor?

Longstreet might have taken a hit, but he rallied fast and came after Seth with deadly intent.

Seth spoke his spell, and fire streaked from his palm, catching Longstreet in the face. Seth rolled, desperate to get away. Longstreet screamed in pain and fury, and flung out one hand, pinning Seth to the asphalt.

Seth figured he had enough energy left to cast one more spell. He called to any ghosts in range of his waning power, summoning them. The temperature plunged, and gray images flickered into sight, dozens of them, agitated at the urgent call. *He's a killer,* Seth tried to send his thoughts. *Stop him!*

The ghosts rallied to his cry, swarming around Longstreet. Some of the spirits probably welcomed any chance to mete out vengeance. Others, grown restless over time, needed little prompting to take out their agitation on a target.

Longstreet swore and shouted as he struggled through the wall of ghosts, intent on finishing Seth. A flash of silver glinted in the moonlight, and the thin, razor-sharp tendril of Teag's steel whip curled around Longstreet's wrist, cutting deep. Longstreet cursed and tried to free himself. A dented metal bucket sailed through the air from somewhere to the left of Seth, slamming Longstreet in the head, and Seth guessed that Dylan had stuck around after all.

Bleeding, injured, and angry, Longstreet turned on Seth with a growl.

Seth staggered to his feet, spent but still fighting. Longstreet raised his arm to cast a killing spell, as Seth lifted his Glock and shot Longstreet in the chest.

Longstreet's eyes widened in surprise. He did not fall; instead, an invisible force kept him suspended in mid-air. Longstreet bellowed a cry of rage and impotence and tried to break free of the power holding him. The warlock thrashed, and his cries grew more panicked and desperate.

Then Seth saw it, a jagged, violet crack of light that opened in the air behind Longstreet, something that hadn't been there before. Seth had seen a rift like that when the other witch-disciples had abandoned their sacrifices mid-ritual. He doubted Longstreet controlled this doorway to…somewhere else.

Longstreet bucked in the grip of the magic, twisting and fighting. The rift flared so brightly that Seth threw up his arms to shield his face, and he slammed his eyes closed.

When he opened his eyes, Longstreet and the rift were gone.

Seth felt light pass over him out of nowhere, just as the shadow had done back in the hospital after their accident. As soon as the light was gone, Seth felt the curse lift. He could breathe freely once again, and while his body still ached, the injuries were a direct result of the fight. His head cleared, and the lingering fever vanished.

It's gone.

What about Evan?

Oh, god. Did the curse break in time to save him?

"Seth?" Teag came around a low cement wall on the other side of the parking lot. Scratches and a bruise marred his face, his ripped shirt and torn jeans suggested a close call with the dumpster, but he was alive, and as far as Seth could tell, otherwise unhurt.

"I'm here. I was afraid he got you when he threw that big bin at you."

Teag managed a tired smile. "It was close, but I dodged."

"Who are you guys?" Dylan stepped out of the shadows, looking haggard and disheveled.

"We fight people like Longstreet, and other monsters," Seth replied, tucking his Glock back into the waistband of his pants. "Thanks for pitching that bucket at him."

Dylan looked embarrassed at the praise. "I don't have a lot of magic, so I need to be creative. Picking something up at a distance and throwing it comes in handy more often than you'd think."

Teag joined them. "You're with the Shadow Coven," he said. Dylan glanced up, startled. "Ian Taylor told us you were missing."

Dylan rubbed a hand on the back of his neck. "The guy grabbed me outside a bar. Bumped into me and must have put a mojo on me because all of a sudden I couldn't keep myself from obeying him."

"He used a hex charm," Seth replied. "They suck."

"I kept telling him that I didn't have any money, and no one was going to pay a ransom. Then he told me he took me for my magic, and he wouldn't believe me when I said my magic ain't worth shit."

Seth gave a dry chuckle. "Oh, your magic is worth a lot. About ten thousand dollars to the guy who bought you."

Dylan looked horrified. "*Bought* me?"

"Supernatural human trafficking ring. Those other members of your coven who disappeared? Blame Longstreet."

"Shit." Dylan's gaze shifted to where Longstreet had vanished. "What happened to him?"

Seth shrugged. "If you want my best guess, his undead witch master pulled him through a rift in space to eat him alive. But...I could be wrong about that."

"What?" Dylan glanced at Teag to see if Seth was joking.

"He's probably right," Teag replied. "Although we're a little fuzzy on the details."

Dylan took a step back. "Um...thanks for the rescue and all, but I need to be going."

"Try not to get kidnapped again," Seth said as Dylan took off. He knew that if they needed to find Dylan, Ian could make the connection. "What happened to Sorren and Donnelly?" Teag asked.

"A rather nasty undead uprising," Sorren said from behind them. They turned to find Sorren and Donnelly walking toward them. Sorren lifted an eyebrow at the still-burning SUV. Other than some streaks of dirt on his white T-shirt, the vampire didn't look like he'd been in a battle.

Archibald Donnelly, on the other hand, had the look of a man who had started a bar fight and roundly trounced his opponents. Donnelly, a big, broad-shouldered man with a bushy mustache and Victorian-style sideburns, seemed entirely too pleased with the night's activities, with a glint in his eyes and a flush to his face that said he enjoyed every minute.

"We found the airstrip overrun with zombies—and badly magicked ones at that," Donnelly said. Leave it to a necromancer to be picky about how the undead were summoned. "Longstreet must have used a cut-rate spell to raise them, and then left them to be ordered about by a chap named Mikey, who had no skill at all as a necromancer, and was a god-awful troop commander, lucky for us." He looked like the fracas was the most fun he'd had in a long while.

Sorren's expression was one of put-upon forbearance at Donnelly's enthusiasm. "We think that either the airfield was a trap, or some scheme of Longstreet's went belly-up at the last minute, and he left Mikey holding the bag."

Seth frowned. "Mikey—he's the guy Ian thinks hexed his brother to let Longstreet use the gang for his own purposes."

"That won't be a problem any longer," Donnelly said, clearing his throat. "He's been taken into custody. It was that or let the zombies eat him." He glanced at Sorren. "I was overruled."

Seth's eyes widened. "Holy shit. There's witch jail? Like Azkaban?"

Sorren chuckled. "Not exactly. The Alliance has facilities designed to detain supernaturally-powered offenders to keep them from committing more crimes. But I assure you, it is far from a medieval dungeon."

Seth knew that Sorren was a centuries-old vampire, and Cassidy had said Donnelly was a high-powered necromancer. But listening to the two of them made Seth feel like he'd interrupted the weirdest buddy flick ever.

"So both Simon's vision and Travis's vision were correct...just different from what they expected," Teag said.

Sorren nodded. "Yes. Different threats. And while Longstreet posed a significant danger, I think it best that Archibald and I handled the undead." He looked around at the parking lot and the aftermath of the battle, including the downed henchmen. "We'll handle the clean-up. It appears you were successful."

Seth and Teag chuckled tiredly. "We're alive, we saved the kidnap victim, and Longstreet got sucked through a rift," Teag recapped. "I'm not exactly clear on how that last part happened."

"I separated him from his amulet when I shot him in the hand,"

Seth said. He walked over to where the ring lay and picked it up with a stick, not wanting to touch it. Sorren took it and tucked it into a pocket. "But he was juiced up from killing Blake Miller, so I wasn't sure we could take him by ourselves. Unless, somehow, Cassidy and Evan found his anchor and destroyed it?"

"That may be," Sorren replied. "Have you talked to them?"

Seth and Teag shook their heads. "We really just finished here—haven't quite caught our breath," Teag replied.

Seth pulled out his phone and turned the volume up, checking for missed calls or texts. There was just one, from Evan. *Fading. I love you.*

He looked up, panicked. "I need to get to Evan. Now."

11

EVAN

"WHERE IS HE?" SETH'S VOICE CARRIED FROM THE KITCHEN. HE SOUNDED like he was one breath away from completely flipping out. Baxter bounced and hopped around his feet, barking incessantly.

"He's in the living room. He's been resting since we burned down the cabin," Cassidy told him and scooped Baxter into her arms.

"Since you...Jesus, you destroyed Longstreet's anchor?"

"It's a long story. Go see him."

"I'm right here." Evan stood in the doorway, with a fuzzy blanket clutched around his shoulders like a cape. He still felt sleep-addled, but he woke feeling much better than before. The effects of the curse were gone, leaving him only the normal bruises and injuries from recent fights.

"Evan. Oh, thank God." Seth rushed toward him, opening his arms to pull him into a hug, then stopped short.

"The curse—"

"It's gone." Rowan replied from behind Evan. "It lifted about half an hour ago. I assume that means you were successful in dispatching Longstreet?"

Seth figured Teag could tell the story. He grabbed Evan and yanked him into his arms, holding onto him like he would never let go. "I thought I'd lost you," he whispered with his face pressed against Evan's neck. "Longstreet said you were almost dead."

"He obviously underestimated the stubbornness of a Malone." Evan didn't want to add to Seth's worry by telling him—just yet—how near a thing it had been.

"You beautiful, wonderful, stubborn-ass man." Seth pulled back just far enough to kiss him, and Evan didn't care who was watching as the reality of the situation sank in.

The curse was gone.

They survived—and they could touch again.

A round of applause and good-natured cat-calls from their new friends greeted them when they stepped apart, and Evan blushed. Seth grinned and took an exaggerated bow. Evan felt giddy with relief and whipsawed by the sudden shift from despair to elation.

"Kell and Maggie made a big batch of chili, and it's been in the slow cooker for hours, so let's all sit down, eat, and catch each other up on what's happened," Cassidy told them. "And for the record, I think everyone deserves a drink—or three."

Seth took Evan's hand, tangling their fingers together in a firm grip. Everyone gathered in the living room, and Teag appointed himself unofficial bartender. Evan set the fuzzy blanket aside, now that he could sit close against Seth. Seth kept one arm tight around Evan as he called Toby with the good news, holding the phone so Evan could also hear.

"Good job," Toby said, relief clear in his voice. "We knew you could do it."

"Your hex sign helped," Seth replied.

"Glad to hear it. Now go celebrate. You've earned it," Toby told him.

Gradually, the whole crew filed in—Sorren and a big man Evan didn't recognize, Rowan, and Father Anne. Kell and Maggie filled bowls and brought a tray of warm cornbread to the table. As they ate, they took turns recounting their piece of the action. Teag opened a secure video chat on his laptop so Beck, Logan, and Ian could join in from the safety of the St. Expeditus compound.

"You must have burned the cabin after Longstreet showed up to hand off Dylan to his buyer," Seth said. "Teag and I hit him with special weapons to weaken his magic, but he was still winning until you destroyed his anchor. It was close. Too close."

"With Mikey and Longstreet gone, it broke their hold on Curtis, and he's back to his old self," Ian reported via the video chat. "It's going to take time to fix the damage Mikey did, and weed out the people who were in the group just to make trouble. But Curtis is a good leader. I think they'll be okay."

"You're not going back?" Evan asked.

Ian looked pained. "Not for a while. Maybe never. It depends on how things go. Curtis wants me to come back, but there are others who aren't as forgiving. We'll see."

Evan felt bad that Ian was exiled for doing the right thing. Then again, Beck faced a very similar situation.

"I'm glad Longstreet is gone—permanently," Logan said, with a defiant glint in his eye as if he thought someone might object. "For Blake, and all the others."

Beck slipped a comforting arm around Logan's shoulders and leaned forward so he was fully in the camera frame. "Do we know any of Longstreet's clients from his relic and trafficking operation? As long as they're out there, that piece of the problem will find another source."

"You and Logan were looking for a research project," Father Anne observed. "Sounds like a worthy one to me."

Beck grinned. "We're on it."

Sorren cleared his throat. "The Alliance will make it a priority to stop the trafficking and the relic trade. So we will appreciate your help."

"Are Beck and Logan..." Seth murmured to Evan.

"It's new."

Sorren wasn't finished. "Rowan and Archibald and I agree that we need to rectify the training gap that has forced those outside the main covens and old families to resort to gangs to learn the craft and protect themselves. I know that Simon and Travis have done similar things with their Skeleton Crew and Night Vigil. We'll be discussing options and coming up with a pilot program."

"You're not going to get the old families' approval?" Father Anne asked with a grin that made it clear she was instigating.

Sorren smiled and let the tips of his fangs show. "I am older than the old families. Over the years, I have done many favors. The time comes when favors are repaid."

Evan didn't doubt that Sorren and the others would find a way to fix the problem.

"I want to figure out how Beck and Logan and I—as well as Travis and the others—can help you two with the witch-disciple problem," Teag said, leaning back in his chair and savoring his tumbler of bourbon. "You've still got more of them to chase down, and you shouldn't be in this alone. You have friends—and friends of friends."

Seth squeezed Evan's hand, and Evan returned the squeeze. Seth swallowed hard and nodded. "That would be great. It's wonderful working with all of you."

"We're just sorry we didn't realize what was going on until now," Cassidy said. "But Teag's right—we've got connections everywhere. And now that we know what we're looking for, Beck and Logan, Travis, Simon, Erik, and the others can do the same kind of research they did on Longstreet to help you with the other disciples. Where are you heading next?"

Seth and Evan exchanged a glance. "Cleveland."

"Just send us what you know, and we'll help you dig," Beck said.

"I can help coordinate with Ben and Brent," Teag replied. "And you know Simon and Travis are in. Erik, too."

Evan's heart swelled, realizing that somehow, against all odds, he and Seth had gone on the run, just the two of them, and discovered a large, extended found-family, one that also included Toby and Milo, Seth's mentors. A family that accepted them just as they were, without trying to change them or make them pretend to be something they weren't. Who understood the truth and were willing to stand with them. He blinked back tears, overwhelmed.

"The Alliance has contacts in many places," Sorren said. "I'm sure I can make some connections."

"So does the St. Expeditus Society," Father Anne added. "In fact, someone I went to seminary with is in Cleveland. I'll make some calls."

"I've been looking into your rote magic," Rowan spoke up. "As I told Evan, I think it's more a case of finding a way to harness otherwise latent natural magic. I think I can help you with a few more useful spells, now that I understand more about how it works. It shouldn't take long to teach them to you." She glanced at Cassidy. "I'm betting we can come up with some charms that can also temporarily boost your power without causing bad side effects."

"And I'm going to weave some new healing and protective pieces for you." Teag shifted in his chair as if he had settled wrong on muscles that ached from the fight. "Every little bit helps, right?"

Seth looked at them and shook his head, speechless. "I don't know what to say, except thank you. That all sounds wonderful."

Evan closed both of his hands over Seth's. He had never seen their mission to stop the witch-disciples as the bleak quest it had once seemed to Seth. But then again, Seth had started out alone. Coming to Charleston was turning out to be the best thing that could have happened to them—even if they did almost die.

"And I haven't forgotten promising that Teag and I would take you on a foodie tour of the city," Cassidy added with a wink. "So even though your truck is fixed, plan on staying a few more days, and we'll show you around."

They said goodbye to Beck, Ian, and Logan on screen. Now that they'd gotten the debrief and logistics out of the way, conversation turned to lighter topics.

Rowan recounted several instances of spells gone wrong that left them all laughing hard. Pretty soon everyone had joined in with tales of misadventures involving magic, supernatural objects, or paranormal events. Sorren entertained them with colorful stories of some of the situations he and several of Cassidy's ancestors had encountered, which made Seth laugh until he almost snorted his drink.

Evan sat on the couch, snuggled into Seth's side, grateful and aware of every touch, something he'd never take for granted again. He felt so happy to be a part of this group, celebrating a win in a business where victories came dear, relaxing among people he trusted, and still a bit gobsmacked to find out that he and Seth apparently did have a bit of magical ability after all.

This was the family he'd missed for far too long, he thought, sipping his drink and listening to the laughter and the good-natured teasing. If he was honest with himself, he'd never felt this sense of belonging, even with his birth family back before he'd come out, when he was still trying so hard to be the person they wanted him to be. Every danger on the way was worth it, for this wonderful sense of acceptance, to find these comrades in arms.

The gathering didn't begin to break up until after midnight, long after the chili was gone, and the bottle of bourbon was empty. Seth and Evan helped Cassidy, Kell, and Teag clean up. Maggie planned to stay the night and volunteered to sleep on the couch since Seth could move back into the guest room with Evan.

"I should head back to our place," Teag said, putting the last of the glasses in the dishwasher. "Anthony will be coming back tomorrow morning from his continuing ed retreat. I bet I'll have more exciting things to tell him than vice versa!"

"I can drop you off," Rowan offered. "I'm going that way." They headed out, with promises to call in the morning to start setting up all the things they'd discussed. Cassidy shut the door behind them and sagged against Kell, who wrapped his arms around her.

"Busy day?" Kell teased.

They all burst out laughing at the absurdity and understatement, as if the tension finally found an outlet, and they were helpless to stop until their sides heaved and tears ran down their faces.

"I'll take that as a 'yes,'" Kell said, looking amused.

Cassidy stretched up to kiss him on the cheek. "I'm beat. Let's crash." She turned to Seth and Evan. "Just turn the lights out when you come up. I'm going to cook us a victory breakfast tomorrow you won't want to miss."

They retreated up the stairs, leaving Seth and Evan alone. Evan looked around, thinking how comfortable he had become in such a short time. When he first arrived, he thought maybe the wardings were the cause of the warm, safe, cozy feeling the house imparted. Perhaps that was true in part. But now that he'd gotten to know

Cassidy and her friends, he realized that it was because the house wasn't just a home; it was also a sanctuary for a wonderful family of the heart.

Seth leaned over and nuzzled his ear. "We can touch again." His voice, low and husky, went right to Evan's cock. Despite everything they'd been through that day, it appeared his dick was definitely up for a long-overdue reunion.

Evan cupped Seth's cheek and kissed him, slow and lingering at first, then with more heat until the slip of tongue and the slide of teeth turned frantic.

"Need you," Evan panted.

In response, Seth took Evan's hand and placed it over his own rock-hard bulge. "The faster we get to our room, the sooner we can both be naked."

They paused just long enough to turn out lights and check that the front door was locked, then raced quietly up the steps. Evan closed the door behind them, and Seth pinned him against it, kissing him from his jaw down to his neck, nipping at his shoulder through his T-shirt, and humping himself on Evan's thigh.

Seth's hands slid beneath Evan's T-shirt, exploring his abs, stopping to tweak the hard nipples. "Off, now," Seth growled.

Evan raised his arms, and Seth yanked the T-shirt over his head. Evan slid his hands across the outside of Seth's shirt, and then up underneath, tracing the muscles and the scars, appreciating the strength and the warmth. Seth reached down and pulled the shirt off in one movement.

All that skin...and Evan could touch it. He buried his face in the place where Seth's neck met his shoulder, taking in the scent of him. Seth carded his hands through Evan's dark hair, nuzzling his cheek against the silky strands.

Evan let his hands roam. His cock ached, and his balls begged for long-overdue release, but right this moment, Evan marveled in the feel of Seth's skin, the dusting of blond hair on his strong pecs, the dusky trail from his belly down below his waistband. He let his hands glide over Seth's sides, then up to his strong shoulders and down his powerful biceps, like he was blind and memorizing the territory.

Seth chuckled. "I have never been so thoroughly felt up in my life. Now can we go to bed before I die of blue balls?"

Evan rolled his eyes, but he knew that Seth's hands had made just as thorough a reconnection with his own torso, as if they were both making sure the other was real and alive and *here*.

"Off," Evan ordered, unbuckling Seth's belt and flicking the button of his jeans. Seth maintained eye contact as he did the same, and as they both shimmied out of pants and briefs, Evan thought the look added a whole new meaning to "eye fuck."

Evan let his gaze take in all of Seth, the broad shoulders, abs that tapered to a sexy Adonis belt 'V' and muscular thighs that put all kinds of naughty thoughts in Evan's mind. A glimpse of Seth's rounded ass had pre-come dripping from Evan's cock and made him groan loud enough that Seth clapped a hand over his mouth.

"We're not alone, remember?" Seth warned, and Evan nodded. He licked Seth's palm and nipped gently at the calloused skin.

"Fucker!" Seth hissed, withdrawing his hand, but his tone was fond.

"That's the idea, the sooner, the better."

Seth stepped back and pulled him toward the big four-poster bed. Evan's cheeks heated as he saw Seth's appreciative gaze sweep over him, taking in the view from head to toe, pausing to appreciate the rigid cock standing up from a dark thatch.

"Less looking, more fucking," Evan urged, hungry for this with an urgency he hadn't felt since those first fumbling, desperate days of puberty.

Seth jerked the comforter and covers out of the way, leaving pristine sheets. He swept Evan up in strong arms and deposited him on the plush mattress, joining him seconds later to lie alongside.

"Tell me what you want," Seth asked as he trailed one finger from Evan's breastbone to his naval, making his abs tremble, then down lower, following that happy trail, only to veer along his hipbone, down to the cleft between leg and groin.

"Everything." Evan's breathy voice made no secret of his desire as if Seth hadn't figured that out from his stiff, dripping cock.

"*How* do you want it?"

Evan wanted it every way they could do it, now that the curse was gone and they could touch again. But he also knew that after what they'd both been through today, they were only going to get one round, regardless of recent deprivation.

"Want you in me, now."

"Your wish is my command," Seth replied with a sexy smile, before dropping down to take Evan's cock in his mouth, all the way to the root, sucking and licking his way up his swollen shaft before diving down again, until Evan felt the tight heat of Seth's throat.

"God, Seth—" Evan meant to warn that he wasn't going to last, but language failed him, and all he could manage was a gurgle as his hands clenched around fistfuls of bedding and his back arched.

Seth came off him with a filthy *"pop"* and a knowing grin. "Just warming you up."

"I'm really, really warm. Now fuck me already."

"Bossy bottom."

"Always." The truth was, they both enjoyed switching, and flip fucks were a wonderful way to spend a lazy day between hunts. But right now, Evan needed the connection that only came from being filled.

Seth reached up to rummage in the kit bag on the nightstand until he found the lube. He slicked his fingers and pressed one into Evan's tight pucker. "Gonna make it good for you, babe," he murmured, chuckling as Evan fucked himself impatiently on Seth's finger. He added a second, making sure to sweep across Evan's sweet spot, and that almost made Evan come right then if Seth hadn't grabbed the base of his cock and given it a good squeeze.

"Seth...do it already. I'm dyin' here," Evan groaned.

Seth stilled and met his gaze. Evan saw his fear and worry, and the strain of the past days, with no walls between them. "No. No, you're not. Not anymore."

Evan bucked his hips, needing to pull Seth out of the dark place he had gone. "C'mon babe. Wanna feel you."

Seth snapped out of his thoughts and added a third finger. Evan caught his breath at the stretch, welcoming the burn. Like the arousal, it was proof that he was alive, that they were together, rid of the curse. *Still here.*

Evan could see that Seth's cock was leaking a steady stream, and his pupils were blown wide and dark. Seth lifted one of Evan's legs and rested it on his shoulder, moving into position, rubbing the head of his prick against Evan's ready hole.

"God, you're beautiful." Seth put one hand on Evan's hip and slid in all the way until he was balls deep, fully seated.

Evan arched, overwhelmed by the feeling of being so full, and cried out at the drag of Seth's cock over that spot as Seth pulled back, nearly out, and slid home again, harder this time.

"Yes," Evan groaned, curling his other leg around Seth's thighs, encouraging him to go deep.

Seth set a fast rhythm. It had been too long, and neither of them were going to last. A sheen of sweat slicked Seth's shoulders and back, and a few strands of blond hair fell across his forehead.

Evan rose to meet him with each stroke and reached to take himself in hand. Seth batted his hand out of the way and closed his fist around Evan's cock, jacking him in nearly the same rhythm as his thrusts in Evan's ass.

It was too much—all the emotions and sensations crashed through Evan and he came, choking back a yelp as his body shuddered, and he spilled over Seth's fist. Seth followed seconds later, biting his lip to keep from crying out as he gave one final thrust and filled Evan's ass with his come. He slowed, then went still, remaining connected, and leaned forward to press a kiss to Evan's lips.

"I love you," Seth whispered.

Evan brought his leg down to wrap both around Seth's waist, holding them together. "Love you, too." He reached up to run his fingers through Seth's hair. "Needed this. Needed you."

Seth kissed him again. "So did I." With a grunt, he pushed up and away. "But we should clean up before we stick together."

He brought a warm washcloth back from the bathroom, and Evan appreciated how tender Seth's touch was as he wiped them both clean, something so simple and so intimate. He put the cloth in the sink and came back to join Evan, pulling the covers up around them.

Evan snuggled into Seth's arms, resting his head on that strong chest. "I was thinking...once we spend a couple of days here with Cassidy and Teag seeing Charleston, and we get the truck back, what if we took the long road to Cleveland?"

Seth made a soft, contented noise that Evan knew meant his lover was beginning to drift off. "Yeah? You have something in mind?"

"We could go up the coast, see the ocean. Maybe stop in Myrtle Beach and visit Simon and Vic, like they've been telling us to do. Catch our breath before we dive back into the action."

Seth pulled Evan closer so that he was lying on his side, pressed against him. Evan slipped his arm around Seth's waist. They'd get too hot to spend all night like this, but it was Evan's favorite way to fall asleep.

"Works for me. I like that idea. Time off. Gives us a chance to catch up on what we've missed."

Evan's reply was a lick and nibble at the pert nub next to his mouth that sent a shiver through Seth's body. "I'm all for getting caught up," he said, his voice sleep-rough. "Doing without gave me all kinds of ideas."

"Oh yeah?" Seth sounded interested, despite being half asleep. "Like what?"

"Can't tell you. Have to show you." He kissed Seth on the chest. "Now go to sleep, and we can start on those new ideas in the morning."

"Promise?"

"Promise."

AFTERWORD

Charleston is one of my favorite places, and I love sharing it with you in these books. While some of the locations are altered for the sake of the story, I draw a lot on local history and legend to create a story rooted in the city's storied past.

All of my modern-day series cross over with each other, and characters make cameo (and sometimes bigger) appearances in each other's series, both the books written under my Morgan Brice (urban fantasy MM paranormal romance) name, and those under my Gail Z. Martin (urban fantasy) name.

Some of the side characters you met in this book have their own series. Simon Kincaide and Vic D'Amato star in the Badlands adventures, with a sexy psychic medium and a hot homicide cop hunting down supernatural killers in Myrtle Beach. Erik Mitchell and Ben Nolan headline my Treasure Trail series, with a former art fraud investigator and a cynical Newark ex-cop fighting Mob ghosts, old scandals and a cursed hotel in Cape May, NJ.

Ex-priest and former Sinistram asset Travis Dominick and ex-soldier, ex-FBI, ex-cop Brent Lawson team up to hunt demons in Pittsburgh in the Night Vigil (Sons of Darkness) series. Cassidy Kincaide (Simon's cousin) and her crew get cursed objects out of the wrong hands and save the world from supernatural threats in the Deadly Curiosities series. Beck and his demon box curse happen in Deadly Curiosities #4, Inheritance, which also features an in-person visit from Simon and Vic. The Night Vigil and Deadly Curiosities series are written under my Gail Z. Martin pen name.

ACKNOWLEDGMENTS

Thank you so much to my editor, Jean Rabe, to my husband and writing partner Larry N. Martin for all his behind-the-scenes hard work, and to my wonderful cover artist Lou Harper, and to Mindy and Leslie for their help. Thanks also to the Shadow Alliance and the Worlds of Morgan Brice street teams for their support and encouragement, and to my fantastic beta readers: Beth, Carole, Chris, Donald, Gregg, Jason & Sherry, Jennifer, John, Laurie, and Sandra, plus my promotional crew and the ever-growing legion of ARC readers who help spread the word, including: Amy, Andrea, Anne, Ashley, Barbie, Belinda, Beth, Carr, Carrah, Cheryl, Colleen, D'Niche, Darrell, Dawn, Debbie, Elizabeth, Grace, Ida, Jamie, Janel, Jessica, Joscelyn, Karolina, Kimerley, Lexi, Linda, Lisa, Manda, Mandy, Mary, Melissa, Patricia, Patti, Raven, Rosalind, Sandi, Shey, Susan, and Xochitl—couldn't do it without you! And of course, to my "convention gang" of fellow authors for making road trips fun.

ABOUT THE AUTHOR

Morgan Brice is the romance pen name of bestselling author Gail Z. Martin. Morgan writes urban fantasy male/male paranormal romance, with plenty of action, adventure, and supernatural thrills to go with the happily ever after.

Gail writes epic fantasy and urban fantasy, and together with co-author hubby Larry N. Martin, steampunk, post-apocalyptic adventure, Roaring Twenties monster hunters and horror comedy, all of which have less romance and more explosions.

On the rare occasions Morgan isn't writing, she's either reading, cooking, or spoiling two very pampered dogs.

Watch for additional new series from Morgan Brice, and more books in the Witchbane, Badlands, and Treasure Trail universes coming soon!

Where to find me, and how to stay in touch

Join my Worlds of Morgan Brice Facebook Group and get in on all the behind-the-scenes fun! My free reader group is the first to see cover reveals, learn tidbits about works-in-progress, have fun with exclusive contests and giveaways, find out about in-person get-togethers, and more! It's also where I find my beta readers, ARC readers, and launch team! Come join the party! www.Facebook.com/groups/WorldsOf-MorganBrice

Find me on the web at https://morganbrice.com. Sign up for my newsletter and never miss a new release! http://eepurl.com/dy_8oL. You can also find me on Twitter: @MorganBriceBook, on Pinterest (for Morgan and Gail): pinterest.com/Gzmartin, on Instagram as Morgan-

BriceAuthor, and on Bookbub https://www.bookbub.com/authors/morgan-brice

Enjoy two free short stories set in my Badlands series. Read *Cover Me* here for free: https://claims.prolificworks.com/free/iwZDEP9Z and *Restless Nights* here: https://claims.prolificworks.com/free/js6x0fq8

Support Indie Authors

When you support independent authors, you help influence what kind of books you'll see more of and what types of stories will be available, because the authors themselves decide which books to write, not a big publishing conglomerate. Independent authors are local creators, supporting their families with the books they produce. Thank you for supporting independent authors and small press fiction!

EXCERPT | BADLANDS

SIMON

AT THIS HOUR OF THE MORNING, THE BOARDWALK GHOSTS WERE SILENT. Simon Kincaide stared down the nearly empty, broad beachside walkway and breathed in the ocean air. Flags flapped in the breeze, waves pounded the shore on the other side of the dunes, and seagulls swooped. The tourists hadn't yet woken.

Simon looked, out of habit, to the places the spirits favored. The old man with his bicycle and his dog wouldn't appear until late afternoon, cycling down the boardwalk. Kevin, a dreadlocked man in his twenties, liked the stairs that led to the beach, perhaps near the spot where he drowned. Two children in Victorian clothing, spirits so faded that they could not even remember their names, would skip past near sunset. Other ghosts came and went, but Simon could set his watch by those appearances. Not everyone could see the ghosts—most of the people milling along the boardwalk could not and never would—but Simon did.

Sebastian Simon Kincaide had known he wasn't like other kids when he realized nobody else could see and hear the spirits he considered regular playmates. Discovering he got glimpses into the future from time to time made him even less like his friends at school. Figuring out that he was gay was just the icing on the cake. That all happened long ago, but the sense of being an outsider never really went away, Simon thought, not even now at age thirty-five, with a prosperous business and a few bestselling books to his credit.

He worked the key in the front door. Grand Strand Ghost Tours, a small shop on the Myrtle Beach boardwalk, shared a building with a beachwear shop but had a coveted location between the legendary Gay Dolphin Gift Cove and the popular Myrtle Beach SkyWheel mega-Ferris wheel. Simon paused in the doorway, letting himself enjoy a moment of pride and satisfaction in the business it had taken three damn years to build.

Simon collected the mail, pocketed his keys, and locked the door behind him since the shop wouldn't open for another two hours. He switched on the lights and music, then went to the back to start a pot of coffee.

His phone buzzed, and he answered. "Hey, Seth. What's up?"

Seth Tanner chuckled. "You haven't had your coffee yet, have you?"

"I'm working on it." Simon held the phone between his shoulder and ear as he readied the coffee maker. "What do you need?"

Seth sighed. "I'm looking into a vengeful ghost problem near Breezewood, up in Pennsylvania. Salt and iron aren't doing the trick, but I'm sure it's ghosts, not demons, so exorcism won't work, either. Got any ideas?"

"Find the anchor object the spirit is tethered to," Simon recommended, measuring out the coffee. "Might not be near where the appearances are happening. Have an officiant from the deceased's faith tradition say a blessing and urge the ghost to move on. If nothing else works, there's a banishment ritual, but it's brutal on the spirits. And no matter what you've seen on TV, don't get yourself arrested trying to dig up the grave to salt and burn the bones."

Seth chuckled. "I knew you'd have the answers. You're a rare medium, Simon. Well done."

"Ha, ha. As if I haven't heard that one before," Simon groaned, rolling his eyes. He pressed the button, and the coffee maker chugged to life.

"Seriously, thanks," Seth replied. "Send me the bill."

"When I have to do some research, I'll charge for the time. This, I can give you off the top of my head. Next time you're in the area, stop in and we'll do dinner. Your treat."

"You're on," Seth replied and ended the call.

Simon headed out to the main room and started to get the shop ready for business. Shelves in the front held books about ghost stories from all over South Carolina and the Lowcountry, but especially those with tales of spirits, pirates, or old scandals of the Grand Strand. Prominently displayed were the three books on local folklore and ghosts that bore his name as author. The glass case by the register held gemstones and silver jewelry for healing and protection, colored candles, and sealed bags of the most common dried plants and flours used in rituals and aromatherapy. Shelves behind the cabinet held an assortment of candles in tall glass holders with pictures of saints on the front. In the back, a table and two comfortable chairs supplied a homey place to do appointment-only psychic readings, and the table could expand to hold six people for a full séance.

A rack on top of the counter held brochures about the Grand Strand Ghost Tours that Simon led four nights a week, as well as the "Pirates and Scoundrels" special tours and the "Lowcountry Legends and Lore" talk he gave twice a month at Brookgreen Gardens. The large sign on the wall behind the counter advertised ticket prices for the tours and special events, with a prominent reminder to "ask about rates for private spirit readings and séances."

Display racks offered t-shirts with the Grand Strand Ghost Tours logo, while others bore catchy phrases like "Ghosts Gone Wild," "Grand Strand Spook-a-palooza," and his favorite, a cartoon of a ghost holding a beach drink that read "Chillin' Out." The nearby shelves that held cups, stickers, and shot glasses with the same designs were a concession to tourist tastes.

Simon straightened some of the merchandise when his phone rang again. "Mark! You're up early."

Mark Wojcik grumbled something in response, and Simon grinned. Mark hated mornings even more than he did. "No, I'm up late and still haven't gone to bed," Mark muttered. "And I'm bruised from head to toe after I got my ass kicked by a were-cougar before we brought it down, so forgive me if I'm not Mr. Sunshine."

Like Seth, Mark was a real-life hunter of things that went bump in the night; part of a loosely allied group of people who by talent or personal tragedy found themselves initiated into a shadow world most people could live happily never suspecting. Simon's gifts as a medium and clairvoyant—and his training as a folklorist—made him a part of that hidden network, and his research skills provided a second stream of income.

"I finished the research on the kelpies you asked for," Simon replied. "Sent the files to the secure share drive."

"Okay," Mark said. "That's what I was calling about. I'll shoot the payment back atcha. Thanks."

Simon ended the call and ran a hand back through his shoulder-length brown hair. Four years ago, if someone had told him that he'd be making a living taking beachgoers on ghost tours, giving readings, and selling tchotchkes, he'd have laughed. But how he'd ended up on the Grand Strand was not funny at all.

Three and a half years ago, Dr. Sebastian Kincaide held a professorship at the University of South Carolina in the Humanities Department, teaching folklore and mythology classes and writing scholarly articles on legends and lore. He kept his abilities as a medium and clairvoyant hidden, although his long-time relationship with another professor on staff had been openly acknowledged, especially after he and Jacen had announced their engagement.

Even now, the memory brought a sour twist to Simon's stomach. Emerson Baucom Tallmudge, the father of one of his students, turned out to be not only a donor and a board member for the university, but a hard-core fundamentalist as well, of the "thou shalt not suffer a witch to live" variety. Apparently, after he'd gotten a glimpse of his son's textbooks for the class, Tallmudge got his dander up and lobbied the board to be rid of such an "evil influence." Simon thought he had successfully placated the board, citing the importance of classical mythology in a well-rounded education, but then Tallmudge found evidence online that Simon admitted to being able to talk with spirits, and everything came crashing down.

The board dismissed Simon with a severance package that told him they also thought Tallmudge's complaints were bullshit, but in the end, the prospect of an endowment beat out standing up for one of their faculty. Then Jacen broke off their engagement, too afraid that Simon's dismissal would compromise his bid for tenure, and Simon's world went up in flames.

Alone, unemployed, and unable to find another teaching job, Simon drifted down to Myrtle Beach, intending to stay for a week or so to regroup and lick his wounds. When his aunt offered to sell him the cottage in Myrtle Beach where he was staying, Simon took it as a sign to rebuild his life from the ground up. He put his folklore background to use writing a book on local ghosts and used the self-published book to leverage himself into jobs as a tour guide, haunted attractions actor, museum docent, and speaker while he put his plan together. Grand Strand Ghost Tours wasn't just a shop; it was Simon's howl of defiance at a universe that had fucked him over.

And which was still doing so, since the coffee maker had not only failed to produce a cup of java-rich goodness, but had sent a gush of murky water and wet grounds all over the floor.

"Shit." Simon grabbed a handful of paper towels and began mopping. The smell of burned electronics told him without needing to use his psychic gifts that the coffee maker was dead. He dropped the machine into the trash on top of the sodden towels, ordered a new one on Amazon with expedited shipping, and then contemplated the prospect of a morning without coffee.

"Screw that," he said, glancing at the clock. He locked up, turned out lights, and headed for Mizzenmast Coffee.

Before he'd made it half a block, his phone buzzed once more. This time he smiled at the number that came up. "Hi, Cassidy. Everything okay?" His cousin, Cassidy Kincaide, ran an antique store in Charleston, just two hours south of Myrtle Beach. They hadn't been close growing up, but now that Cassidy had discovered her own ability to read the history of objects by touching them, they had bonded.

"Fine. Just busy. Mostly regular stuff, but some of the other too, if you know what I mean." Cassidy's shop proved to be the perfect opportunity to get cursed and haunted objects out of the wrong hands.

Simon and Cassidy often talked over whatever weird or supernatural situation they were currently navigating. Not to mention Cassidy had a gorgeous gay Weaver witch best friend as a partner in her supernatural escapades. It was another sign of the universe's contempt for Simon that Teag was already taken. "Is the store open yet? Can you talk?"

"I'm heading for coffee," Simon replied. "What's up?"

"I've got a carved mahogany trinket box with the name '*Jeremiah Holzer*' engraved on the bottom," Cassidy said. "There's a pretty nasty curse on it. I think Jeremiah was from the Myrtle Beach area, but Teag and I can't find anything about him online, and I thought maybe you could check some local archive stuff for me."

"Sure," Simon agreed. "How urgent?"

"We've got the box quarantined, so it's not doing any new damage, but two people were injured from the curse, and I have a feeling there's missing information that we need to break the bad juju. So, the sooner, the better."

"I'll work on it tonight, after the tour," Simon promised. "Say 'hi' to everyone for me."

"When are you going to come to Charleston? You know we've got the best restaurants on the Southeast coast," Cassidy replied. "Plus, Teag and Anthony have a couple of cute guys in mind they think you might hit it off with."

Simon cringed, glad Cassidy couldn't see his expression. Even after three years, he wasn't sure he was ready for a new romance. Perhaps he never would be. "It's the busy season," he begged off. "But maybe this winter. Or come visit me. Roads go both ways, you know."

"It's tourist season here, too," she reminded him. "But we'll get together soon, one way or another. And thanks for the research."

"You got that haunted painting off my hands," Simon replied. "I owe you." He hung up, but couldn't shake the melancholy that had settled in. A couple walked past, hands clasped, talking quietly, and an ache he didn't want to acknowledge flared in his chest. As much as he feared being hurt again, Simon couldn't deny the fact that he missed being in a relationship, having someone to wake up with every day and fall asleep with at night. For a while, he'd buried himself in his work, and that had dulled the loneliness. Now that he was no longer in survival mode, the evenings were not completely filled with busyness, and the nights stretched long.

Simon chuckled at his fears. *Here I am, backing up people who hunt real monsters, and I'm too chickenshit to go on a date. I need to man up and...man up.*

EXCERPT | TREASURE TRAIL

ERIK

"IF THE SHOW PROPOSAL GOES THROUGH, IT WILL REALLY PUT *TREASURE Trail* and Trinkets on the map!" Corinne Scott had the bouncy enthusiasm required of an agent, and it came across as clear over the phone as it did in person.

"It's exciting, but let's wait before we break out the champagne," Erik Mitchell protested. He had been dealing with the chaos of unpacking boxes and living out of a suitcase for two weeks, since his move to Cape May, New Jersey, and the complete uprooting of his life. "If they're counting on using my supposed notoriety to sell the show, they might be disappointed. There's a lot I can't talk about—and it's mostly the exciting parts."

"You traveled the world stopping art and antiquities fraud," Corinne continued, undeterred. "It's like something out of Indiana Jones."

Erik winced. Much as he loved those movies, Indy was more like the kind of guy he helped bust for swiping relics. "Um…not really. I spent a lot of time in the back rooms of museums going over old stuff with a magnifying glass. And I only got shot at a few times."

That was enough. A collector with a very rare Fabergé egg music box wanted Erik to authenticate the egg for the buyer. Unfortunately, there were other interested parties, and they all brought more muscle than brains. The deal went sideways when they decided to negotiate with guns; all hell broke loose, and Erik nearly died. He ended up with a concussion, a bullet wound in his shoulder, and nightmares verging on PTSD.

"This wouldn't be anything so dangerous!" Corinne was in full sales mode now. "It's only six episodes, and it's the local PBS station. All the crimes have already been solved. You're just on camera for the expert cameos, and to toss out some advice on how to avoid buying fake art or accidentally stealing priceless relics."

The longer Corinne talked, the more Erik became convinced the whole TV show was a colossal mistake. He had relocated to Cape May from Atlanta to get away from the sensational—and dangerous— aspects of his old life. Sure, chasing down art fraud had been his dream job, like something out of a thriller novel. His younger self had relished the constant travel and intermittent danger, and the work paid well—in headlines and in a very healthy salary.

Then there was the clusterfuck bust and Erik's injury. He realized that he was ready to move on, settle down, and step out of the spot-light. He'd thought his boyfriend, Josh, would be happy about the change. Then he got home a few days earlier than expected and found Josh banging Erik's personal assistant on the dining room table.

After all the shouting and tears were over, Erik found himself single and lacking an assistant. He'd decided right then to leave his old world behind. That meant getting out of Atlanta, out of the apartment he'd shared with Josh, and going somewhere he could get a fresh start.

He surfed real estate sites and found a beautiful Victorian in Cape May at a great price. Even better, it was part of a package deal and included an established antique store on the main floor, inventory included. Suddenly, the daydream Erik had indulged about starting a blog on trendy antiques and running a boutique service for designers all came together. The next thing Erik knew, he was standing in front of his new home and business with the keys in his hand, wondering whether he'd lost his mind.

Now, he was certain that the answer was "yes."

"Let's see if the proposal even gets interest," Erik protested. "And if it does, it's going to depend on what they actually want, and we'll take it from there."

"Party pooper," Corinne joked. "Fine. I'll let you know when I hear from the producers. But I'm telling you, Erik, this would be a great way to start your new business off with a bang!"

That's what I'm afraid of.

Corinne conveniently seemed to forget that some of the thefts, forgeries, and smuggling rings he'd helped bust had ties to the Mob and the cartels, or left a trail of pissed off billionaires who were used to getting what they wanted. Death threats had been common, and for a while he'd had a bodyguard. While Erik wanted his new venture to succeed, he didn't want to attract the wrong kind of attention.

"Look, I need to finish what I'm doing," Erik said. "Call me when you hear something. And…thanks." Corinne might be exasperatingly upbeat, but she had stuck by Erik through all the changes in his life, and she had been a good friend—especially when there was a commission in it for her.

Erik ended the call and slipped the phone into his pocket, turning to look around the downstairs of the grand old house. It had been updated by the prior owner to create a shop on the first floor and an expansive living area on the second and third floors. Boxes and packing peanuts littered the floor, along with crinkled paper shred. He sighed, completely overwhelmed.

"It can't be that bad." Susan Hendricks, Erik's new next-door neighbor, looked up with a grin from where she sat on the floor, helping to unpack some of the items Erik had shipped from Atlanta. His condo and office had been full of antiques he had bought in his travels, but he'd decided to sell them all and start over, using his personal collection as part of the inventory for Trinkets. "You've got some real pretty pieces here."

"I'm just feeling a little out of my depth," Erik admitted. Susan was probably the same age as his mother, but far more energetic and approachable. Her short salt-and-pepper hair framed a youthful face, and he suspected her wardrobe of T-shirts and yoga pants saw real gym time. She'd been the first person other than his real estate agent to welcome him to Cape May, and won him over with her genuine friend-liness and no-bullshit attitude.

"I couldn't help overhearing," Susan said. "There's nothing wrong with spreading things out instead of doing everything all at once. You don't have to say no or yes...you can say 'later.'"

That sounded like the best thing Erik had heard all day. "Thank you. You're a genius."

Susan laughed. "No, I've just felt overwhelmed a time or two myself, and I'm happy to pass along the tricks that worked for me, for what it's worth."

If I just take one room at a time, it might be all right, Erik thought. The front parlor was the main showroom, and the furniture was already in place, providing plenty of places to display the additional inventory he had brought with him. He bent down to pick up a vase, trying not to wince at the thought of the pricy piece sitting on the floor.

"You might change your mind about only being open by appoint-ment," Susan said as she carefully unwrapped a vintage tea set. "The folks who visit Cape May have refined tastes—and money."

Erik figured he would get everything safely off the floor and out of boxes and rearrange them for maximum impact later.

"I know. Just trying not to bite off more than I can chew. I want to get the blog up and running because that will not only bring people into the store, but it should attract decorators and curators looking for the perfect piece. If I can attract those folks, they'll be steady business even in the off-season." Given his knowledge and reputation, Erik's collection was likely to attract attention from museums looking to round out their collections, and designers searching for eye-catching and unusual items for their clients' homes. He could make more money with less overhead.

"Sounds like you've thought everything out," Susan said, wiping some stray paper fibers from an inlaid music box.

"Not really, but it's nice of you to say so." Erik felt like he'd been careening from one major life decision to another since he'd woken up in a hospital in Antwerp with a concussion and a gunshot wound, and decided the paycheck and fame weren't worth dying for. Now here he was, relocated, single, a new homeowner, taking over a business and finding his way in a vacation town he vaguely remembered from a few trips when he was a kid. He'd been outrunning his dumpster fire of a life, and Erik was ready to slow down and try to find some kind of new normal.

"Have you done anything except unpack, move furniture, and work on your website since you got to town?" Susan raised an eyebrow to tell him that she already knew the answer.

"Guilty as charged. But there's so much to do, and…"

"And you know what they say about all work and no play," Susan said with a grin. "You need to go out, meet some people, let the town get to know you. Maybe meet a cute girl—or guy," she added with a wink.

"Definitely guy," Erik replied.

"Well then, you've come to the right place. Cape May is very welcoming. My son is probably a few years younger than you, and he and his friends never seem to have any trouble finding dates."

Erik's escape plan hadn't been quite as headlong as it sometimes felt. He'd done his research on Cape May, a town he visited several times vacationing with his aunt, uncle, and cousins when he was in middle school. He remembered the beach and all the classic Victorian houses—and the ice cream. When he went looking for a place to relocate, he checked out the town on a whim and discovered it was gay-friendly and eclectic. While that was definitely true of his former home in Atlanta, the same couldn't be said about everywhere else in Georgia, or in his native South Carolina.

At thirty-five, Erik was ready to put down roots, settle in, and settle down. He never really liked hookups, even before his relationship with Josh, and while Josh's betrayal had rocked Erik's confidence, he still hoped that there was someone out there for him.

"Don't worry. All in good time," Susan reassured him. She got to her feet with a gracefulness that only came from hours of asanas and dusted herself off. "Let me help get everything up on shelves, and by then the meatloaf in the slow cooker will be done. I don't know about you, but I'm starving!"

"It does smell good." Erik knew he'd lucked out with a neighbor like Susan. She had refused any pay for helping him unpack and insisted on bringing over dinner. He'd been wary about her friendly overtures at first, but she quickly won him over.

"It was one of Keith's favorite recipes," Susan said, and her smile grew wistful. "Nothing fancy, just good comfort food." She had mentioned her husband's death to Erik not long after they met, and they had commiserated about how scary it was to get back into the dating game.

"I just bought ice cream, so I can at least contribute dessert," Erik said.

"Sounds like a plan," she answered. Together, they made quick work of moving the antiques out of harm's way and cleaning up the packing materials. Then Erik led the way into the next room, where the slow cooker sat on the table, along with the paper plates and plastic utensils Susan had brought. A two-liter bottle of soda and red cups made for a picnic-style supper.

Susan filled plates while Erik brought chairs. He had to admit that the smell of a home-cooked meal made the place feel more welcoming. He'd been surviving on takeout subs and pizza delivery.

"Tell me about Cape May's ghosts," Erik asked as they sat down to eat. "I've read that local ghost whisperer's books, and I've got to admit, I'm very curious."

Susan wiped away a bit of tomato sauce. "Oh, there are plenty of them, enough to go around, if all the tales are true. It's almost a point of pride to claim you've got a resident ghost."

Erik ate and listened as Susan recounted what she knew. Most of the stories told of victims of swimming or boating accidents who never left, or jilted lovers who died of grief or by their own hand. The fierce storms that had pummeled the beach town added a few more spirits to the tally, as did old local scandals.

"But you know, I think the biggest ghost story in Cape May isn't a 'who.' It's a 'what,'" Susan said with a conspiratorial smile. "A big old hotel that took up two city blocks—the largest hotel in the United States when it was built back around the turn of the last century."

"A hotel?"

"The Commodore Wilson Hotel was quite the showplace back in the day, and everyone who was anyone stayed there. But the hotel was snake-bit from the start. Or cursed, maybe. Ruined everyone who owned it and seemed to be a magnet for tragedy."

Erik vaguely remembered seeing the hotel mentioned when he had researched Cape May, but hadn't seen anything that resembled what Susan was describing. "Where is it? I can't believe I missed it!"

She paused to take a few bites of meatloaf. "Oh, they finally tore it down years ago. It was a grand place in its prime, and it was a shame to see it fall into disrepair. In the end, no one could afford to fix it, so they brought the hotel down with dynamite, and the whole town held a wake."

Erik made a mental note to do some online digging. The Commodore Wilson sounded like the sort of hotel he always sought out when he traveled, a place with a rich history and the kind of architecture no one could afford to build anymore. "You said the place was cursed?"

Susan shrugged. "Maybe that's not literally true, but it sure seemed like it. Five owners went bankrupt. A mobster got gunned down in the lobby. Several celebrities committed suicide there. Its real heyday was probably during Prohibition and the Second World War, but it was still *the* place to be seen into the seventies. Then a shady televangelist bought it and brought all his followers in for big events. It was all fun and games until he up and vanished, leaving a pile of debt and a bunch of pissed off followers—and a lot of unpaid taxes."

"Did they ever find him?" This story was better than anything on the History Channel.

"Nope. Hard to imagine someone who'd had his face all over TV like that could just disappear, but everyone figured he probably went to Brazil or somewhere else without extradition," Susan said. "If so, I guess he was smarter than that TV preacher from South Carolina. He went to jail."

Erik remembered. He'd grown up in Columbia, South Carolina, and the infamous preacher's scandal had unfolded when he was a child, but it had been impossible to live in the state and not know. For a while, it seemed like all anybody talked about.

"Wow. That's a lot of excitement packed into one building," Erik said. "But I hate to see landmarks like that destroyed. They're a part of history."

Susan grinned. "Oh, the Commodore was so much a part of this town's history I swear it's like a ghost itself. Everyone who grew up here had a story about the hotel—working there, wedding reception, going to prom, drinking too much in the bar, spotting someone famous. And after it closed there were paranormal investigators and urban explorers—and local kids who dared each other to go inside and bring out a souvenir."

She sighed. "You should have seen the crowd when they finally sold off all the Commodore's stuff. People who used to live here or stay at the hotel came from all over the world to buy a memento. Monogrammed china sets, silverware, knick-knacks, even the metal fobs for the room keys. It was quite the media circus."

Erik grabbed another slice of meatloaf and gestured for her to continue. "Sounds like my kind of event."

Susan raised an eyebrow. "Actually, you'd have been right at home. Even at the end, there were rumors that some of the artwork and antiques were fake. So many of the hotel's owners were strapped for cash, I wouldn't be surprised if they'd sold the originals and put good forgeries in their place."

"It happens more often than you'd imagine," Erik replied. "I've had to break the news to European nobility that their 'priceless' Monet or Rembrandt was just a very good copy."

Susan sat back and took a sip of her soda. "So, you're interested in ghosts? See any yourself?"

Erik hesitated, but figured that in a place like Cape May, where the local spirits were practically celebrities themselves, it wouldn't hurt to tell the truth. "I've seen a few," he admitted, although the real number was more than he could count. "Guess it goes with knocking around museums and historic old mansions. I can't talk to them or hear them say anything, but I've seen some things I can't really explain."

He didn't mention his odd hunches, the ones that always seemed to know the forgeries from the real deal. They were never wrong. Erik also didn't mention his second sight, the way some objects gave him flashes of their history, showing the world as the object had seen it, a window in time.

Thank God that didn't happen with everything. But it occurred often enough that he usually wore gloves to handle new acquisitions, until he could check them privately to avoid an embarrassing incident. He'd only told one person about that ability, Simon Kincaide, a grad school friend who was a psychic medium. Simon had understood. Erik knew others wouldn't.

"I believe. In ghosts, I mean," Susan said. "There are plenty of things about the world we don't understand. Seems a little arrogant to think we've got it all figured out, don't you think? I don't understand why some people can see ghosts and others can't, but I know enough people who have that I can't dismiss it."

Erik relaxed a little. Susan set him at ease. Most of his friends in Atlanta and on the cases he had worked were situational, so when they weren't forced together by circumstances, the connection withered. He could count the friends who didn't fit that pattern—Simon included—on one hand. It felt good to make a new friend who liked him just for being him.

"So every now and then, I pick up a hint of a drawl from you," Susan said, going back for another small slice of meatloaf. "I get the impression you're not a Jersey boy."

Erik usually didn't say much about his family, but he appreciated that Susan hadn't just Googled him. "I'm from Columbia, South Carolina. State capital and all that. But I've been gone for a long while, and I've lived in New York, London, Rome, and Atlanta. I think the accent comes out most when I'm tired." Or stressed or hurt, he didn't bother to add. Josh had always chided him when his drawl slipped out, calling him a "redneck" and spewing bigoted stereotypes.

And yet, I sat there and took it. So what does that say about me?

"Your parents must be so proud. I imagine they'll be the first to tune in if your TV show comes through."

Susan meant well, but she didn't know his family. "My sister was an Olympic athlete—brought home two silvers and a bronze in gymnastics—and now she coaches. If the TV is on at home, it's usually because Macy has a televised meet."

"That sounds exciting." Susan didn't press for more, and Erik got the impression that she read between the lines.

When Erik was growing up, Macy was being groomed for gold medals. All of his parents' time and money went toward coaches, lessons, and going to competitions all over the country and later, the world. That usually meant no one was around to go to his high school plays or other events. Erik had worked part-time jobs and gotten scholarships to put himself through college and graduate school. He loved his sister, and he did his best not to hold his parents' favoritism against her, but they weren't really a close family.

"How about ice cream?" Erik asked. It wasn't the smoothest segue, but it worked to get past an awkward moment. It wasn't Susan's fault that a question normal people could answer without blinking was such a minefield for him. Even now, with all his accomplishments, Erik had to remind himself that he wasn't as invisible and replaceable as his parents' indifference always made him feel.

"Count me in!" Susan replied with a grin. "And I know it's still off-season, but once everything opens up for the summer, there are some fantastic local ice cream shops that make everything from scratch. I'll have to take you!"

"You're on." He ran upstairs to get the ice cream out of the freezer and returned a few minutes later with a scoop and bowls.

"I'm really looking forward to seeing the town wake up from its winter nap," he said as he set out generous portions of vanilla bean for both of them, finishing off what was in the carton. Once he got settled, he'd have to see about adding toppings to his grocery list. "I know a lot of shops and restaurants close in the off-season. I'm looking forward to getting the whole Cape May experience!"

He had fond memories of the seaside town with its stately Victorian homes and yellow-striped beach tents. Aunt Karen and Uncle Jim included Erik whenever they could in their vacations, saying it was because he was the same age as their boys. Now that he looked back on it, Erik guessed that they were doing their best to make up for his parents' indifference. Their visits to Cape May had left a lasting impression.

"Oh, you'll love it," Susan gushed. She was definitely the town's biggest booster. "I mean yes, there's more traffic. But there's also a lot more energy. Plus even more theater and music, live bands in the bars, fireworks—I wouldn't want to live anywhere else!"

They chatted about favorite kinds of ice cream and desserts, fun topics without any stress. Once Susan scraped her bowl clean and licked every drop from her spoon, she sat back with a satisfied sigh.

"This has been fun. Thank you."

Erik gave her a perplexed look. "You volunteered to spend an afternoon helping me unpack and brought dinner. I owe you a big thank you!"

Susan shrugged. "I enjoyed the company and got to see some lovely antiques up close. I stay pretty busy, but it's nice to get out. Tank and Ziggy are good company, but the conversation gets a little one-sided." Erik had already met Tank, the bulldog, and Ziggy, the black cat.

"Anytime," Erik said. "This was fun." Once he unpacked his kitchen boxes, he'd have to find the few recipes he could make well enough to serve to company and repay the favor.

Susan helped clean up the garbage and went to grab the slow cooker. She divided the leftover meatloaf and put half into a plastic container for Erik. "Here. It makes great sandwiches."

"I never turn down good food," he assured her. "Thank you—for everything."

She grinned. "You're very welcome. Don't forget it's Friday night—why don't you wander into town and see if there's anyone worth meeting? You never know if you don't try!"

With that, she was out the door and across the yard. Erik watched out the window to make sure she got in safely, still thinking about her words. Before he could second-guess himself, he pulled out his phone and downloaded a dating app. As soon as the app registered his location, he uploaded a photo and sketched out a quick bio.

He hesitated, staring at the photo, worried it might not attract interest. He considered his looks fairly average, and he hadn't devoted enough time to the bar or club scenes to gauge his effect on other men. He hadn't had difficulty finding casual boyfriends in college and graduate school, but then he'd connected with Josh and taken himself off the market.

His light blond hair had a bit of a wave no matter how he styled it. Erik had always considered his blue eyes to be his best feature. They were dark like sapphires, and he thought they made up for other unremarkable features. At five foot ten, Erik wasn't short, but he wasn't terribly tall, either. Running and lifting weights kept him in good shape, although he doubted anyone would mistake him for an underwear model. His build remained on the slender side, even now that he was in his mid-thirties. He'd discovered long ago that he preferred men who were taller and more muscular, and had found that interest was often returned.

Erik paused. He really wasn't looking for a quick fuck. The appeal of hookups had gone cold in grad school. Trying not to overthink this, he dismissed the profiles that made it clear they were "one and done." Whether they were telling the truth, a few of the profiles indicated they wanted friends with benefits or were willing to start slow and see where it went.

For once, his intuition wasn't telling him a damn thing as he looked through the remaining profiles. He picked one for "David," a good-looking man with dark hair, a muscular build, and the promise of intriguing tattoos peeking from beneath the sleeves of his T-shirt. Then Erik gathered his courage and hit "send."

ALSO BY MORGAN BRICE

Witchbane Series

Witchbane

Burn, a Witchbane Novella

Dark Rivers

Flame and Ash

Unholy

Badlands Series

Badlands

Restless Nights, a Badlands Short Story

Lucky Town, a Badlands Novella

The Rising

Cover Me, a Badlands Short Story

Loose Ends

Night, a Badlands Short Story

Treasure Trail

CPSIA information can be obtained
at www.ICGtesting.com
Printed in the USA
LVHW111644270322
714534LV00001B/88